Unsuspected

A Fictional Story Based on Yup'ik Oral Legends

Unsuspected

A Fictional Story Based on Yup'ik Oral Legends

PO Box 221974 Anchorage, Alaska 99522-1974
books@publicationconsultants.com—www.publicationconsultants.com

ISBN 978-1-59433-342-2
eISBN 978-1-59433-343-9
Library of Congress Catalog Card Number: 2013931862

Manufactured in the United States of America.

Dedication

Unsuspected is dedicated to Susie, Aaron, Esther, Chelsea, Stephanie and Dante, elders, friends and family.
Quyana to Aan, Lillian, Olinka and Terry

Acknowledgement

I express my sincere gratitude to my editor Ms. Marthy Johnson

Table of Contents

CHARACTER NAMES

Aan	Tatu's mom, also means mom
Aat	Patu's victim, Guk's son, also means dad
Aatiin	Tatu's father
Akim	Eli's father
Anuksua	Tatu's elderly relative
Apaq	Tatu's friend
Arii	A little girl
Arupak	Elder from Nanvarnarlak
Atmak	Guk's wife
Ciuk	Guk's baby
Cung	Leader of the warriors
Cuuk	Elder from Nanvarnarlak
Eli	Tatu's friend
Guk	Tatu's leader/friend
Iis	Guk's daughter
Ipuun	Guk's friend/ Warrior from Tulukar
Iriini	Warrior from Tulukar
Kaluk	Tatu's friend
Kauki	A warrior from Tulukar
Kulun	Warrior from Paimiut
Kumak	Patu's victim
Maurluq/Maurlu	Tatu's grandma
Napaq	Trapper's brother
Nuk	Elder from Tulukar
Patu	Shaman
Qay	Elder from Tulukar
Qum	Teriikaniar leader
Quuk	Shaman
Tatu	Main character
Tuma	Guk's friend/warrior
Tut'ggar	grandson
Uam	Kaluk's father
Apa/Apii	Tatu's grandpa
Uquv	Guk's son
Urraq	Elder from Tulukar

PLACES

Atmaulluaq	Atmautluak
Anarciq	(A place downdriver)
Cuukvaggtuliq	(old village site)
Gali	(a place down Kuskokwim)
Kasigluq	Kasigluk
Kakeggluk	(old village site)
Kwiggluk	Kwethluk
Masercurliq	Mountain Village
Nanvarnarlak	(old village)
Naparyallruaq	Napakiak
Napaskiaq	Napaskiak
Niugtaq	Newtok
Nunapicuar	Nunapitchuk
Nunaacuaq	(old village site)
Paimiut	(old village site)
Qasgirayak	(old village site)
Tulukar (Tulukarnarlak)	(old village)
Qaluuyaaq	(old village site)

Rivers and Lakes

Kakeggluk River	
Kuicaraq River	
Nanvarnarlak Lake	
Pitmiktalik River	
Kusquqvak River	Kuskokwim River
Taklirlak Lake	
Tulukar Lake	
	(Tulukarnarrlak Lake)

Tribes

Teriikaniar People
Inuguaq People

Other words and meanings in this book

Agaa	Oh no
Aka	Ouch
Maqivik	Steam bath house
Maklak	Shoes
Qasgiq	Communal men's house
Wugg'	Awesome

THE REAL PEOPLE

The land was young and fairly new to the people. It was summertime and the tundra was soaked from the fresh rain. On this particular hill, a shaman and a Yup'ik man were hunting each other.

The Yup'ik man had his bow ready. The shaman was weaponless, but had his wits. After the ferocious battle, the shaman was on his knees trying to catch his breath. As the shaman was catching his breath, his mouth started gurgling out some blood.

The Yup'ik man walked in front of the shaman and fired his last arrow at the shaman's forehead. From his arrow's impact, the shaman finally fell down backward, but there were so many arrows in his back that he didn't hit the ground. The shaman was finally dead for sure, the man was thinking to himself.

The man's grandfather had once told him: "Everyone remembers the good times, but they never forgot the unsuspected moments."

The central Yup'ik people are located in southwestern Alaska. They have lived, endured, adapted, and survived in the upper part of the world for thousands of years. With their knowledge of the land and the wisdom of their ancestors, they were able to survive there.

They called their land *nuna* and it was mostly made of tundra and trees. The winter months were extremely long and the land was mostly covered with snow. From spring throughout fall, it flourished with life. This priceless land had a variety of animals and plants that fed them. The short summer season made it impossible to cultivate the land. Unable to cultivate the land, the Yup'ik were solely hunters, fishers, and gatherers.

The Yup'ik elders are the educators in their region. The region was unforgiving and extremely dangerous, so the elders' sole responsibility was to educate their people. It was most critical to use the knowledge gained from the elders to survive the harshest winters and the common starvation that sometimes plague the people.

Like most of the indigenous cultures throughout the world, the Yup'ik had shamans. Shamans had their own special roles and they could be either female or male. To cure the people, most shamans were healers who were experts in medicinal plants. They had the ability to heal their patients with their touch. Some believed that shamans possessed supernatural powers. The shaman's reputation depended on how they treated the people. Most shamans treated their people very well, while some took advantage of them. Depending on what shamans did, they left their mark wherever they went and whomever they touched.

Male and female roles were varied and divided in the villages. The males hunted, gathered, and protected their people. The females also hunted, gathered and took care of their children. The women brought the men and the boys' food to the *qasgiq* and cared for their clothing. Both genders greatly depended on one another to live.

Most precious to the Yup'ik people were the children. Believing in reincarnation, names were given to a newborn of a person who had recently died. When boys reached a certain age, they moved out to the qasgiq and learned from the men. The girls were left with their mothers or with other women to learn. The children were taught the correct way to live and behave in their world.

The children were the lights of their world and like the shining stars above them, some faded and some touched them. Their light had to be strong, so the people protected them closely and trained them very hard. Spread the light and anyone could see the beautiful magnificent land they called harsh.

In the center of every Yup'ik village was the center of their universe, also called the *qasgiq* (communal men's house). The qasgiq was basically made from wood, grass, tundra and clay, gathered from the surrounding area. The qasgiq was partly dug down under the ground to keep the wind from blowing inside. The qasgiq was an important piece of the Yup'ik world and it was used in many ways.

The qasgiq was a community center for all the members of that village to gather and to hear the news. It was also a place for men and boys to learn the ways of Yup'ik life. It held great feasts and many ceremonial deaths or weddings. The qasgiq was a multipurpose home and it was even used for steam bathing.

To get inside the qasgiq, the people had to crawl in. Either a grass mat or fur hide was used as a door. Once inside the qasgiq, there was enough space for about fifty people or more. The floor was made of wood planks and grass. All around the side of the qasgiq were benches, which also became sleeping areas for men and boys.

The fireplace was located in the middle of the qasgiq. Above the fireplace was a window and it was made of animal guts. The window could be opened for the smoke to go out or closed during the day for the people to have light to see. Hanging on the ceiling were the traps and tools they used. To see at night, the clay lamps with oil were lit.

Circling around the center of their universe were individual sod houses. Much like the qasgiq, the semisubterranean sod houses were also made of materials from the surrounding areas. These homes were typically for families and for women and children to live in. The women cooked meals, mended furs, sewed parkas, and maklaks (fur shoes) in these homes.

To tell the stories, the Yup'ik danced and sang to the people. Their circular animal skin drums and their ancient songs told them the stories of their past, how they lived and who they were. Many such stories would be told this way and this was one of them.

DANCE FEST

It was wintertime and the snow was slowly falling all around the area. The full moon was out and the weather was freezing. On this night, two people were walking toward the desolate Yup'ik village called Tulukar. One was a boy and the other was a man. As the boy and the man were getting closer to the village, every step they took broke the snow crust that just hardened this night.

By the Tulukar qasgiq, four warriors were guarding the entranceway from any unwanted people. As they stood guard, they began hearing the crackling noise from the human footsteps. The warriors pinpointed the noise and saw two people coming in this late. As ordered, they got their weapons ready and stopped them.

The Tulukar qasgiq was filled with many people. They were celebrating their catches from the summer and fall. The festival's purpose was to bring the people together and to honor the fish and game that fed them. They believed that the animals had spirits and if they didn't respect the animals, the animal spirits wouldn't freely give themselves to them and they would face starvation.

For three days now, the people were dancing and singing the ancient rituals. The dancing and singing were their heart and soul. It was a time of peace that the people enjoyed for many, many years. Giving thanks to the animal spirits, the people danced in great numbers.

In this last day of their great feast, eight elders, five men and three women, were sitting in the back of the qasgiq. Surrounding the elders were ten warriors and they were there to protect the people, especially the elders. This big gathering attracted many uninvited guests, so the elders had also placed four guards outside to stop them.

As the people danced and rejoiced, one of the clay lamps that lit the qasgiq fell down and broke into pieces. The people closest to the shattered lamp quickly turned it off and cleaned up the mess. For many people, the clay lamp was just an object, but to some people it was more than that.

One male elder noticed the clay lamp that had fallen and broken into pieces. Knowing what the sign meant, the elder muttered to his fellow elders, "The lamp fell and broke into pieces; something bad is coming our way."

The elders knew they were well protected, so they looked at each other and waited patiently. Patience was one of their keys for survival and so they waited. Sometimes their people patiently waited for days for their catch. Their winter was cold, long, and dark. The never-ending winter darkness stressed most of their people. So patience is what they had learned to endure all their lives.

As the festival was about to end, Patu and a young boy showed up in the qasgiq. Knowing that Patu was a great shaman; everyone in the qasgiq ceased what they were doing and quickly sat down to the side. As Patu's presence was known, the elders looked at each other, but said nothing. Something bad had entered the qasgiq and the elders knew it was Patu.

Showing great concern, one elderly woman did not want the kids to see what this shaman could do, so she nicely told them to go out. Knowing the shaman's reputation, whoever was afraid of this shaman went out with the kids. Those who were left in the qasgiq began to focus on Patu.

The shaman Patu arrived from the sea they say. When the Yup'ik first saw Patu, he was wearing a parka and pants made of loon feathers. It was never known where exactly he came from, but from a land unknown to the people.

Nobody liked Patu and nobody wanted him, so he never seemed to care what he looked like. Patu was chubby and his small beady eyes were always puffed up from giggling a lot. His face was brown, wrinkled, and leathery looking. His hair was dark black and long, and it always looked a mess. Like his hair, his mustache and beard grew unevenly.

Patu was a healer and a good one too. With his touch, he cured the sick, mended their torn muscles or their broken bones. He deceived the people's eyes, foretold the future, and ritualized to multiply the catches.

This shaman was powerful and everyone knew it. The most powerful shamans could kill people in their sleep and Patu was one of them. In people's dreams, some say, he came in forms of animals. Violating people's dreams and scaring them, he wasn't liked very much.

Like the rest of his kind, Patu went from village to village to help or taunt the Yup'ik. The shaman traded anything for his services. This was his way of living with the people, but soon the people started dying or getting very sick when Patu showed up. Knowing that he was not helping them, the people didn't want him around the village anymore. His presence was like a curse and more of an annoyance to the people. Then this day, for some reason, he decided to pay a visit to them.

In the middle of the qasgiq, with his face looking down, Patu began to smile at himself. He reached up with his right hand and covered his mouth. Covering his mouth, he started giggling to himself. His devilish giggle always made the people very uncomfortable and he knew it.

Patu's roughed-up loon parka seemed old and dirty as he started wiping his hands on it like a long-lost pet. Without saying anything, he took off his loon parka and gave it to the young boy, who was his student.

Patu's student never seemed to smile at anyone. The boy, who seemed about ten years old, was disturbingly dirty and it looked like he hadn't washed himself for months. He was wearing a muskrat parka and pants and his garments showed the signs of wear and tear. He didn't seem to be well fed, because his eyes were deep and dark in color. Patu probably beat him up a lot, because the little boy's cheek was bruised and darkened.

This sorry-looking student was taken when he was very young. His parents were brilliantly smart, but he was sick a lot and needed a lot of care. Noticing the kid was strong-minded, Patu had taken him under his care and trained him.

As Patu gave his parka to his student, the young student grabbed it and went over to the entrance of the qasgiq. At the entrance, to keep the wind from blowing in, a grass woven mat was hung. When the young student reached the entrance, he removed the grass woven mat and replaced it with Patu's parka.

To protect the shaman, the changing of the mat was done to shield off other unwanted shamans who tried to get in. Patu knew when he summoned his spirit, other shamans would want a taste of it. So his parka was enchanted to stop them from entering.

After replacing the grass woven mat, the shaman's student gazed at the people and he finally spoke up, "No one leaves or enters the qasgiq."

After the young student warned the people, he took out a stone knife from his parka and placed it down by the entranceway. After placing the stone knife, the student sat down and focused on Patu.

The elders' council was unusually nervous at the shaman's presence. The uneasiness of elders was felt by the shaman. Feeling the fear, Patu opened his eyes wide and gazed at the people. The elders noticed his awkward-looking eyes and they immediately shied away from him.

When everyone settled down, an elder by the name of Urraq began to speak to the shaman. "Patu, what brings you here? Tell us what news we need to hear so badly?" asked Urraq.

Without answering Urraq, when Patu heard his name being called upon, he began to dance and sing. To get into his trance and to call upon his spirits or demons, this shaman danced and sang to the people. This was his way to summon his demon, who was beyond this realm.

When Patu's dancing and chanting began, without warning, his student flew off from the entrance-way and he landed on his back. At the unexpected loud thud, everyone in the qasgiq was startled and they immediately focused upon the student.

On the floor, the student realized that he got pushed and he quickly got up and yelled at his master, "Patu, someone's trying to get in!"

When the boy yelled out, the rest of the people started getting nervous. Their eyes focused on the qasgiq's entrance-way, but no one was there and no one came in. Suddenly, Patu's parka started moving violently and a loud flickering noise was heard from it, but the wind didn't seem to blow in. As the noise got worse, coming from the entrance-way, everyone heard a woman's voice seemingly trying to enter the qasgiq.

"Aah! Open up and let me in!" the woman cried out from behind Patu's parka.

Hearing the womanly voice, Patu ran over to his parka and grabbed the stone knife and poked his parka once. After poking his parka, the uninvited guest ceased to try to enter for a brief moment.

Grinning, Patu looked back at the boy and shouted, "Another shaman!"

The shaman or whoever was behind Patu's parka started to scream again, "Aaaah! Ah!"

Knowing what to do, the student ran over to one of the warriors and asked him to give up his weapon. The warrior looked at the elders and when one of the elders nodded to him, the warrior surrendered his weapon. The boy grabbed the spear and ran over to Patu and gave it to him. At the entrance, Patu took hold of the spear and raised it up. He was now ready to strike and cleared his throat. His student backed off to see what would happen next.

Pointing the spear at his parka, Patu shouted out, "Next time, I'm going to strike you to death if you try that again!"

When Patu warned the intruder, the intruder ceased suddenly and got very quiet. Satisfied with the result and with a big grin on his face, Patu relaxed and he slowly backed off from the entrance. Whatever it was, behind Patu's parka, seemed to be gone...for now.

After the entranceway incident, Patu threw down the spear and went back to the middle of the qasgiq. He had a couple of tattoos on his face and on his back. The tattoos were made of lines and shapes that people didn't understand. His back was scratched and some of his scratches were still bleeding. The scratches on his back, they would say, were made by his demon that he summoned so much.

Then showing the motions of the earth, wind, and fire, Patu began to dance and chant again. He started off dancing slowly by turning his whole body around and showing all his tattoos to the people. His strange chanting was a language these people didn't understand. It was said that his chants were really old and only he knew what they meant.

When the curious people tried to figuring out what the tattoos were, Patu would turn and move, going in circles, and leave them wondering what they were. What the people didn't know was that one of Patu's tattoos was a portal to open up the middle world.

As Patu was chanting and dancing, he suddenly yelled out, "Drums, where are my drummers!"

Hearing Patu's request, the people closest to the drums picked them up and began beating. At first, the beats were slow and then Patu slowly quickened his dance. The drummers followed his rhythm and they started to hum and sing.

When everyone's heart began to flow with the rhythm of the drums, Patu started summoning the spirits. He quickened his dance and the whole qasgiq cooled down drastically. The hot and steamy qasgiq was cooling and the people could now see the clouds forming on their breaths.

When the air cooled down, some people in the qasgiq started going in a trance-like state of mind. Unable to hold it back, the possessed people began to scream uncontrollably. When the possessed people got ecstatic, the others who were not possessed quickly took hold of them and tried to calm them down.

The elders and the warriors watched the frenzied people in the qasgiq. The elders had to stay focused, good spirits or bad; they didn't like to mess with them. No shaman was to be trusted, especially Patu. They had to keep calm and they didn't want to let down their guard at the moment or their people might die.

The singing suddenly stopped when Patu yelled at them, "Tie me up! Tie both of my arms and legs!"

After yelling at the people, Patu went down on his belly and started growling softly at first, but then his growling got louder and louder. His mouth was now beginning to foam as his breathing got erratic. When the people didn't budge at his orders, he screamed again, "You better tie me up into a ball or you will all die!"

Hearing the word *die*, the men closest to Patu quickly grabbed some ropes and tied him tight. Patu's growling got worse and worse until his eyes got strained and became bloodshot red. After tying up this shaman, the men backed off and sat down again.

On his belly now, Patu's ropes around him began to break from his frantic movements. Seeing the ropes shearing, without warning one of the men jumped out and grabbed Patu on top of him. As soon as he touched Patu, the man buckled down and fell off him. The other men and women were shocked to see this and gasped. Out of the crowd, one of this man's friends grabbed the limp man to remove him, but he too stopped in his tracks and fell down beside him.

The two collapsed men weren't moving or breathing as the shaman kept growling and twitching violently. The frightened people in the qasgiq closest to the shaman backed off as far as possible from him. The people were thinking that if they touched the shaman, they too might get the same fate as the two men on the floor.

The elders and the warriors had to take caution after what they had witnessed. One of the elders nodded his head to the warriors and they picked up their spears. All the warriors then pointed their spears at Patu. One warrior, with his spear ready, slowly walked toward the shaman and stopped. The bold warrior just looked at the shaman and waited for the elders' orders to kill him. Finally, such an order came to him. "If the ropes break, kill him!" demanded one of the elders.

Patu was still on the ground and heard the elder's threat and got mad at them. He gazed out with his bloodshot eyes and yelled at them, "I see you all! You're all going to die!"

After yelling at the people, Patu started calming down. His head was face first on the floor and he was now breathing heavily. The horrified people, who were holding their breaths, began sighing in relief when Patu calmed down. The ropes still held the shaman, but with more of his fits, the ropes could get loose and a lot of people would possibly die.

Patu finally gasped to breathe and calmed down. With his forehead on the floor, he was now groaning in pain and his eyes were still shut. His mouth was still foaming heavily and the dirt from the floor was now collecting over the shaman's face.

Finally, Patu came around and seemed to get his senses together. He opened his eyes and turned his head to face the elders. His eyes were normal white again. Gazing around at his surroundings, Patu noticed the two men beside him. He raised his head slowly and pleaded to the elders, "Elders, let me loose, I got what I needed!"

Gaining more consciousness, Patu studied the two lifeless people beside him. The two men didn't seem to be breathing and they looked dead. He knew what to do, but right now he was too exhausted; yet he had to react to save them and time was of the essence.

After taking a deep breath, Patu shouted again, "Untie me now, if you want these two to live!"

Patu didn't care if these two died, but he was with the elders, warriors and everyone else who was watching him. He needed to gain the trust of these Yup'ik, so he could get anything he wanted from them. He had no sympathy for these people whatsoever. *Fools who dare to touch me should die!* Patu thought as he disgustedly looked at the two lifeless men beside him.

One male elder, closest to Patu, took out his stone knife and carefully cut the ropes. After freeing Patu, the elder backed off and sat down again. This elder, fearing that he might have touched the shaman, looked at his hands carefully. Feeling nothing, he muttered to his fellow elders, "I'm good, I'm OK."

Freed from the ropes, Patu immediately stood up and took out a feather from his pants. Holding the feather, he raised the feather up and quickly showed it to the people. After showing the feather, he placed it on one of the lifeless men's mouth. After placing the feather on the man's mouth, with his fist Patu pounded the man's chest twice. On the second try, the helpless man began to spit out blood and started to breathe again.

With the same results, Patu revived the other limp man beside him. Both of the men were now on their knees coughing and coughing until there was no more blood to be seen. When the men came to, Patu told them that they shouldn't eat any feathered birds for a year or they would die. One of the men who got choked that day, tested Patu's warning and choked himself to death on bird soup. When the people checked what choked him, the man's mouth was filled with blood and feathers.

Everyone in the qasgiq was uneasy from the current events, but sighed in relief when the two limp men began to move around. The people were awed to see what had happened to the two men and how Patu saved them. After saving the men and still on his knees, Patu told the elders that he needed to talk to them alone.

ELDERS ALONE

After saving the two men, Patu stood up and gazed at the terrified people and started to giggle again. The tension was high with these people and he could feel it and loved it. After feeling the fear in the air, Patu motioned his student for his loon parka.

Getting orders from his master, the student got up and grabbed the shaman's parka and brought it to his master. As the boy gave Patu his parka, for no reason Patu pushed the little boy off and the boy hit the floor hard. On the floor and grimacing in pain, the little boy just lay there for a while. He realized that he got pushed down and when he didn't get hit again, the boy shook it off. He slowly got up and sat down beside his master.

The little boy was always getting hit by his master and he was used to it. Most kids would probably have cried if they got shoved like that. This little boy just sat there like nothing happened to him. This was nothing compared to what Patu would do when they were alone.

In the qasgiq, the people gathered themselves and began to move around. Some people looked at the boy and felt sorry for him. This was no way to treat a boy and they tried their best not to show any emotions for him, fearing that Patu would notice it.

"You all heard this shaman, everyone out, except the elders and the men!" Urraq ordered his people.

Getting their orders, the rest of the women started moving out of the qasgiq. As people were heading out of the qasgiq, they smiled at the little boy and tried to show him their comfort and care.

The little boy just looked at the floor and let everyone pass him. If he looked at these caring people, Patu would notice and he would get a beating later. It didn't take long for the women to get out of the qasgiq. To the little boy, his people showed too much love and he wasn't used to it. It was very uncomfortable for him to receive such love.

When the ladies went out, the shaman began to chant again. As Patu chanted, the room was getting colder and colder again. This time, Patu's chants were powerful, because all the fire from the lamps went out. For a brief moment, there was total darkness in the qasgiq and then the lamps lit up again.

When the lamps lit up, everyone's eyes got blurred for a second. People started looking around to see if everything was still there. Something was unusually different in the qasgiq. Something seemed to be out of place. They all looked at Patu and focused on him.

Patu never moved, but this time, he was wearing a mask made of wood. No one had seen him or his student carrying the mask in. Patu's mask looked like a loon with two arrowheads on it. The masks he wore were always the same, but when they concentrated on it, they could see what they were made of.

When the shamans danced with masks, the mask revealed either flying birds, moving animals, or swimming fish. Most often, the mask told a story with the motions. On the mask, a person could tell what was to come by seeing what they had on them.

Last time, when Patu danced for the people, a lot of people had noticed Patu's mask had whitefish on it. When spring came, the people started catching a lot of whitefish. This time, Patu's mask was surprisingly different, because it had two arrowheads on it. The arrowheads were the sign of hunting, but hunting what?

The first dance was to call upon his demon. The next dance, with the mask, was to foretell the future. Wearing a mask now, Patu snarled at them and shook his head violently and stopped. Snarling and violently shaking his head at the people worked for him, because he could feel the fear in them again. When Patu stopped shaking his head, he screamed, "My drummers!"

When Patu ordered for his drummers, the elders looked at each other and one of them said, "Watch closely and don't let down your guard. This is going to get interesting."

The drummers started beating again and they started off slowly until they began to beat as one. Once the smooth sound of the drums began beating like their hearts, the drummers steadied and let it flow.

In the middle of the qasgiq, Patu started chanting again. With his feet this time, Patu started pounding the floor harder and harder, seemingly trying to open up a portal. Every step he took, the drums followed him. When Patu picked up his pace, the people started hearing eerie shrilling sounds from the shaman's direction. The drummers, hearing the shrilling sound, began beating loudly. Then all of a sudden, the people heard a loud *CRACK!* Hearing that, Patu and the drummers automatically ceased what they were doing and everything got super quiet.

Patu was now looking up at the ceiling. Then, very slowly, he started looking around his surroundings for a while. He seemed to get scared and went on his knees. On his knees, he started crawling in circles and looked around.

The people were thinking that Patu was looking into the future, but they weren't sure. When Patu was looking around the qasgiq, people started hearing the shrilling sounds again. The shrilling noise was quite faint and it slowly dissipated and stopped. When the shrilling ceased, Patu got up and took off his mask and threw it in the fireplace, where it slowly burned.

After Patu threw his mask away, his face was sweating heavily and he was trying to catch his breath. He hunched down on both of his hands and knees and looked at the people. He smiled at them and shook his head no. Looking into the future took a lot of his energy away.

The people started thinking of what just had happened and what they had just seen and heard. The elders were thinking about the two arrowheads on Patu's mask. They began deliberating on this issue. Most of the time they used arrowheads to hunt big game. The shrilling noises were too faint to tell and it could be anything to them.

As the elders tried to get a meaning of it all, Patu was still gasping for his breath and started coughing. Getting his energy back, he finally relaxed and started giggling again. Hearing Patu's giggle, the elders stopped talking and looked at the shaman.

After getting everyone's undying attention, Patu said to them, "What will you give me, if I tell you what wars are to come in the future?"

Hearing what Patu had to say to them, the elders thought about it for a while. Living in peace was a wonderful thing for them. War was the last thing on their minds and it should be avoided at all costs. Now they knew the shrilling voices were of men, men crying in pain. War brought a whole lot of pain to them.

War was the word that everyone there didn't like to hear, Urraq had to respond, "Wars, what wars? We live in peace, what do you want in return for your information?"

Patu looked at Urraq and started to laugh at him and cynically replied, "You all saw what is to come and what makes you think I need anything from you?" Patu pointed at every elder there and continued, "I take what I need and if anyone doesn't agree with me, I kill them. I don't even need to fight to kill them. You've seen what happened to the two men who tried to bind me. If I need anything anytime, you have to obey me or people will die!"

The elders looked at each other and got nervous at the threat, but one bold elder didn't flinch. The elder, with his calm tone, made the other nervous elders relax. That was Urraq and he responded to Patu, "I don't mean to be rude, but we can't let you kill or torment a person as you please. We depend on one another for living, because that is who we are and we can live without you. We, Yup'ik, are capable of doing anything."

Urraq was tired of this shaman and his threats. Patu wasn't as important as he thought he was. What he had to say was to protect his people and he wanted to protect them from this high-caliber, evil shaman.

Patu was trying to get his free meal from these people, but he got crushed by Urraq's words. His eyes winced and looked at Urraq. He could see himself stabbing Urraq a couple of times and killing him. His wishful thinking wasn't going to happen as he looked around the room.

These two men started staring at each other for a while and neither ever blinked. Patience had never been Patu's strength and his face began turning red with anger. He was mad at Urraq and everyone could tell. As these two people stared each other down, the other elders began to speak simultaneously on the current matter. The topic of war made everyone uneasy and this topic was taken seriously.

Urraq was calm and not threatened by Patu's threat as he gazed at him. Being the second oldest of the council, Urraq had lived too long and nothing scared him these days. He had lost most of his relatives in the past and Patu had probably taken some of them. He never flinched at his threat and never even broke a sweat.

Way back in the qasgiq, the oldest of the elders by the name of Qaluksuk, noticed Patu was staring down at one of his elders. In his final days, he wasn't about to lose any of his people. So the old man, with his worn-out body, struggled up to his feet. The rest of the elders noticed Qaluksuk standing up, so they moved out of the way and let him face the shaman. The respect of the eldest was crucial…disrespect the eldest of this world and you would get stepped on.

When the elders moved away, Qaluksuk yelled out to the shaman, "War! Long ago our ancestors killed everything from insects to people, but you killed more people than war!" Qaluksuk was furious and the oldest of the elders didn't take things lightly. He wasn't going to let this shaman scare any of his people. He knew they were scared, except one of his men. The old man was mad at their weakness and he showed it to them. Qaluksuk paused for a bit and then he raised his arms and pointed at Patu and continued, "You! Of all people! Patu! We don't need your help! You're nothing!"

When Qaluksuk stopped speaking, the free meal just evaporated from the shaman's mind. The power Patu had over these people was no more and he knew it. He knew what they were going to do next. Looking at the old man and hearing his tone of voice, he was in trouble.

Qaluksuk was very old and he had lots of gray hair. Like every other elder in the village, his face was wrinkled and brown. He had been born in the tiny village of Paimiut. In his young days, Qaluksuk's old village had been hit by famine and everyone in that village died, except for him.

In order for Qaluksuk to survive, his mother had cut up dry fish into little pieces. She told him to take one piece a day until spring came. She wanted him to slowly protract the outer skin's fat of the dried fish and have it last all day. Then when spring came and the rain began to fall, he was told to drink the water from the puddles. Then he should wait for the people to pass from upriver. If one of them asked him to come with them he should go.

After giving their last request, Qaluksuk's parents lay down on their bed. Then a couple of days later, Qaluksuk's parents had stopped moving and starved to death. To see such a dreadful sight was hard for Qaluksuk, especially at the young age of seven. For him to survive seemed bleak, but he kept his mother's words and followed them.

Qaluksuk spent the long days and nights all alone. The only thing that kept him alert was someone telling him to stay strong and never to give up. He knew everyone in that village was dead, because he had gone to check on them. Sometimes, he could hear people talking and when he went on to check on them, no one was there. After multiple times of hearing people, he stopped listening to them. Qaluksuk knew he was living with the dead and he was the last one left alive.

When spring came and the ice melted away, thankfully, a kayak appeared from up river. When Qaluksuk saw the kayak, he blinked his eyes a couple of times to see if he wasn't imagining it. Sometimes when he saw people, he would happily get up to see them. Strangely, as he approached these people, they would disappear from in front of him. Seeing the kayak, he blinked his eyes couple of times and the kayak was still coming toward him. When the kayak finally beached, he looked up at the sky and then back at the kayak again. The kayak seemed to be real and it was still there. Looking closely at the people, he noticed it was his relatives! Never knowing they were real, he didn't get excited. Like the rest of his encounters, the people might just disappear and leave him.

Coming from upriver, his relatives finally landed at Qaluksuk's village. Weak and unable to stand up very well, Qaluksuk slowly etched his way down to the kayak. The man, in his late twenties, got out of his kayak to meet him. This man was Qaluksuk's relative!

The man walked over to Qaluksuk and stood beside him. The man then finally touched Qaluksuk's arm. When the man finally touched his arm, Qaluksuk felt weak and collapsed. To his relief, this man was real and he finally got touched by real human hands. The stress of living alone for a long time finally caught up to him. He lay down for a while to revive his energy. The touch of a human hand was very strong for him and he had not felt it in a long time.

His relative looked down at him and sat down beside Qaluksuk. Qaluksuk tried to give this man a smile, but he had no energy for it. Finally, the man asked Qaluksuk if anyone was around. Qaluksuk told him that everyone was dead, except for him.

Hearing the dreadful news, his relative checked the sod houses, to see if he had eaten the people, but Qaluksuk had never touched anyone. After checking Qaluksuk's dead parents, to his disappointment, his relatives still left him for they were starving too.

Qaluksuk was hunching down as he watched his relative row downriver. He was hoping they would change their minds and return for him. His relative kept rowing and rowing farther away and eventually, they disappeared from his view. Still, he kept believing that they would show up to get him, but they never did.

Qaluksuk was getting weaker and weaker as the days passed. Still, he was drinking the water from the puddle, which was keeping him alive. After drinking a lot of water, his stomach started rejecting it. As Qaluksuk tried to drink the water, he would vomit it out. If he couldn't drink the water, Qaluksuk knew he would die for sure. So Qaluksuk gave up hope and waited.

Qaluksuk had been out of food for days when a young couple stopped by, but they were not his relatives. When the kayak beached, the man got out of his kayak, while his wife stayed behind. This man asked Qaluksuk the same questions as his relative. After Qaluksuk told the man what just had happened there, the man also checked the sod houses and when he saw the occupants were not eaten, the man trampled the sod houses and buried them as they were. After trampling the sod houses, the man headed back to his kayak.

Standing beside his kayak, the man said to his wife, "I like this little boy."

The man was impressed that this boy had lived this long. Usually, the whole village starved to death after a great famine like that.

The man looked at Qaluksuk and smiled at him and then said to his wife, "I want to keep him as my own."

Upon hearing those words, Qaluksuk closed his eyes and began to weep, but he didn't want to show it to the man. He had to be strong or this man might not take him. Qaluksuk wiped the tears from his eyes and tried not to show his weakness. The man noticed Qaluksuk's tears and went over to him. He then put his hands around him and said to him, "Hey, little hunter, you're going to be OK. It's OK to cry."

Without saying anything, his wife took out a dried fish and cut a little piece and gave it to Qaluksuk. After some quick small bites, Qaluksuk was asked to go in their kayak. Qaluksuk, without arguing, happily went with them.

Years later, Qaluksuk grew up and became a great hunter and gatherer. Then one day, one of the relatives who had left him for dead, told him that he should move in with them and where he was staying now were not his relatives. He looked at his relative and said nothing to him and stayed with the family who saved him.

After the ordeal around his area, Qaluksuk helped as many people as he could and became a well-known person. With his knowledge of what he'd been through, Qaluksuk was well respected and honored. Everyone who passed through Tulukar loved to see the great Qaluksuk.

In the qasgiq, the elders and the men had never heard Qaluksuk speak so loud before. When the other elders thought Qaluksuk had stopped speaking, they began debating to see if they should obey Patu or not. Patu was a great shaman and the elders didn't want anything bad to happen to them or even to their families.

Irritated by his people's ranting, Qaluksuk raised his arms and asked for his spear. Hearing Qaluksuk's request, the rest of the elders immediately stopped their quarrels and began focusing on Qaluksuk. Up until now, he hadn't asked for his spear for ages. When Qaluksuk asked for his spear, it usually meant that someone's going to die that day. The leader of the warriors quickly grabbed Qaluksuk's spear and gave it to him. Qaluksuk's spear was made of spruce tree, but blackened in color with an ivory (walrus tusk) tip.

The great Qaluksuk was now holding his spear. As Qaluksuk and Patu gazed at each other, everyone got quiet and nothing was heard. The rest of the warriors got their spears ready and waited for Qaluksuk's orders.

Fearfully, Patu started to chuckle and smiled at Qaluksuk. He knew what the spear meant to these people, so he began to speak. "The great Qaluksuk's spear…I didn't know you still had the strength to lift it. But before you make any decision, please do listen to me." The shaman had his arms open to let Qaluksuk know that he had no weapons of any sort. He was trying to let them know that he was harmless and small. Then with the nicest smile he can muster, Patu continued on and said, "The two men that tried to stop me are the two armies growing. One of the armies comes from a land unknown to this people. This threat will keep going along the coast and kill all the men they go against. The other army will come down from the great easterly mountains, also unknown to this people. They will also be killing the people they come across and they will come down this way and annihilate you all."

After Patu foretold the future wars, everyone was shocked. *Would* there be two wars? Everyone was thinking. *One war* was one thing, but two wars? A lot of people were going to die!

Patu and everyone in that qasgiq were surprised at what Qaluksuk had to say next. The old man didn't waste his time thinking about what he just heard from Patu and yelled at him, "I warned you last time not to kill people, but you and your mouth are threatening my people with future kills!" Qaluksuk then pointed his spear toward the warriors and then at Patu and continued, "Feed this one to the dogs!"

Even when Patu had just been sentenced to death, he looked around the qasgiq and started laughing. When he stopped laughing, he raised his arms and what he said next surprised some people. "Dogs?" he paused for a bit and continued, "I like dogs."

Urraq wasn't going to give the shaman the last word and said to him, "Patu, you just killed yourself," and then he gave the shaman a little smirk.

Getting orders from the great Qaluksuk, the armed warriors quickly approached Patu with caution. Knowing what Patu could do, they had to be extra careful with him. One of the warriors, by the name of Iriini, grabbed Patu's arm and he wasn't afraid of anyone or anything. He had seen a lot of things in his life and he didn't trust or like this shaman one bit.

Getting his arm grabbed, Patu felt insulted and whisked Iriini's hand away and swore at him, "Iriini, touch me and you die!"

When Patu whisked his hands away from Iriini, Iriini used his spear and hit Patu on the back. When the shaman got hit, he immediately fell down to the floor.

Patu's back was in pain and he immediately yelled out, "Aka . . . my back!" and he began to rub his back for comfort.

"Shut up, Patu! Get out now, before I kill you myself!" Iriini warned Patu as he looked down at him.

When the warriors took hold of Patu, the other men grabbed his student. The warriors had to make sure the little boy wouldn't do anything to them. As far as they knew, the little boy could do them harm too. When they grabbed him, the shaman's helper cried out, "Patu, don't leave me!"

Patu looked at the dirty little boy, but said nothing to him. The warriors pushed the little boy and told him to shut up. Patu was now surrounded by armed men and his student was useless. Iriini and another warrior were now holding Patu.

Patu looked at Iriini and said to him, "Like you said, I'll kill you myself, but wait…" He paused for a while and continued, "There will be a bee and this bee will sting you and then you'll die."

Threatened by his words, Iriini hit Patu again and the shaman fell down again. On the ground now, Patu groaned in pain and gritted his teeth. The warrior roughly grabbed him and stood him up again. After they got hold of him, they escorted Patu over to the entranceway and threw him down again.

By the entranceway, Iriini shouted out to the guards outside, "Whoever is guarding the entrance, Patu's coming out, take him!"

Patu went on his knees to crawl out of the qasgiq. When he was crawling out, he took something from his parka and ate it quickly. As he swallowed it, Patu started breathing heavily.

Iriini noticed Patu's erratic breathing and kicked him. Iriini didn't like this shaman and he was glad they had sentenced him to death. He told him to get out again and this time, Patu listened to him and crawled out.

Iriini knelt down and got ready to crawl out after Patu, but stopped for a moment. Iriini was taking in what Patu had just warned him about. *What about the bee sting?* Iriini wondered if it might be true. He shook it off and followed after the shaman. The threat was still in his mind, but it was wintertime and summer was a long ways to go. The bees were little and easy to kill. *The bee sting is nothing compared to my spear,* Iriini thought.

As Iriini was crawling out, he noticed that Patu wasn't in front of him as the shaman was supposed to be. He was thinking that Patu had gone out already and the men got a hold of him. *That shaman's dead.* Iriini's mind trailed off. This shaman had to be killed, and he started crawling after him.

Outside the qasgiq, the men heard that Patu was coming out and they were ordered to take him. So the warriors got their spears ready waited for him. No one wanted to touch a shaman, but they were ordered to take him, so the guards waited for him cautiously.

UNSUSPECTED

S tanding outside the qasgiq, the four guards were able to see the village outlines. The weather was still cold and the full moon was shining upon them. This night, the guards had gotten very edgy after hearing a lot of crying. What spooked them the most was, they heard a loud crack coming from the qasgiq. After that, the eerie shrilling sounds seemed to be everywhere. It didn't take long till they heard that Patu was coming out and they wanted them to take him.

Receiving orders to take Patu, the guards got their spears ready and waited for him. Then all of a sudden, a black dog jumped out of the qasgiq and looked at the guards. Surprised to see a dog, the warriors jumped back, because they were expecting Patu. The black dog just looked at them and ran away. In that unsuspected moment, the guards couldn't help but breathe out again. The warriors got their thoughts together and waited for Patu to come out. This night, nothing was normal and it was quite unusual for them.

As they waited for Patu, one of the warriors muttered out quietly, "Ruff," and upon hearing this, the rest began to chuckle at the sarcasm. They stopped chuckling when they heard someone coming out of the qasgiq.

Taking caution, one of the guards warned the rest, "Everyone be careful, this is a powerful shaman," and they tightened their grips and waited.

Coming out of the qasgiq, a man appeared wearing a parka that their men wore, but it wasn't Patu's loon parka as the guards expected it to be. Looking at the man and his parka, the warriors had to take caution, because this shaman was a trickster and they grabbed him.

As Iriini came out of the qasgiq, he got grabbed by the guards. Stunned that he got grabbed, he started punching, kicking, and screamed out at them, "What are you guys doing? It's me, Iriini, and where's Patu?"

The guards looked at each other and threw the screaming man down on the frozen ground. There was no way Patu could have passed them and they had to be very careful. They were ordered to take Patu when he came out, so the warriors weren't easily going to let go of him.

"Hey, it's me! Iriini! Let me go, and where's Patu?" Iriini screamed again

One of the warriors turned Iriini around and said, "They said Patu was coming out, but we saw a dog and then you!"

Still taking caution, the warriors kept their spears on Iriini, because he might be the shaman taking a different form. They weren't going to take any chances, especially with a shaman of this caliber.

Hearing the commotion outside, the other warriors from the qasgiq came out and checked the guards. They also carefully checked the person they were holding and it wasn't Patu. Knowing it wasn't the shaman, they ordered the guards to release him. The other men asked the guards what had happened and also asked which way the dog went. The dogs from the south end of the village started barking and the warriors pointed in that direction.

"Was that a dog? Did the shaman turn into a dog?" One of the warriors asked.

Standing still, the warriors began focusing on the barking dogs. None of the people outside that qasgiq breathed for a while. The dogs ceased barking and quieted down. The silence set in that area and nothing was heard.

When the dogs ceased barking, Iriini told his men to stand down and he went back inside the qasgiq and told the elders what just had happened. After reporting to the elders, he went back out and told the warriors to track the dog.

As ordered, the warriors followed the dog tracks all the way to the end of the village and stopped. At the end of the village, the warriors agreed that it was too late to track it. All they could do was think about what had happened.

"Did you see that dog?" One of the warriors said to anyone who was there.

"It was a dog," someone replied.

Surprised and confused, the warriors decided to head back to the qasgiq and report to the elders. Once inside the qasgiq, the guards explained what had happened and what they just witnessed.

Hearing the bizarre news, Qaluksuk ordered the men to stand down and prepare themselves to track down Patu the next morning. He also ordered everyone to stay in their homes, because the shaman was out there and no one was safe.

After a restless night, the following morning, three chosen trackers followed the dog tracks. The weather was cold, but it was decent enough to run. The trackers were expert hunters and they knew the area very well.

The trackers followed the dog tracks until the sun was in the middle. As the trackers investigated these particular tracks, the dog tracks rested and when it appeared to stand up, its tracks became human footprints. The human footprints then seemed to walk in circles and then somehow it turned into dog paws again. The dog tracks then started running off again.

The trackers had never seen such a thing before, so they got excited to chase it. Knowing if they caught it, they would have a good story to tell. This thing that they were chasing was very unusual and unheard. Amused at the tracks, the trackers kept on pursuing it. The dog tracks were running toward the south, following the trodden path trail that led up to the next campsite. The trackers ran all day and never came close to that thing. Whatever it was, it didn't seem to be human and it was moving fast.

When they stopped to rest, the leader looked at his men and told them that they were running out of daylight. The leader wanted to head back home for safety reasons. They had the weapons to kill it, but Patu was also good with weapons. Disappointed, one of the trackers was willing to chase it, because he felt they were getting close to the shaman. The leader did not want to take any chances, so he decided to head back home without the shaman.

The trackers marked Patu's last location with some twigs and they headed back to their village. On their way home, tired and hungry, the trackers halted and took out some dried smoked fish and started eating. All day, they'd had a lot of questions in their minds about what they were chasing and kept it to themselves. It was hard for them to go home empty-handed. Curious about what they were chasing, the trackers began to speak.

"What is he?" one of the hunters asked his companions.

"I don't know, but he is not human. The tracks are really strange and I've never seen tracks that change like that before," the other tracker said as he gorged his food down.

Without much to say, when they finished eating, the trackers got ready and took off toward home again. This time, the leader picked up his pace. It was getting dark, but like yesterday night, the full moon gave enough light for them to keep running.

As they followed their tracks back home, suddenly, in front of them they saw what looked like a man. Not knowing who or what it was, the tracking party stopped and sat down quickly. The trackers cautiously examined the figure in front of them and they slowly got their weapons ready and waited. This could be the shaman they were looking for!

Finally, after a while of examining the figure, they saw the figure moving toward them. For precaution, the trackers raised their bows and aimed at the figure. Before it got too close, the tracking leader yelled out, "Move and you're dead!"

The figure hastily sat down and stayed still. The air was quiet and they could not hear any movement that came from that area. After a brief uneasy moment, the figure finally responded, "I'm Cung! Our elders sent us to check on you!"

The tracking leader sighed in relief to hear their people and stood up. His other two trackers lowered their weapons and got up too. They were glad it wasn't Patu as they all breathed out in relief.

The relieved tracking leader had to yell back, "Cung! The ice just melted away when I heard your voice!"

Relieved that these were men from their village, the whole tracking party started chuckling and relaxed. They gladly walked over to Cung and sat down in a circle with him. As they sat down, the trackers told Cung and his men what they had seen. After a quick briefing, everyone got up and started running toward home again.

When the search party got closer to the village, the dogs began to bark at them. Everyone in Tulukar was up and anxiously waiting for news. When they entered the village, the three trackers were quickly escorted to the qasgiq.

"You guys catch that thing?" someone in the crowd asked them.

"What was it?" Someone in the crowd asked again and continued, "You guys kill him?"

Empty-handed, the disappointed trackers just shook their heads and went into the qasgiq. Inside, the three trackers knew they had to sit in the middle of the qasgiq to report. The people were eager to hear what they had seen and if they had killed Patu. The elders were already there and the shaman's student was bound to the side. In the middle of the qasgiq, the trackers sat in a straight line looking toward the elders. When the trackers settled down, the women immediately served them some meat.

"Eat and drink and replenish your energy. Report to us what you've seen," the elder said as the trackers received their meal.

Everyone there was now focused on the trackers. The tracking leader took a bite and after chewing and swallowing his meal, he looked around the room and gave them his fake smile. He could tell everyone was anxious to hear news, so without waiting to finish his meal, he gave them his report.

"I've never seen any tracks that change like that before. This thing is not human and it's something bad. We went south following the river that leads to the next campsites. The tracks were hard to find at some snowdrifts, but we were able to track it. The tracks turned back to human footprints as it seemed to rest. After it rested, it ran around and turned back into a dog and started running again," the leader said and he looked around, but no one spoke up. Hearing no questions for him, he started eating as fast as he could.

One of the trackers stopped chewing his food and swallowed his meal. The tracks they'd been chasing were just bothering him and he had to get it out. He looked at the elders and reported, "These are very strange tracks. I've never seen tracks like that before. I think we had a chance to catch him, but it was getting dark, so we decided to head back and that's when we met Cung and the other party you sent us."

When the trackers stopped reporting, the elders looked at each other and asked each other if anyone in the past had ever encountered such a thing. Someone in that qasgiq had to know something. If no one had ever heard such a thing, it was going to be interesting.

Disappointed that this thing wasn't caught and killed, one elderly woman spoke up, "Whatever it is, it's not human, and it shouldn't be human. I've only had some dreams about them, but nothing like this, not in real life. No human being can ever do that unless it is something else, something bad. No one can change forms and even the animals themselves can't do that."

The elderly woman thought about it for a while. She was hoping someone would agree with her. In the back of her mind, she remembered a lady with a tail who showed up at the festival one time, but the people had chased her off. She looked around the room and when no one spoke up, she slowly looked down. This lady with a tail was seen at some villages, but they had all chased her off, she thought, but then she shrugged it off and said nothing, because she had to see it to believe it.

No one in the qasgiq spoke for a while and no one responded. When the trackers finished their meal, they went to the side and sat down. Around the qasgiq, everyone was quiet, probably thinking if Patu was a human being or a dog. Then Urraq motioned to the bound student and ordered him to the middle of the qasgiq.

When they received the orders, the warriors shoved the shaman's helper to the middle of the qasgiq. Standing in the middle of the qasgiq, the scared little boy looked at the elders. When he was ordered to sit, he sat down and looked down at the floor. The little boy had too much respect to look into the elders' eyes.

The elders observed the scrawny little boy for a while and the interrogation began. "Did Patu ever teach you to kill us?" one concerned elder asked the little boy.

The boy looked at the elder and thought about the question and responded, "No, Patu just taught me how to chant and dance and also to sing to the animals, so the animals will come back to our area, but not killing human beings." The shaman's student paused for a second and continued, "One time, Patu sang a song to an otter that was in a water hole. The otter came out of its water hole and it showed no fear. The otter came up to him and then Patu clubbed it to death."

The shaman's helper had to be careful with his words, because his life was on the line. The elders and everyone in the village was jittery and he knew it. His shaman was powerful and he had once been told to pierce a spear into Patu's body. The spear went in one side and out the other. To his surprise, Patu never seemed to get hurt or even bleed from the spear. The shaman's student didn't want to say more than what he had to say or these people would kill him for sure.

Qaluksuk was listening to what he had to say. Looking at the little boy, he was reminded of himself when he was younger, all alone and scared. This little boy was no threat to him, but he had to ask.

"Hey little one, look at me," and when the boy looked at him, Qaluksuk continued, "Have you ever seen Patu change forms?"

The shaman's student just sat there for a while and thought about it. His master had never changed forms, but he knew he was powerful enough to do such a thing. The student cleared his throat and replied, "I don't know, I've never seen him change before. I've never really thought about it and he surprised me today on what he can do."

The elders had questioned the student enough and they weren't getting the answer they wanted from him. The elders ordered the shaman's student back to the corner. The elders began debating if this young man was dangerous to them or not. They ordered Patu's student to sleep in the qasgiq for a couple of days to see what happened to him. Why Patu had chosen this young boy was unknown. The young boy probably had the ability to change too. So, during his stay, this student was watched very closely.

The elders ordered the people of Tulukar to stay in their homes and to stay alert, for Patu might come back and kill some people. They also ordered the people not to mention his name, fearing that Patu might hear them when his name was spoken. Shamans tended to hear everything when people talked about them.

The days passed with no incidents and the weather was getting colder. The elders decided that Patu was gone for good and had left his trainee behind. Still edgy from the incident, some people said they saw Patu around, but they weren't sure if it was him or not. For a month that year, everyone was cautious to see anyone roaming around that area.

The shaman's helper was sent back to his parents, but still the boy was watched very carefully. When the little boy got older, he pierced a spear through his body and died.

Still edgy because of the incident, hearing that Patu might be lurking around, the elders ordered the warriors to visit the neighboring village of Nanvarnarlak. From there, they were to bring one of the elders. It was crucial for the Tulukar elders to talk to an elder from Nanvarnarlak.

This time, Iriini and three other warriors went out and headed toward Nanvarnarlak. There were a couple of small camps along their way and every time they stopped at the camps, Iriini told them about Patu. The occupants of the camps told the warriors that they'd seen the shaman, but he had left the same day as he came. The warriors moved on until they reached Nanvarnarlak.

NANVARNARLAK

Iriini and his warriors finally reached the village of Nanvarnarlak. Nanvarnarlak was located at south of Tulukar. These people lived by a big lake, which they had named after the village. The lake was about two miles wide and three miles long. Nanvarnarlak had whitefish and pike in the summertime. The never-ending fowl games that fed in that lake were seen from spring through fall.

At the edge of Nanvarnarlak village, Iriini and his warriors were met by warriors from Nanvarnarlak. After they confirmed who they were, the Nanvarnarlak warriors led Iriini and the rest of his group up to their qasgiq. In their qasgiq, Iriini and his warriors met with the elders and told them about Patu and what had happened in Tulukar.

One of the Nanvarnarlak elders, named Cuuk, talked to the Tulukar warriors and told them their side of the story. Cuuk was the eldest of the village and he had lived at Nanvarnarlak all his life.

When the warriors settled down, the food was prepared for them. Iriini and the warriors started eating some dried whitefish with *akutaq*. While they were eating, the people there were anxious to hear the news. Later on, the qasgiq was getting overcrowded, so the elders kindly told some of the people to go out. There was no need for fire in the qasgiq, because of the heat from the people was enough. When Tulukar warriors finished their meal, they began to get into their business.

After everyone settled down, Cuuk began his story: "Patu came by last month and stayed with us. When Patu arrived, the people started getting very sick. Being concerned for their people, the elders decided to invite two shamans to check what was going on in the village. Quuk was another shaman that was invited to the qasgiq."

Cuuk asked the Tulukar warriors if they knew about Quuk and when they didn't acknowledge, he told them the story of how Quuk had become a shaman.

Quuk was born in Nunaacuaq, a tiny village near Nanvarnarlak. He grew up normal at first, but when he was looking for mouse food, he changed his status for life.

Around Quuk's area, mouse food was gathered during fall, after the top ground froze. *In order to find the mouse food,* you have to look around on tundra or grassy areas. Usually, it could be found by locating their burrows. The mouse dropping were usual indicators that there was a food cache nearby. It could be found by pressing down your feet on the ground. The pressure from the stepping process would usually cave the ground down. Then if anyone thought they found it, they then tried their luck and dug it out. When digging in the area of the mouse food, some found nothing or just the nest of mice. Some people got lucky and found the mouse gold. Like a squirrel gathering nuts, mice gathered the edible plants and stored them underground for winter.

Depending on the family size of the mice, they gathered one to five pounds of edible plants. Once the finding were gathered, they took it home and the chef cleaned the edible plants with water. Depending on the chef, it could either be served raw or cooked and mixed with oil and berries. Once the dish was ready, it was usually gone before the chef got a taste of it.

On one of his favorite mouse food sites, Quuk got lucky and found mouse droppings. He looked around carefully and he eventually found a soft spot on the ground. With mouse gold in his mind, he started to dig out the dirt. When he opened one spot, thinking it was the cache, instead he saw different types of insects that were bunched up together. As the weather started to freeze over, to keep warm, insects tended to gather in one spot.

Looking at the insects, Quuk remembered what his elders told him about insects that gathered like that. He was told that when he finds a nest of insects, he had to put both of his hands on top of them and let them move around till the insects disappeared. This was done to get healing powers.

Curious about it, Quuk was about to place his hands on the nest of insects. He hesitated at first, but then he gathered himself and reached down and closed his eyes and shut them tight. His hands felt the insects move around and then his hands began to tingle. The tingling intensified and went throughout his body and stopped. When the tingling stopped, he opened his eyes and looked down.

The insects were now gone and nowhere to be seen. Quuk stood up and inspected his hands and wondered if it was true. He clinched his fists and felt the heat from his hands. His hands started to tingle again. Feeling the tingling, Quuk got scared and questioned himself, *what have I done?*

When Quuk got home, he told his mom about his encounter. After learning what Quuk had done, his parents decided to send him to the qasgiq. At the qasgiq, the elders gave him a small twig of a willow tree, which was broken in half. Then the elders told him to put his hands on it. As Quuk was ordered to, he reached out and grabbed the willow tree and covered the broken part of the twig. After a while, when he opened his hands, the broken willow tree was one again. After the elders had tested him, Quuk started healing people with his hands. From that day forth, the other shamans wanted to train Quuk, but since he was a good healer, the elders declined their requests.

After telling the story of Quuk the shaman, Cuuk continued, "Patu usually doesn't stay for long and since he was there for a while, they also invited Quuk. In the qasgiq, Patu and Quuk looked at each other and Patu stood up. Both of the shamans were edgy and they didn't seem to like each other. The elders ordered Patu to sit back down. As ordered, Patu sat back down and he didn't say anything. Someone asked Quuk why our people were getting sick, because they never had it as bad as since Patu arrived."

Cuuk reached down and took a rope that was lying down beside him and started wrapping it around his wrists. He seemed to be troubled as he was talking about this story. His face seemed nervous about something that had happened next.

Iriini noticed Cuuk's nervousness, so he reached over to his hand and said to him, "Go on Cuuk, and finish your story."

Cuuk's wrist was getting red from tightening the rope around it. He looked at Iriini's hand and relaxed a bit. He took a deep breath and continued, "Quuk stood up and checked the sick man that was there in the qasgiq with us. He inspected the sick man closely and seemed to notice something. He looked over to Patu and then he said to us, 'Look! Can you see the string on him?' We couldn't see what Quuk was talking about and told him no, but somehow, he reached down and took hold of the imaginary string and said again, 'Whoever is getting this man sick is attached to this string.' With that being said, Quuk started pulling the imaginary string back and forth. As he was pulling the imaginary string back and forth, Patu started rocking back and forth."

Without him thinking about it, Cuuk's body was moving back and forth and then he stopped. He looked at the warriors and shook his head no to them. Looking worried, Cuuk muttered out, "*Agaaa* (Oh no)."

Cuuk gathered himself and he took a deep breath again. He hesitated at first before he resumed the story. He remembered what happened next, but he still couldn't believe it, but he had to continue and it needed to be told. Cuuk looked around and then he continued, "When Quuk stopped pulling the imaginary string, he took out his knife and cut the imaginary rope. When he cut the imaginary rope, Patu stopped rocking and then he stood up. Patu got mad at Quuk and tried to stab him. Quuk moved away from his strike and then Patu ran out. At that instant, everyone got scared and jumped up in that qasgiq. We yelled to the warriors to stop Patu, but we were too late. The warriors outside saw a dog and they waited for a person. Patu got away turning into a dog and fled. The warriors followed Patu's tracks and he kept on changing too. They lost Patu when his tracks hit the Qusqukvak (Kuskokwim) River. We ceased tracking him from then on. After that incident, the sick man and the others got better."

Exhausted from telling the story, Cuuk finally relaxed. He was now rubbing his wrist and checking it out. The men, who were listening to his story, started looking around. Cuuk gave them his best smile, but he eventually stopped and looked down.

Iriini knew the village of Nanvarnarlak was in fear. Nothing like this had ever happened before and Patu was the first one. Looking at Cuuk, he knew it put a lot of fear in him.

ARUPAK AT TULUKAR

After Cuuk told the story of the familiar incident. Iriini and the warriors decided to head back to Tulukar. Iriini brought one elder from Nanvarnarlak to meet with the Tulukar elders. One of the elders, by the name of Arupak, was chosen to go with the warriors.

Arupak's life was very simple. He got along with everyone in his area. Like some of the elders, he preached to the kids to behave and to treat everyone as equal. He especially loved it when his people worked together. In his area, Arupak was known to bring tranquility to everyone. He was an important part of the elder council and that was why he was chosen to go.

In order for Arupak to travel to Tulukar, he had to use his dog team. Arupak was old and he needed the dogs to travel far. He decided to use a long sled, so the dogs would run slow and easy. He didn't like the small sled, because the dogs would find it light and they would run fast and make the bumps seem bigger than they were.

In this area, most of the Yup'ik families had three dogs and a person was lucky to have four to five dogs. When a person needed to go on a long run or gather wood, they had to use ten or more dogs. The extra dogs had to be collected from their relatives or friends. Using dogs, the burden of hauling heavy items was easier and efficient for them. So the dogs were also important part to the Yup'ik.

Iriini, Arupak and the rest of the group followed the same trail which they had used to go to Nanvarnarlak. The travelers stopped at campsites to eat and to replenish their strength and they continued until they reached their destination.

Once they reached Tulukar, Iriini escorted Arupak to the qasgiq. The elders of Tulukar were not at the qasgiq as expected, but it was daytime. The elders of that village were probably with their families.

At the qasgiq, Arupak was served cooked rabbit meat. The rabbit meat was much easier to chew for him. When Arupak finished eating, he decided to lie down to rest. It had been a long trip for his old body and he was glad he had traveled by a dog team. His old body couldn't handle the long runs anymore, but when he was called upon, he had to go for the good of his people.

Arupak was full and his eyes got tired and he started to relax. Looking around the qasgiq, he saw the fur beds and smiled at himself. His body needed the rest, so he slowly went over to one of the empty beds. The bed was soft and comfortable to the touch as he relaxed and lay down. The rabbit meal was doing its job as he started to feel warmer inside of him.

Lying down on the bed, Arupak decided to take a quick nap before he talked to the other elders. His back muscle had a knot that irritated him. He moved around and tried to find a sweet spot, but it was still uncomfortable. The bed was soft enough for him to stretch his back, but it didn't help much. Still feeling the knots on his muscle, Arupak muttered, "Where's the healers around here?" but no one responded.

Arupak closed his eyes to rest. He heard voices outside and they were coming in to the qasgiq. These voices were loud and obnoxious and he knew it was the elders. Being sent here and for the good of his people, Arupak smirked to himself and pretended to sleep. *The guest* of this qasgiq always made the elders mean, he said to himself. Even though his eyes were still shut, he could feel someone heading straight toward him. He kept his eyes closed and waited for this person.

As the elders of Tulukar began to come in, one elderly man walked straight to Arupak and said to him, "Who's this old man! This man is sleeping on my bed like a little baby! Does he not know its daytime? Can someone wake him up?"

As this man was talking about him, Arupak kept his eyes closed. He knew that if he made one little move, he would get mauled. He was a guest and he tried his best not to react to this man. Any small reaction would send him to his doom. Knowing the consequences, he kept his eyes closed and it was a huge mistake.

The man beside Arupak continued, "Someone shake him! This Nanvarnarlak man might be dead!"

This time, upon hearing the word *dead,* Arupak cautiously opened his eyes, looked up, and was disappointed as he said, "Oh, it's you. I'm surprised that you're alive and I thought you were dead. I heard that your woman killed you, because you couldn't make love anymore." And Arupak began to laugh hysterically at him.

The old men began to chuckle at being insulted by this man. Urraq had to retaliate and grabbed the old man and said to him, "Wait, hold on, don't get up, you old man! You might break your bones! Quickly, someone give me a stick, I think this little kid needs a spanking!"

Arupak couldn't stop laughing now as Urraq took a small stick and hit Arupak on his leg. Getting hit in the leg and still laughing, Arupak slowly got up and faced him.

"It's been a long time *iluq* (cousin) and it's good to hear your beautiful voice and to see you alive," Arupak said to him with kindness and tried to make peace with him.

Urraq was chuckling too as he squinted his eyes and looked at his cousin. It was a long time since they had seen each other. He was happy to see him still alive and breathing too. Urraq, trying to show kindness to his cousin, gave him a hug and said, "It is good to see you too, *iluq*."

Being cousins, Arupak and Urraq teased each other a lot. They were the last of the cousins. Without hesitation, Arupak then grabbed the stick from Urraq. When Urraq turned around and tried to run away, Arupak whipped his cousin's leg, *Whap!*

Being old and too slow, Urraq cried out, "Aka!" in pain as he got hit with the stick. Urraq began rubbing his stinging leg and turned around to face his cousin. Making peace wasn't going to be easy. Without warning, Urraq went over to Arupak and they grabbed each other. The old cousins were trying to wrestle, but all they could do was hold each other.

"OK, stop it! Stop it!" having enough, Arupak pleaded as he tried to control his laughing.

The people there were amused by these two. They knew that every time these two faced each other, they brightened the qasgiq with laughter and they teased each other relentlessly. The two cousins were always entertaining, because they tried to best each other.

Finally, everyone stopped laughing and sighed under their breaths. The two cousins were wiping off tears from laughing and finally calmed down. Making peace was always beautiful.

The rest of the elders started to come in and one by one they said their welcome to Arupak. As the rest of the elders slowly came in, one of them asked Arupak if he had eaten already. Arupak nodded yes to him.

Arupak looked around and everyone was in circles by now. One of the seats seemed empty. Fearing the worst, he asked for Qaluksuk, "Where is the owner of this seat?"

The elders looked at Arupak and said nothing. The elders seemed to be sad now when Arupak asked for their great elder. The elders stayed quiet and stayed put. Silence always made everyone nervous, even an elder like Arupak.

From the back of the qasgiq, a familiar figure slowly sat up. The figure of the man started throwing the fur blankets in every direction. Whoever it was, he was mad. Everyone was now concentrating on this figure of a man.

"Cross-eyed people can't see anything, even when they're just in front of them!" The figure said jokingly.

The figure was Qaluksuk and he slowly got to his feet and smiled at Arupak. Arupak's eyes squinted at Qaluksuk and smiled back at him.

"Ah, it's you, I am very happy now and you're back from the dead. Only the great Qaluksuk can do that," Arupak responded happily.

Everyone in that qasgiq started to chuckle again as these two greeted each other. The elders finally settled down and waited for their eldest. Qaluksuk slowly went over to his seat and sat down with them.

When everyone had greeted Arupak, the elders started getting into their business. They talked about Patu and what had happened when he took off on four legs. When they saw the shaman again, Patu was to be killed on sight. After the elders agreed on Patu, their final real business topic was war.

Arupak didn't know what had happened at their dance festival, so the elders told him about the wars to come, but they didn't know when the war would start. The elders had some small conflicts with other tribes, but not a full-blown war. Fearing their people would get annihilated, as soon as they were able, the elders decided to train the boys.

Most of the boys in the villages were young and were able to get trained. The elders decided to concentrate on the next boys and train them for war and nothing else.

The next day, after the meeting, the message was sent to all the Yupik in that area. It was crucial to start the training that following season. The parents of the boys were to be notified that the warriors would be collecting them next fall.

Sadly, the great Qaluksuk and the two teasing cousins, Arupak and Urraq, never got to see the kids train that fall.

PINK MICE

In the tiny village of *Atmaulluaq (Atmautluak),* three ten-year-old boys were killing mice and scaring little girls. They didn't know they would be training for war that year.

Atmaulluaq was a small village and it was called after a backpack that was found in that area. Atmaulluaq was a small tributary to the Pitmiktalik River. It was located just about five miles south of Nanvarnarlak. Most of the people from Atmautluak came from that surrounding area for the abundance of whitefish.

In this tiny village, there were seven sod houses and a qasgiq in the middle. All the homes were filled with families. It was a nice little village for the kids and everyone.

Without much responsibility in life, one of the three boys' minds started thinking. In one hand he was holding four baby pink mice that he'd found when he was scrounging around the area. The four little pink critters were squirming around his hands and without thinking about it, he threw them at an old woman.

Being hit by the unknown objects, the old woman looked around. One of the objects found its way to her neck. Whatever it was, the object started moving around her neck. She immediately reached up and grabbed it. The foreign object was mushy to the touch and she was thinking it just might be mud.

She looked around and spotted the boys and yelled at them, "Stop throwing mud around and get away from here!"

The boys just stood and stared at her. She was happy that they weren't throwing mud anymore, but listening to her. The mud, as she thought, began moving around and she quickly looked at it. Being old, her eyesight wasn't good enough and she brought it up to her face to inspect it. The old woman was now facing the unknown object and noticed what it was and she screamed, "Ah!" and jumped up!

The little boy who had thrown the pink little babies said to his friends, "I think they were lying to us when they said she was an elder, because I don't think the elders can jump that high."

Laughing hysterically, the three mischievous boys ran away from the scene and they all ended up by the riverbank. The boys with their endless energy were playing all day and they finally lay down to rest. The boys then looked at the beautiful blue sky and dreamed big. Life was just too plain easy and fun for them. At the end of the day, they knew they would get into trouble.

It was springtime and the river was flooding all over the area. The mice that lived in lower lands were escaping to the higher grounds.

One of the kids was Kaluk; his fathers name was Uam, and he was one of the three boys that could run faster than his friends. Like the rest of the troublemakers, he had black straight hair, brown eyes, a small nose, and a sharp-looking chin. He had a wicked sense of humor, quick-witted, and he was liked by many. Kaluk always made fun of people though and that got him beat up at times. In his family, he was the youngest of the boys, so the spoiled little brat tended to get away with anything.

The other culprit was Eli and his father's name was Akim. Eli was taller and bigger than the rest of the boys. He had features like the rest of the boys, but his chin was much wider. He was also the younger one of his family, but from his older brothers, he took his punches and hung in there. Other kids weren't lucky to have families that loved them and took care of them and he was one of those kids. Even though his brothers treated him aggressively, he was nice to his friends and his family. Being born first of the three, he was a leader type and every time his friends were with him, something always seemed to happen.

The last of the three boys was Tatu. He was the quiet one, but when Eli and Kaluk started these types of incidents, he was always right there in the middle of it. Tatu's hair was like the rest of the little kid's. He had brown eyes and a small chin. He was the younger one of the three and they grew up together, like brothers. He was the one who had thrown the pink baby mice at the poor old elderly woman.

After a long day of terrorizing everyone, Tatu was in trouble, as he was lectured by a woman. She was grilling him with the same words he had heard for so many years. "Be nice, treat everyone with respect, stay out of trouble, you watch yourself and it's entirely your fault. It wouldn't have happened if you hadn't been there," she would say to him.

This woman had straight black hair and her eyes were light brownish in color. When she glanced at the sun, her hair brightened in color. Her elegant hair was long and braided. Her rosy cheeks shone as she smiled. Her nose was straight and perfect. Tatu would say, "Aan!" every time he saw his mother.

Aan was originally from Tulukar and it had been arranged for her to be married to his dad, Aatiin. She moved to Atmaulluaq, to be with her husband. Like many mothers in this area, Aan was very beautiful.

Just after Tatu's parents had gotten married, he was born on the coldest day of the year. Everyone was surprised that he made through the harsh winter. His mother told him that he almost died a couple times, but somehow made it through.

Like the rest of the women in that area, Aan was skilled with furs and grass. She and the other women were always preparing meals for everyone. The women had never-ending chores and once they rested, they told stories to their children.

Tatu loved his mother very much, because her hands seemed to fix everything she touched. Her hands were small and delicate, but they were very strong. She fed him, clothed him, washed him, told him stories and comforted him with her hands.

His mother loved to tell him stories about the birds, the animals, and why they called them so. She would sing to him to keep him calm. He never seemed to be bored when he was with his mother.

Aan gave Tatu a simple rule to follow. His mother told him that he should listen to his elders, especially his grandpa and also his dad, for they would give him the tools of wisdom in life.

Like the rest of the people, his dad had black hair and brown eyes. Aatiin's mustache was rough and his body was rugged. He had unusually long arms and he told his son that his arms were made that way to give him a good hug and lift him higher than anyone in that area. Tatu's dad was a relentless hunter and a gatherer. Everyday, his dad was out hunting, either checking his black-fish traps or other traps that he set. Aatiin gathered wood for his family and Tatu's grandpa. If Aatiin got mad at Tatu, he knew he was in trouble. His dad never seemed to get mad at him for no reason. His dad's unending love and attention was good for him, so he tried his best to listen to him.

Like the changing weather they got around at area, Tatu and the other kids were very unpredictable, so everyone watched them closely. Every time Tatu broke the rules, he got scolded by an older people or his parents. After they scolded them, the parents would tell the kids that they weren't really scolding them, but they wanted them to learn and they were just correcting them.

As the water receded, the weather started to get warm and the birds started showing up. The tundra was covered in snow, but it was turning brown and small birds were now everywhere. The changing of the scenery was always nice after the long winter.

When the summer hit its peak and the people started catching a lot of fish, Aan came up to Tatu and talked to him. She knelt down in front of him and took hold of his arms. When Aan got Tatu's attention, she told him that he was to move out to grandpa's house to help him and his grandpa would gladly take him in.

After she talked to him, Tatu gazed into his mother's eyes that he had seen for so many years and knew she was serious. He didn't say anything at first, but he was saddened to hear that from her. He told her that he didn't want to go and live with his grandpa, but he wanted to stay with them.

Slowly, the tears from Tatu's eyes started flowing uncontrollably. He tried to hold the tears back, but he couldn't help it. She was sad too and he could tell, because as she tried to smile, tears were falling down her soft beautiful cheeks. "It was for the best," she said at the end.

After their little talk, her mother got up and gave him a bowl. The bowl was Tatu's and she had fed him with it for so many years and told him to take it with him. Tatu took his bowl in his hand and inspected it. The bowl was worn out and he had used it as long as he could remember. His bowl has had two red lines around the inside of it, but the lines were now gone. On the outside were designs of animals and fish. On the bottom of his bowl was a foot mark of a raven. The raven's foot mark was meant for good luck for him. As he ate some soup with it, he tried to finish it all, just to see the raven's feet.

When his dad caught whitefish or pike, Aan would feed him the biggest fish eggs, anything smaller was not for him to eat. She'd tell Tatu as she fed him, "May your catches multiply by many."

When it was time for Tatu to move out, his dad came up to him and told him that he would be OK and they would see him daily. Moving out of his house was a big step for him. Moving out was going to be hard and he loved the comfort of his home. Tatu felt a lot better if both of his parents would see him often.

He took the stuff he needed and slowly walked out the door. Once outside, it was nighttime and people were getting ready for bed. So he went over to his grandparents' sod house and stopped at his entranceway. He waited outside his grandpa's home for a while and then he got on his knees and crawled inside.

Inside his grandpa's home, Tatu noticed a fire burning in the middle of the house. His grandpa's home was very much like everyone's, but with an abundance of furs on the bed. His grandparents were sitting down on the homemade seat of fur. His grandma was sewing something and his grandpa was making what looked liked a black fish trap.

Tatu called his grandpa either, Apa or Apii (grandpa). He also called his grandma Maurluq or Maurlu (grandma) for short. His grandparents both called him Tut'ggar (grandson), instead of Tatu.

Apa was taller than anyone in that village. Everyone listened to him, because he had a deep low voice when he spoke. He had gray hair and his face was weathered and wrinkled. His long eyebrows were his trademarks in that village.

Tatu's grandpa was well known to predict the weather and his predictions were very accurate. When anyone wanted to know what the weather would be like, they would come to him and ask him for his prediction.

Apa wasn't the type to sit there and waste his life away. He was always moving around and doing something. Most of his time was spent in the qasgiq, either teaching other kids or making tools, traps, nets, arrows, or other equipment they used.

Maurluq was a master furrier, as were all the elderly women in that village. She also had gray hair and her best feature was her wonderful smile. When she smiled, she would seem to light up everything and everyone. The wrinkles in her face told people that she was a loving person.

Some days, the women gathered around his grandma and they mended clothes or make clothes for others and she would tell stories all day. Aan used to join her and keep her company and she learned a lot from her.

Maurlu also prepared food for the kids and she would order Tatu to send some food to the qasgiq. The kind elderly woman always seemed to be busy.

Standing by the entranceway, Tatu had to stay there until he had permission to move, so he waited patiently. He didn't move or even tried to make any noises as he waited. His grandparents noticed that he entered and smiled at him. Being noticed, Tatu still waited until he had the permission to proceed.

"Who's this by the entranceway?" his Apii asked him.

Apa and Maurlu were both looking at Tatu with curiosity. They knew who he was, but they had to ask. Their eyes were blurring as they got older. Kids to them seemed alike these days.

To see him better, Maurlu squinted and got very happy and said, "It's our Tut'ggar (grandson)! Come in and sit by us."

As Tatu was ordered to do, he went over to his grandma and sat by her.

Maurlu looked at Tatu and brushed his hair, "You look like your dad and you've grown so big now," she said to him and smiled.

All Tatu could do was smile back at her. His grandpa stopped what he was doing and looked at his grandson. "Oh! It's you! How's my little Tut'ggar doing these days?" his Apa asked him.

Tatu gave them his best smile and told them that his mother had told him to move in with them and help them out with the chores. Seeing that they were old and slow, Tatu knew he would be busy all the time. It wouldn't bother him a bit to help them out, because he knew that he would learn a lot from his grandpa and receive grandma's good cooking.

Hearing Tatu's reason, his Apa smiled at him for a while and he had to tell him the real reason why he was moving in with them. Apparently, his parents had never told him about the wars to come, so he had to tell him. "Yes, you're here to help us and learn. I also have to train you to become a warrior."

Hearing what his grandpa had to say to him, Tatu was very surprised to hear those words. *Me? Become a warrior?* Tatu thought, and he let it drain into his mind for a while. He had seen warriors before and they always seemed to be running and hunting. Deep inside of him, he was scared to hear that, because he was just a boy and the warriors were big, tall, and fast. He knew the warriors could run for a long time and they never seemed to tire. The warriors were good with their weapons and he was just starting to learn how to shoot the bow and arrow. *How would I become one, if I didn't kill anything bigger than mice or little birds?* Tatu was thinking to himself.

Tatu was still deep in his thoughts when his Apa brought him back to reality. "Hey, little hunter," he said to him.

Tatu looked at Apa's gray hair and his stern face and said to him, "Apii, I don't want to be a warrior. I want to stay here and help around the house." He tried to plead out with his grandpa of becoming a warrior.

His grandpa told him the reason why he had to train him. "I know you want to help us out and you will. Not too long ago, a shaman went to Tulukar and predicted the wars to come. All the elders agreed to train the boys. So I'm going to have to start training you."

His grandpa loved him, but he needed to train him hard. He wasn't thinking of right now, but he was thinking of the war. Eventually, he had to give him his first training, and that would shock him. Harsh as it might be, he had to train him hard.

"In order for your body to get used to the cold, you have to sleep on the porch. When you wake up early, you need to immediately go out and check the weather. Warriors always sleep outside," Apii said to him.

After chatting with Tatu, his grandpa told him to go out and sleep on the porch. It was hard for Apa, but he had to do what he had to do. The light of his world was his grandson and he loved him very much. The first day of training was always hard, especially sleeping on the porch at a young age.

Knowing that he had to go, Tatu slowly got up and faced them both. The fire now seemed farther and colder to him. He really didn't know what to think now and he was shocked to hear it from his grandfather.

Tatu's comforter, Maurlu, looked at him and said that he would be OK and that his father was trained the same way. She always comforted him when she spoke. She assured him that he was going to live through it. That was comfort enough for Tatu to hear, but it was going to be a rough night for him, a long cold night.

Tatu turned around and slowly walked out of there. He found himself on the porch and the porch was dark, cold, and creepy to him. The porch floor was just made of mud and wood planks. Tatu didn't like being alone. He stood there for a while and then he went to the corner and started crying silently. He had the urge to run to his parents' sod house and sleep on a nice piece of warm fur blanket, but he didn't want to disappoint his grandpa, so he stayed put. As soon as he stopped crying, his eyes started feeling heavy and he fell asleep.

Shivering, Tatu woke up in the middle of the night and his body was curled up into a ball. In the dark, he reached out and started looking for a blanket. He was hoping that he would be at his parents' home, but he remembered that he was still on the porch. Realizing where he was, Tatu moved closer to the entranceway and curled himself back into a ball to conserve the little warmth he had left. Why would Apii let me sleep at the porch? Tatu thought and then he closed his eyes and fell black to sleep.

The reason his grandpa let him sleep in the porch was clear when he woke up the next morning. That morning, his whole world turned upside down. The world of comfort was no more for him.

Whack! Something stung Tatu's back. He was still cold and he was still curled up in a ball. Whack! Another whip hit his legs and it stung more than the first strike.

His leg was still stinging and he thought, *I think it's just the cold*, but he was wrong. He reached over and felt around, but he didn't feel the cold. He thought he was dreaming, but then he got hit again, Whack*!*

After getting hit again, Tatu heard someone yelling, "Hurry up and get up!"

Another whip hit his back and he felt the sharp pain again, "Aka! (Ouch), that hurts!" Tatu cried out.

Tatu realized that it was his grandpa's voice and he was hitting him with something hard. He had his hands over his face now and looked around and saw his grandpa. His grandpa didn't seem too happy with him.

"Get up now!" Apii yelled again.

Getting yelled at, Tatu had to come back to reality, because he didn't know that he'd slept like dead mouse. Awake from the blows, he cleared his vision and looked at his Apa. His grandpa was holding a twig from a willow tree.

Tatu got his senses together and his Apa showed him the stick, he was hitting him with and said to him, "Every morning, I'm going to hit you with this twig. So you better be awake when I get out. If I swing at you, you better learn to move away from my blows. I want you to learn to avoid the blows, so it will be an instinct for you and your body. I want your body to move off from anything that tries to hit you. Now, get out there and check the weather!"

Afraid he would get hit again, Tatu walked out observantly. When he got outside, he checked the weather. The weather seemed warmer outside the porch. He looked at the sky and observed it. The sun was inching its way up. *It's going to be sunny*, Tatu thought, *sunny and warm!*

As days grew to months, the twigs his grandpa was holding got bigger and longer. It was hard at first for him to adjust, but then his body learned how to move before his grandpa hit him. When he was sound asleep, he instinctively felt the blows coming at him and he would move away from his blows. His Apii stopped hitting his grandson as the days passed by. He was learning fast and that impressed the old man. Every time his Apa went out with a stick, he was already up and out of the porch and predicting the weather.

To keep himself warm, Tatu started collecting grass and used them as mats and a blanket. Apa surprised him one time when he changed his timing. He had to adjust again and when he heard him crawling out to hit him, he moved away and his old man missed him. After missing Tatu with the stick, his grandpa told him that he was learning. Then the old man would go back into the comfort of his sod house. He didn't mind, he felt comfortable at the porch, thanks to the grass he had collected.

Sleeping in the cold wasn't miserable for Tatu anymore, but some days he felt lonely, when he thought about his parents. He saw his parents all the time, but not as much as he wanted to. Some days when he went out to check the weather, his dad came by and talked to him.

Apa had a lot of stories his parents had never told Tatu. His grandpa told him long stories and taught him the ways they lived and believed. One of the pieces of interesting information Tatu learned from his grandpa was the three great deaths that usually happened to his people.

The three great deaths were the epidemic, starvation, and war. These three topics killed and devastated his people.

When an epidemic hit a village, two people would be immune to the disease. The two fortunate people would help the infected people. These two helped the sick by either feeding them, getting them wood, or burying the dead. In order to control the spreading of the disease, the villagers told the people not to travel to the surrounding villages. When the epidemic was over, the two people who had helped the sick would get sick themselves in the end. It had always been that way, two people that seemed to be chosen to help the sick. The people who got better, in turn, would help the two grateful people.

War has been said to be started by two boys. The two boys were playing darts and then one of the boys accidentally popped another boy's eye out. Seeing this, the father of the unlucky boy got mad and threatened to pop the eye out of the boy who did it. Since the father was going to do it, the uncle of the responsible boy told the father to pop one eye out. The father took hold of the responsible boy and instead of popping out one eye, he popped both his eyes with his finger. The uncle got mad and went to the other boy and popped the other eye out. After this incident, with the two boys, the war started. They never knew war, but it is said that it started that way.

Starvation was the hardest one that hit the Yup'ik. The agony of past famines would be repeated over and over from one generation to the next. So being experts on starvation of their land, they concluded that the only solution was to respect the environment. Their environments were water, dirt, and all the way up to the humans. The consequence of such misuse of the environment would only result in famine.

PACK OF WOLVES

The months passed and the subzero winter set in and froze the Atmaulluaq area. Disheartening as it sounded, the people treasured it, because they were used to it. Once the ice froze over the area, three warriors from Tulukar came down to the village of Atmaulluaq. These warriors wanted to talk to the elders from there. They also wanted to see the three kids at that meeting.

That same day, Kaluk, Eli, and Tatu went over to the qasgiq and waited outside. All the boys were wearing muskrat fur parkas and mittens. The kids were to wait outside until they were called in. As the boys waited, the auburn sun was setting and the shadows slowly gloomed the area. The weather started getting chilly for the boys and to keep themselves warm, the boys started pushing each other around for a bit.

Their parents were already inside the qasgiq and Tatu was wondering what was wrong and why everyone seemed so nervous for them. Then he remembered what his grandpa had told him about and why he was training him. He didn't tell his friends what the warriors were here for, but instead, he told them that they were in big trouble for all the mischief they had been doing. In his mind, he was hoping the warriors were just here for food and nothing else.

The time slowly passed as the destined warriors waited. The stars were out now and the temperature was getting uncomfortable. Even thought it was uncomfortable for them, the three friends sat down and waited nervously. Suddenly, from one of his friends, a snowball hit Tatu's chest. The energy they had in them couldn't wait for nervousness. To break the tension, they all started fighting and wrestled each other.

The people inside the qasgiq could hear the restless little boys yelling and screaming outside. Hearing their ruckus, their parents got very embarrassed. *They better take these boys*, one old woman was thinking.

All the fun and games stopped when the elders called the boys in. As they crawled in, the boys pushed each other to see who would go in first. Tatu lost and he slowly started crawling inside behind his friends. Everyone inside the qasgiq quieted down as the boys entered.

Once inside, the boys were ordered to stand in the middle. Everyone in the village seemed to be there. Tatu looked around and saw his parents, but they shied away from his gaze. Their parents didn't look too happy with them and that got him worried a little. Tatu's father, Aatiin, gazed back at his only son and smiled at him. His dad's smile gave him the confidence he needed at that moment. His dad was tough and when a tough man smiled, everything was going to be OK. Destined to become a warrior, the time was here, so Tatu took a deep breath and waited for them.

Standing in the middle of the qasgiq, three big men of war stood up and started walking around the boys. These warriors were rough and tough-looking and they never seemed to smile. It was an uneasy feeling for Tatu and he felt like they were just some prey to them. The warriors ordered them to take their parkas off. Once they got them off, the warriors started checking their bodies to see their physical shape.

Satisfied with the kids, a warrior looked at their elders and said to them, "We'll take them and they seem tough enough." Then one by one the warriors asked who they were and the boys told them their names and the names of their parents. After meeting with the warriors, they sent the kids home.

Outside the qasgiq, the three friends just looked at each other and they all went home with nothing to say for the very first time. Slowly, Tatu walked over to Apa's house. The warriors were here for them and they were going to take him. Trying not to think about it, Tatu started running home.

At Apii's home, the house felt empty and it seemed colder than usual. So Tatu started the fire and waited for his family. The fire was useless and it didn't seem to warm anything that day. The time passed as he patiently waited to see what his parents had to say to him. Becoming a warrior wasn't in his plans. His plan was to stay here and help his grandparents. His grandparents seemed to need him more than the warriors did. He was sure the warriors had a good reason to get him this early.

Finally, after patiently waited for them, Tatu's grandparents came in with his parents. He was told that he would be leaving with the warriors early in the morning. The elders had decided that every available boy was to get trained either at Tulukar or at Naparyalruar (Napakiak). When the time was right, the warriors went to gather the boys and they were chosen to go to Tulukar.

Tatu's whole family was sitting in circles by the fire and everyone was very quiet. The fire was slowly burning and Aatiin added some wood, so he could see his son better.

Apa finally broke the silence, "I've never liked silence and I've never liked a lot of things, but I've liked my little hunter."

That made Tatu smile a little, but not for long, because he was about to go upriver tomorrow morning to Tulukar. Leaving the village was a horrible thought to him. Leaving all his other friends and family was worse.

Aatiin patted his back lightly and said to him, "You'll be training for a while and you will be learning a lot of things from the elders there and I'm proud of you. Your mom and I will come up once in a while to check on you, and I'm sure your grandpa will too. Your Apa talks too much and I'm sure he'll get to talk to you boys."

That made Tatu feel better, knowing they would be checking on him once in awhile. As Tatu's dad finished talking to him, his mother looked at Tatu and called out his name. Tatu slowly looked at her.

Aan cleared her throat and said, "When you get to Tulukar, Tatu, make sure you listen to the elders and warriors there of what they have to say. Try your best in what you do and what they tell you to do. Your first couple of days will be very hard for you, because you'll be missing home. Stay away from bullies and if they pick a fight, just walk away."

Tatu could tell Aan was fighting back the tears as she spoke and she was holding them back. She always told him the dos and don'ts of life. *Don't let me go!* Tatu was thinking to tell her, but if he said it out loud, she would be in ruins. So he didn't say anything to her and kept it to himself. It was a sad moment for all of them.

After talking to Tatu, his parents went home to get his stuff ready. His parents said that they would come by in the morning to see him off. That night, Tatu's relatives and other people of his community came by to comfort him and wished him well. When it was time for him to sleep, Tatu headed out to the porch, but his grandpa stopped him and invited him to sleep with them for the very first time.

Apa asked Maurlu to make Tatu's bed and he took out some dried seal meat and oil. When the meal was ready, Apa called for them, "Where's my wife and my little hunter? Lets' enjoy the warm fire and eat."

They sat together and began to eat the seal meat that one of his relatives had brought over from Niugtaq (Newtok). Apa, in return for the seal meat, had given his relative some whitefish. Trading food had been their custom for a long time. Tatu felt better after eating some much-needed fat from the seal. When he finished his meal, he thanked them and went straight to bed.

The fur bed was really comfortable than the grass mat he was used to. He wasn't accustomed to the warmth and the comfort of the fur, so he took his parka off. Lying in the extremely warm fur bed, he looked at the ceiling and out of the blue, he started to giggle to himself.

At the other side of the house, hearing his giggling, Apa asked him what he was giggling at. Tatu stopped his childish giggle and closed his eyes. Instinctively, he felt something move and he moved away. *Whoa,* Tatu thought and he cautiously opened his eyes and looked at his grandpa. His Apa was grinning, because he had just thrown a stick at him.

Still grinning at his grandson, his grandpa said again, "Tut'ggar, what you giggling at?"

His Apa was going to get his answer one way or the other. Tatu had no choice, but to tell him. He looked at him and looked at the porch and said, "The comfortable fur bed is so warm and soft that it is uncomfortable for me." With that being said, they both started chuckling.

"Hurry up and go to sleep. You'll need a lot of rest tonight. Tomorrow will be a long day for you and you'll need all the energy," Apa said to Tatu and he was smiling away.

Tatu closed his eyes, but he couldn't sleep. That night, he felt his grandpa move and felt him taking a stick again. He didn't move, but this time, he waited for his hit instead. For some reason, his grandpa lost interest and threw the stick down and went back to sleep. His last day of training by his grandpa was over.

Tatu woke up early and his grandparents were still sleeping. Not waiting for them to get up, he put on his clothes and went outside to check on the weather. He was hoping that the weather would turn bad outside. Blizzard or whiteout conditions would be nice for him, so they would stay in the village a little longer. Once outside, he was disappointed. It was a cold, crispy morning and snow was everywhere. The lazy wind was blowing from the north and the sky was going to be clear that day. After checking the weather, Tatu went back inside and got his stuff ready.

His grandparents woke up as he entered and they talked for a bit. His dad and mom came by to wish him well and they also gave him some extra clothes to wear. He had to pack light, because he was going to be running today.

The warriors and his friends came by and waited outside for Tatu. He went out and his parents followed behind him to see him off. It was a sad day for all of them as they gathered together. Tatu's little world seemed different; it seemed way bigger than usual. Everyone in that village gathered around the boys to see them off. The kids bid their last farewells.

Most of the village people were in tears. Even though these boys were mischievous, they were all sad to see them leave. They were going to be missed dearly for they entertained them. One person had tears falling down her face and deep down inside of her, she was jumping for joy to see these boys leave. After a couple of boring days later, she missed the runts.

TULUKAR TRAINING CAMP

The warriors and the boys slowly took off west and paced themselves. As they were farther out from the village, the three boys looked back. Their small little village got smaller and smaller and then it disappeared from their view. They were on their own now and the boys looked at each other and kept on running with the warriors.

Once they got out of the village, the warriors stopped the kids briefly. The kids immediately sat down to conserve as much energy as possible. Seeing the boys sitting down, the warriors walked around them in disgust. As the boys were resting, one of the warriors warned them, "We are going to run and you boys better keep up with us. The slowest shall be killed when we reach Tulukar!"

With that warning in mind, the boys tried their best to keep up as they ran to the next village. It took them four days to reach Tulukar. The warriors picked up more kids on their way and slept as they stopped at every village.

From Atmaulluaq, the warriors went to Nunaacuaq and picked up six boys from there. From Nunaacuaq, they headed to Nunapicuar (Nunapitchuk) and picked up six more kids. Their last destination was at Kasigluq (Kasigluk) and they picked up four more kids. Each time they went out of a village, the warriors warned the kids with the same thing that they told them before. Fearing the worst, the kids tried their best to keep up.

Tatu knew some of the boys from the other places they picked up. When they had their great feasts, he had talked to some of the boys or their parents would know each other. Some of these kids were his relatives and he was glad they picked up the other boys. He had been thinking that there were just going to be three of them from Atmaulluaq heading to Tulukar.

Most of the boys were wearing what they wore. Their marvelous parkas, made by strong women, who had impressively sewed them together with their strong, but delicate hands, they were either made of muskrat, otter, mink or bird skins. It was amazing for Tatu to see what the women could do with their needles. Most of the kids were wearing muskrat parkas that were caught during the spring-, summer-, and fall time. Tatu was wearing muskrat fur skin parka and the inside of his parka was lined with rabbit fur skins. His parka kept him warm all that winter. The designs on the parka were individual, designed by their mothers, and he could tell who was related, just by looking at their parkas.

On the fourth day, the boys finally saw the village of Tulukar. Tulukar was located by a huge lake on the hill that stretched quite a ways. This village seemed big to them. Looking at the sod houses, there seemed to be more people than in the rest of their villages combined.

When they were closing in to Tulukar, the warriors yelled out, "Home, sweet home!" And they sped up and left the kids behind.

Knowing the slowest would be killed, the boys began pushing each other as they rushed to the village. The competition was on, but Tatu got pushed down and he fell on the snow. On the ground, he got up and watched the kids running farther away from him. Doomed, he knew he wouldn't catch up to them.

As the kids were dashing for their lives, Tatu's friends noticed him when he fell down. They scanned back and saw Tatu slowly getting up from the ground. Eli wasn't going to lose one of his friends. He had to react fast, so he tackled one of the kids that were running for dear life. Kaluk noticed Eli jumping on a little boy and he stopped to help him out. The boy that just got tackled was now yelling and screaming. Eli, still wrestling with the boy, looked back and yelled at Tatu to *run!*

When Tatu got yelled at, he started speeding toward them. When he finally reached his friends, they were still holding the little kid. Standing beside them now, Tatu could see the horror in the boy's eyes and felt sorry for the kid.

"What are you guys doing? Let the kid go. Eli, Kaluk!" Tatu asked them.

Being told to release the squirming kid, his friends shook their heads *no*.

When his friends didn't budge at his request, Tatu repeated, "Let the boy go."

His friends reluctantly let the little boy go and the scared little boy got up and dashed toward Tulukar. Lying still on the ground, Kaluk blurted out, "I'm tired and why did you want to let him go anyway?"

"We all are tired Kaluk," Tatu replied and he reached down and heaved his friends up.

Once up, the boys started shacking off the snow from their parkas. It was getting dark and the boys scanned the village. Of all the villages they had been in, Tulukar looked mysterious and spooky to them. Silence was in the air now and silence always made the boys wonder.

As they were looking at the village, Eli said to his friends, "Let's go or maybe we should run back home."

Instead of running back home, they started walking toward Tulukar. Beneath their feet, the crackling snow seemed louder as they stepped on it. Besides the crackling snow, the area was eerie for them.

"You scared, Tatu?" Eli asked Tatu.

Tatu didn't want to answer his question and the thought of dying was not an issue he wanted to talk about. They were still young and learning the world. The curiosity of dying young was never even a thought until the warriors got them. The warriors had already warned them about the consequences. One of them was going to die and they knew it.

"So who's going to die?" Kaluk awkwardly blurted out.

Hearing that question from Kaluk was just awful for his two best friends. The moment was awkward for all of them. Tatu and Eli gave him the silent treatment, as they crept toward the village.

As they were getting closer to the village, Tatu made up his mind and said, "I'll be the last one in, so you guys can start running for it and tell everyone back home that I love them."

Hearing what Tatu had to say to his friends, they didn't listen to him, but they kept walking with him. The other boys, who had taken off without them, seemed to stop and they seemed to be waiting for them. The three friends still took their time and kept on walking together.

From the village of Tulukar, the warriors started yelling at the remaining three boys, "Hurry up and run!"

Getting yelled at, the friends slowly started jogging again. This time, they ran together and reached the rest of the boys. As they reached the rest, they didn't utter a word, knowing that the slowest would be killed and one of them was going to die.

On the bank side of Tulukar, all the boys noticed there were a lot of fish smokestacks and a dozens skeleton kayaks. Still, they scanned the area and saw crowds of people from Tulukar and they seemed to be waiting for the boys. Looking at these strangers, the boys got very nervous and they all looked down to avoid any eye contact with them. The boys were let up the hill and they entered the village. One of the bigger kids in the crowd threw snow at them, but the boys left him alone. There were a lot of sod houses, similar to their own. In the middle of the village was their qasgiq.

When the boys reached the qasgiq, the warriors stopped them. The boys were all nervous, but the warriors assured them that they would not be killed, but they would be trained very hard. The slowest kid was spared and they were relieved and relaxed. Hearing the good news, Tatu looked at his friends and they all sighed in relief.

Being ordered to enter the qasgiq, one by one, the boys slowly crawled inside the qasgiq and bunched up in the center. There were also other kids inside the qasgiq and they were already waiting for them.

The elders and the men were already sitting along the sides of the qasgiq. The men motioned the new recruits to sit down and listen. The men observed the new kids with curiosity and they mumbled out to themselves to see if they could recognize which kid belonged to whom.

Tatu observed his new rich surroundings very carefully. The qasgiq was way bigger than the other qasgiq he had been in before. This building was intimidating and beautifully built. The floor was made of wood planks with some grass mats. At the side of this magnificent building were wooden seats, which also became beds sometimes. On the back of the qasgiq were more grass mats and furs, mostly used by elders for their bedding. On the ceiling, hanging on ropes were tools, spears, and some unfinished blackfish traps. The window was in the center of the ceiling and it was made of animal guts. At night time, the window was opened to let the smoke out from the fire.

When the boys settled down, a man by the name of Qay stood in front of the kids and yelled at them, "Listen up! Everyone, stand up! Stand up now!"

Qay screamed as loud as he could and that scared them all. The boys weren't accustomed to a sound that loud. Hearing Qay scream, they immediately stood up as they were told to.

Qay was tall and skinny. All his life he had trained as a warrior. He seemed to be in his late fifties as his gray hair started to show. On his lower lips were ivory-looking ornaments that looked like walrus tusks. The big man was intimidating to the boys. This man wasn't going to take it easy on them and he was there to make them better.

When the boys stood up, Qay screamed again, "Sit down!"

Surprised that Qay yelled again, all the kids sat down as fast as they could. Qay looked at the other men and motioned to them. The other men went up to the new kids and told them that if they were going to sit, they had to plant their feet always down. Their butts should never touch the ground as they sat.

The new sitting position was very awkward for the boys, but the elders had a reason for it. In this sitting position, the boys could just get up and run and they also wouldn't get wet from the ground. The warrior showed the boys an example and the boys imitated the man.

Qay started asking for their names, places they came from, and who their parents were. It was very important for him to get their names. Without names, they were just little kids to him.

After checking their background, Qay started preaching to the kids. "You little kids are nothing! Worthless! You know nothing of living and hunting game or fish. Your parents feed you, clothe you, and the other men hunt for you to eat. You live, not because of yourself; it's because of us, Yup'ik. If we cast you out alone right now, you would die and freeze to death!" Qay paused to catch his breath and began walking around, then he resumed. "Open your eyes, listen with your ears and always look at our lips when we talk to you! Once you stop listening or watching us talk, you will miss out the important key parts that you will need for you to survive this life."

Qay stopped lecturing for a second and pointed to a boy who was looking around. The other men went to the boy and pushed him and told him to pay attention.

After the boy got pushed, Qay started preaching again, "When you aren't paying attention to us and looking around like him, you're going to miss the wisdom of what we are teaching you. One day when you are lost, fall into icy water, or starve to death, you will not know what to do! That's because you did not pay attention to what we have to say to you. These words, these precious words we use, go way back even before I was born and we learn from them. The old elders were very strict with us and they wanted us to pass them on to you. We wouldn't be living here today if that generation hadn't passed them on to the next!" Qay was sweating heavily when his speech was over.

Most of the lectures were about survival and what they had to do to survive. They taught them to respect nature and their fellow people. The values and standards the elders set were high and it was important to follow them. It was worth learning the world around them and what they could expect from the outside and the inside of their universe.

As the days went by, the elders taught them how to get fish, how to catch and trap animals and birds. They showed the boys how to use tools and what they were made for and what they could do. They learned what hunting weapons were made from and the purpose of them.

The elders drilled them to remember landmarks. It was crucial for the boys to remember landmarks, because someday they might be lost and they wouldn't be able to go back home. Sometimes, in the wilderness, people encountered things that cannot be explained. Some people saw orbs of lights that played with them. Witness of these phenomenal activities said that they were the *ircinraqs* (little people) playing ball. These orbs of lights should be avoided at all cost, because some forgot their way and find themselves in different areas of the land. So to get back home, they needed to learn the landmarks.

The boys learned many brilliant things from their teachers. Especially, how to survive and to be a man. Tatu sometimes dozed off listening to the elders, but he got pushed to the floor just like the rest of the sleepy kids. The elders' lectures were repeated a couple of times to insure they had them in their minds.

When it was time for the boys to eat, the warriors let the hungry little kids out of the qasgiq and lined them up. Their first day was OK so far and no one got killed. Then the next day, the kids were all hungry, thirsty, and tired. As the boys lined up, Qay came by and he had a feather in his hand.

Qay, holding the feather, showed it to the kids. It was a small feather, possibly from a loon's back. Tatu could see the white dots on the black feather. On the other side of his hand, Qay was holding a wooden water container.

Qay, holding the water container, went to the first boy and told him to look up. As the boy looked up, Qay dipped the feather in the water container and he said to him, "Open your mouth."

Once the boy opened his mouth, Qay placed the feather on the boy's mouth and let the boy lick the water from the feather. After the boy licked the water from the feather, Qay moved on to the next boy that was in line. He went to each boy and let them drink that way. When everyone got the taste of the water, Qay said to them, "That is all the water you will get for today."

Flabbergasted, the boys looked at each other and their jaws dropped. *Is that all the water I am going to drink?* Tatu thought and his mind started worrying. His throat was still dry and he was still thirsty from the run. He looked at the rest of the boys and the boys seemed to be disappointed from Qay's words too. At that moment, the most powerful word in this world was *water*.

No more water, Tatu said to himself repetitively and he could see another boy's mouth move up and down like he was probably doing. He was now trying to get his tongue wet and swallow down his saliva. It didn't seem to work for him, but it seemed to make him thirstier than ever. Being denied water was shocking for him.

After Qay gave them a taste of water, he ordered one of the warriors to grab the pack that was on the ground and let the boys look at it. As ordered, the warrior opened the pack and revealed dried fish.

Wow, dried whitefish! It's energy for my body! Tatu thought to himself as he gazed at the meat. He was hungry, but his mouth was still too dry to feed. He looked at his friends and they tried to smile at each other. He just needed a little bit more water and he should be OK.

In front of them, Qay and the other warriors set up a log and they started cutting the food into little pieces. When they were done cutting up the dried fish, Qay went to the first boy and told him to get on his toes. Once the boy was on his toes, he told the boy to look up and open his mouth wide. When the boy opened his mouth, Qay put one piece of dried fish in the boy's mouth and told him to start chewing. Qay fed this boy another slice as the boy finished the first piece of the whitefish. When the same boy let his heel hit the ground, Qay stopped feeding him and went on to the next boy. That feeding style went on till everyone was fed like that.

Tatu held his heels up enough for one piece of dry fish. His legs were dead sore from running and he couldn't hold on for the second piece of meat. When he finally swallowed the dry fish, he reached down and felt his stomach. Not consuming enough meat, he was still hungry. Reality hit him when his stomach wasn't satisfied and he knew it was going to be a long night for him.

On the third day after the elders and warriors preached, lectured, fed, and watered the kids, their attitude changed drastically for the worst. When they were thirsty and hungry on the third day, the trainers set the water pouch in front of them and left it there.

The sweet-looking water pouch was made of seal guts and it just looked so beautifully designed to them. The lovely-looking cork was made of driftwood and it was nicely roped around and closed very loosely. Inside this beautiful-looking pouch was water and everyone knew it.

The struggling little boys licked their lips, but their lips were still too rough and dry. The boys glimpsed at each other and one brave little kid yelled out, "The water pouch is going to tip over! I'll save it!" and he dashed for the water pouch.

The rest of the kids chased after the savior by pushing and shoving each other until one of the boys reached the water pouch. The boy who reached the water pouch first got pushed down. Being thirsty, the kids began fighting for the precious water.

At first, Tatu was going to run for the water pouch, but then he stopped in his tracks, knowing if he did run, he would be fighting someone for the water pouch too. So Tatu stayed put and just watched the action. *Water,* Tatu's thoughts yearned for the cool, clear, smooth taste. Even though he was thirsty, from a safe distance, he watched them fight for the water pouch, but he wasn't alone. There were four other kids staying put with him and they were probably thinking of the same thing. His friends were in the middle of the pile of the thirsty kids and they were kicking and pushing each other.

In this flurry, the bigger ones shoved all the little ones to the side now. One of the big kids had the water pouch and he held it high. The other kids, beside him, tried to take it from him, but this big boy pushed them off. The big boy was no match for the thirsty mob and he ended up fighting for it again.

While they were fighting for the precious water, without hesitating, Tatu ran to the snowy area and grabbed some snow. Immediately, he put some snow in his mouth and let it melt inside of it. As the snow melted in his mouth, he drank the water from it. Everyone who lived in this area knew that they couldn't just eat snow or they would get very thirsty again. The snow would cool their insides real fast, thus making them thirsty for more. Quenching his thirst, Tatu looked around and saw some other kids doing the same thing, melting the precious snow.

The kids stopped fighting for a moment when the water container was opened. Once opened, one of the kids started guzzling it. As the kid guzzled the water, he got hit in the stomach by another boy. The water container flew off and the others grabbed it and after a few moments of flurry, it was all over just as it had started. The most powerful word in this world was now empty.

After a while, the thirst was still in the air and everything got out of hand. The boys started fighting each other for little things that really didn't matter. Hearing the commotion, the man came out again and ordered them to go back in the qasgiq. It was going to be a long night for all of them.

Was it their way for us to fight each other? Tatu asked himself and his mind wandered off. If it was, it was working perfectly, he thought.

So Tatu learned to get some water any way he could. Sometimes he needed to go pee at night and he would end up melting snow instead. Some of the little kids seemed dehydrated and white in color. He told them the secret way to get water and they felt better after a few days.

Qay got tired of such little flurries among the boys and warned them, "You boys better help each other out and work as a team! If you don't work with one another, I'll make sure we bury you!"

When Qay finished warning the kids, the kids tried their best to help each other, but still they fought each other over little things. As days went by, they never walked again, but jogged everywhere they went. The only time they got to walk slowly was when they were in the qasgiq. When the elders and warriors saw the kids walking, they scolded them. The men made sure they got hit a couple times in the legs for just walking around.

A wooden staff was given to the kids on the fifth week of their stay. The staff would become spears when they became warriors. All the warriors had spears, but boys not yet. The kids were nothing to them and they didn't deserve such a dangerous weapon.

The elders told them the reason why they couldn't lose their staffs. The staff was useful in many ways around this area. It was important for them to have it at all times with them. The staff was used to check the thickness of ice. When they got lost, the staff was used to make an air hole in the snow shelter, because if they didn't make an air hole, they would suffocate and die. The staff was deadly when used properly. Their staff became their third leg and the kids carried it everywhere.

WINTER TRAINING

At the training camp, tensions were high due to the lack of food and water. The torturous training got the boys in physical shape. Their legs were getting strong and their bodies were tight. As their attitudes got worse, the elders finally sent them out hunting with their staffs.

The hunting plan was simple. The men were going to split them in four ways, north, south, east and west. Some of the boys were left behind in the village to gather wood. Tatu's team had one guide with them and his name was Guk and he was to lead three of the boys toward the west to hunt some game.

Guk was a rugged-looking man. He was tall and lean. His legs were powerful from running a lot. His face was leathery brown from being outside a lot. He had a mustache and a small growing beard on him. Sometimes, when it got really cold outside, they could tell it was freezing just by looking at his frozen mustache.

Guk was a born leader and he loved to train everyone to their potential. His keen eyes watched the kids closely and figured out their weaknesses. If he sensed a strong one, he would push the kid to his limits.

Guk's family came from Kwiggluk (Kwethluk) River, one of the tributaries along the Kusquqvak River. His parents had moved to Tulukar long before he was born. His parents had decided to move here for the summer and then head back home during the winter. His parent's plan to return home changed when they fell in love with the people, especially the abundance of waterfowl, game, and the wide variety of wild berries and plants that were present in that area. They also had some relatives here, thus making it easier from them to settle. Even though his parents missed the big game, the huge salmon runs, the beautiful people, or the abundance of trees back home, they loved it here.

As the boys gathered around their leader, Guk checked his boys and got disappointed, "This is the sorriest-looking bunch of kids they ever gave me. I strictly requested the best of the breed and they got me the worst-looking ones."

Hearing this from this warrior, the boys tried their best to look decent for him. Guk, being tall and intimidating, started walking around the little critters and asked them who they were and where they came from. The little kids gave him their names and he gave them his. As Tatu and the rest waited for his orders, Guk turned his head and looked over his shoulder to another group that seemed to look much better than his.

Guk was looking at the healthier group and yelled out, "Ipuun! Hey buddy!"

When Ipuun heard his name being called upon, he turned to Guk and responded. "What do you want, Guk? One of the kids died on you already?"And he began to chuckle.

Guk pointed at his little crew and hollered, "Ipuun, can I feed one of the kids to my dogs? My dogs are pretty hungry!"

Ipuun started laughing at his friend's sarcasm. When he calmed down from laughing, he answered back, "Yeah, your dogs look pretty pitiful with their empty bellies." Ipuun started chuckling again and pointed to a small-looking boy with him and continued, "Yeah, you can have this one. No, I think he's OK, he got some little meat in him I think."

Guk and Ipuun started laughing at themselves, but the kids took them seriously. The kids stayed quiet and kept to themselves. For all they knew, these big men of war could easily kill them, if they wanted to, and possibly feed them to the dogs. Being scared of these two men, the boys just waited for their orders.

When the fun was over, Guk turned around and warned his boys, "You worthless kids better keep up with me."

Getting warned by the big man, the kids nodded yes to him. Guk then took off running and the boys followed behind him. The weather was crispy and the wind wasn't blowing this time.

This hunting crew was running west for a while until their leader saw a fox track. Guk and the rest of the boys halted and observed the fox tracks. After Guk checked the fox track, he asked the kids when the tracks were made. The kids scratched their heads and gave him a couple of their best answers. Not getting the answers he wanted from them, Guk got mad. Disgusted to receive all wrong answers, Guk told them to study their own tracks and learn from them.

The little hunters needed to learn fast and the real hunters didn't like mistakes. From Guk's experience, one wrong move and his meal might run away.

Tracking an animal was very important for Guk, so he gave them a little advice. "To learn how to track, you need to start looking at your own tracks. Check your tracks after you make one. Check it later on, then the next day, then a couple days later and then a week later. You will start to tell the difference by looking at your own tracks. You could learn to tell how many hours, days, or weeks ago they were made."

After inspecting the fox tracks, the hunting crew started running again till they saw some willow tree bushes. Guk slowed his pace and told the kids to be very quiet. He stopped before they reached the willow trees and sat down. He ordered the kids to sit down with him and form a circle.

In the circle, Guk said to them, "You worthless little boys have been taught to jog all this time and everywhere you go. This is hunting time and when we hunt, we stalk, meaning that we slow down the pace and sneak in for the kill. There should be rabbits in those bushes and if you guys make a lot of noise, I'll beat you boys myself. I'm hungry and I need to eat. So we split up in two. You two," He pointed at Tatu and to another boy from Nunapicuar, "go on that side of the bushes. This boy and I will take the other side. I will lead and you two will follow me from the other side. Keep your eyes on me and the rabbits in the bushes. Make sure you stop and signal to me when you see a rabbit. Don't try to spook the rabbits, they tend to stay motionless and if you spook them, they run and they run fast. You boys better be quiet and if I even hear a fart, I'll kill you myself. Understand?"

Guk's blazing eyes looked at them and when he was satisfied, they all got up. They slowly headed toward the bushes and paired up in twos. Tatu went to the opposite side of Guk and his adrenaline kicked in. It was hunting time!

Tatu felt light in his toes as they slowly kept going along the side of the bushes. He saw nothing at first, but then he started seeing rabbit tracks and some nibbled spots. This was a good sign for them and they were heading in the right direction. Suddenly, Guk raised his hand and the boys immediately stopped in their tracks. It was the moment of the hunt that got to them all. The heartbeat slowed down, their focus cleared the air and everything got quiet. They slowly breathed in and out and waited for the rhythm of their prey. If they blinked, they knew that they would miss it all.

Whoosh! Guk's arrow went off into the bushes and he jumped forward and cried out, "Ah! What happened?"

Reacting to Guk's disappointment, Tatu dashed forward to see if he hit something, but a rabbit darted out from the bushes. The rabbit was scrambling toward him. Everything seemed to slow down for him, as he watched the rabbit run. He quickly raised his staff and swung at it. As he swung, he adjusted his aim and his staff hit the rabbit on the back of its spine and stopped it. Catching the rabbit, Tatu couldn't believe he hit it. To make sure it wouldn't run away, he pressed his staff down harder. He quickly checked his catch and noticed that the rabbit had big ears and it was a decent size. His partner in the back said something, but Tatu didn't hear him for he was still concentrating on the moment.

Noticing that the rabbit wasn't going to move anymore, Tatu said, "Quyana! (Thank you)," and he took the rabbit by its neck and raised it up.

On the other side of the bushes, Guk saw what happened and he smiled to see such a sight. The first rabbit was caught and Tatu had killed it with a staff. The rest of the boys were happy too and they were awed to see a kill like that.

Guk was very happy at this moment. For the past couple of months, he hadn't been able to catch anything. Like a lot of hunters, he was competitive and if he went home without anything, his friends teased him about it. The long unlucky spell in hunting game finally had broken for him. This little boy had broken his bad luck in hunting and it finally seemed to change. The little boy was now a special fuel to his fire. He would never forget this day and he would get to eat fresh meat. Hunters sometimes couldn't catch anything for months or even years. That is why they shared the meat with others. Looking at the catch, Guk relaxed his muscles and smiled at the boy. The months of not catching an animal disappeared in his mind. *Finally!* Guk yelled at himself as his future seemed brighter.

Guk and the other two boys cut through the bushes toward Tatu and checked his catch. Tatu was still holding the rabbit and he gave it to Guk.

"It's a jackrabbit," said one of the boys.

After analyzing the kill, Guk patted Tatu's back and told him that he never saw a kill like that before. He ordered the kids to sit and he took out his knife and started dressing the rabbit. He took his time with the animal and finally got the fur and the guts out. He then distributed the little meat around, but Tatu declined the meat and told him that it was his first rabbit catch. Tatu knew that it was a tradition not to eat their first kill, so he would be hungry to catch more of them.

As they were eating, Guk told Tatu that his arrow hit a branch and ricocheted. It was a total miss and that was when the rabbit took off toward him. When they finished eating, they thanked Tatu for the meal and they continued on with the same hunting technique. This time, Guk's bad luck changed and he got ten jackrabbits as they neared the end of the bushes.

Every time when Guk hit one, he yelled out, "Got it!" and the boy behind him would immediately fetch it. At the end of their hunt, Guk decided to eat one more rabbit and Tatu finally got the meal that he needed. Afterward, Tatu felt a lot better and a lot energized.

With the dusk in their grasp, Guk decided to head back home. Feeling the joy of the hunt, he let the kids take turns as they led back to Tulukar. It was a good day for hunting rabbits and Tatu had caught one. The successful rabbit hunters got back safely to Tulukar that night and so did the other hunting party.

As Guk's hunting party reached Tulukar, the rest of the boys were already sitting outside the qasgiq. The boys immediately started exchanging stories of their adventures that day. Tatu found out that two of the parties hadn't caught anything and the other party got lucky and caught some ptarmigan. After the boys had gone out hunting, they felt a lot better emotionally. They desperately needed the hunt and the much-needed break from the village. It was fun and exiting for them all.

A little while later, Guk went out of the qasgiq and told Tatu to come with him. Tatu followed Guk to his home and once inside, Guk introduced him to his family. His wife's name was Atmak and Tatu couldn't help it and said, "Hi Atmak!" and she laughed and said hi back to him.

Guk had four kids in his home. His older boy was Aat and he was about eight. Iis was his oldest daughter and she was about seven. His next sibling was a five-year-old boy was Uquv. Their smallest and cutest was baby Ciuk.

To settle down, Guk asked Tatu to sit down and dine with them. During their meal, Guk told him where his family came from. He also told him about his unlucky spell that had lasted couple of months. When Guk was finished with his background, he asked Tatu about his parka, "Why does your parka have two white spots on the back that look like eyes?"

So Tatu told him the story of his parka.

TATU'S PARKA

The fire was burning lightly as Tatu drank his water. Guk and Atmak were facing him by the fire. The three of his older kids were sitting next to him and listening to what he had to say. The kids loved to hear stories, especially from a stranger who visited them.

Tatu took a big breath and told the story of his parka. "It was summertime when I was just a little boy, I was playing hide and seek with the other kids from my village. I decided to hide in the tall grass and knelt down and kept quiet. I stayed still to avoid being detected and then something bit my back and it started pulling me backward. Whatever it was, it wasn't making any noise, but it was trying to drag me back. It was painful for me and when I looked back, I saw a big black dog as big as me. I realized that the dog just pounced on me from behind. I started to panic and tried to crawl forward, but it kept trying to pull me back with its fangs and his front legs. Unable to escape, I started yelling as loud as I could, so the dog could let me go or have my friends hear and help me out. Luckily, the other kids heard me crying and came to my rescue. The kids saw the dog and knew that I was in trouble. So they started throwing sticks at it. Eventually, the dog let me loose and I crawled away to safety as fast as I could and stood there with the kids. The dog just stared at us and then it ran away. The kids checked my back and I was bleeding from the bite. After the incident, I told my parents what had happened to me and they found out about the owner of the dog. My mom checked my wounds and she said that I would be OK. They caught the dog and tied it up. I told my mom to kill it, but she said, 'No, we will kill it, but not right now, because you have to heal first before we can kill it.' I got mad

85

and went to see the dog. I was carrying a big stick when I reached the dog. The dog seemed to realize that it was me and its tail curled up to its belly and it started crawling around in fear. Seeing the dog crawling around, I knew it was scared of me this time, but I felt sorry for it and left. I knew it was a condemned dog and it would eat its last meal. That same day, my mom patched the back of my parka with two white rabbit furs. It kind of looked like eyes, but it's a bite mark of a dog. Ever since the dog's bite, I've been having the marks for years and my mom told me. 'A dog will bite you in the back when you're not looking, but if you confront it face to face, it's going to get scared and run away.' "

When Tatu finished his parka story, Guk and the rest of his family were just curiously looking at him. The kids went behind him and checked the bite marks and began touching them. The kids were probably imagining the dog biting Tatu.

When Tatu didn't add more details about the incident, Guk smiled at him and said, "It was an interesting story, a dog bit you in the back and you're alive? Some dogs kill poor little kids around here, when they get really hungry. So we try to keep them tied up and feed them. Tell me about your parents."

Tatu told them about Atmaulluaq and his family. The Atmaulluaq people had relatives all over the surrounding villages, even at Kuskokwim River area and along the coast.

After getting to know more about him, Guk told him that he went to Atmaulluaq and got some kids from there and they were really a nice bunch of kids. After they talked a little more, Guk promised Tatu to take him near Kasigluq and fish for whitefish.

Living close to the villages, Tatu told Guk what his grandpa had told him about the neighboring villages. His grandpa told him that most of the people from Nunapicuar moved to Atmaulluaq. To the west from Nunapicuar was Kasigluq and it had the best white fishing spots. In these close villages were many relatives of people in Atmaulluaq. After talking about those interesting places, Guk looked at Tatu and said that it was time for him to go back to the qasgiq.

"OK, let's go," Tatu said to Guk.

They both went out of the house and the stars were out as they headed toward the qasgiq. They slowly walked down and reached the qasgiq. The kids were still outside and Guk told Tatu to join them.

The kids were looking at the stars silently. They were busy thinking of their homes and plenty of food and water they could have had. When they realized that Tatu got there, the kids started moving around and asked where he was and what he was doing. He just told them he had some little dried fish to eat and some water and told stories at Guk's place.

One of the big kids came up to Tatu and asked him, "You got some water on you or some food?"

Tatu told him no and the boy didn't believe him and said that he was lying to him. The boy started patting down Tatu's parka and didn't find what he was looking for. When the boy didn't find what he was looking for, he continued, "You should have stolen some water or some food."

Hearing the word *stealing* Tatu told him what his mother said to him once when he stole something from a neighbor. "If you steal something from somebody, your finger tips will form a mouth and what ever you touch will be eaten from your fingers."

When Tatu finished talking, the rest of the boys were looking at their fingers. Happy that these boys were now concentrating on their fingers, he went over and sat down by his friends, Kaluk and Eli. As Tatu sat down, Eli grabbed his hand and examined it.

Eli was still examining Tatu's hand and then he shook his head no and said to him, "So where's your food and water, Tatu?"

Tatu whisked his hand away from him and responded, "It's in my stomach, you idiot," and the boys started chuckling.

The boys were still waiting outside when Guk finally came out of the qasgiq. He wanted to talk to Tatu and asked him to go with him. They went a little ways out from the boys and when they were alone, Guk told him that he talked to the elders and that he could train with him and his group. Guk also told him that other kids would get the same training, but he was to go with him the next morning.

Hearing the news, Tatu thought about it for a while, but then got scared. These were real warriors and he was just a little boy, Tatu was thinking. If he went with them he could learn more and probably have more fun. Their training was mostly discipline and how they should be functioning. Tatu made up his mind and said yes to him. That sounded a lot better for him than fighting other kids for water anyway.

Tatu was anxious to get out of the training area and he was restless all that night. He told his friends that he was going up north to hunt fur-bearing animals. Hearing the good news, his friends were saddened. "You should go," they both agreed.

Early next morning, Tatu woke up and he also woke his friends. They talked for a while and it was going to be hard for Tatu to leave his friends. The thought of going up north without his friends was scary, but it sounded better than being there. His friends told him to watch himself and made sure he came back. Tatu said his goodbyes and then he went out.

Tatu went out of the qasgiq and the stars were still out. The morning cold opened his eyes and then he went to the north end of the village, but no one was there. *What if they already left me?* Tatu thought and he took his chances and waited for them. He was getting cold when three figures of men headed in his direction.

THIRSTY AND HUNGRY

Patu was all alone in the wilderness. It was wintertime and the weather was cold and snow was everywhere. He was getting desperately thirsty and hungry for attention. After the men had chased him away from Nanvarnarlak, he kept away from the Yup'ik.

Patu ran up the Kusquqvak River and came upon some human tracks. He knew that the tracks were from trappers and hunters from a nearby village. Desperate for attention, he decided to visit them, especially an old man from that village who owed him attention.

Back when Patu was not a threat to anyone, before his killings began to get hold of him, he was called to a village of Elai. There, he was summoned to a man who had problems with his stomach. The man was old now and his name was Kumak. Patu examined Kumak's stomach and diagnosed that Kumak had an infection in his intestines. He opened him up and cleansed his intestines and Kumak got better in less than a month.

Patu knew where Kumak's sod house was, so at night he paid him a visit. It was really dark out as Patu entered Kumak's home and to his surprise, no one was there. Inside the sod house, he lit all the lamps and checked around. He went to the bed and smelled it. Smelling the same man he was looking for, he smiled to himself.

Satisfied that this was Kumak's home, he checked around and saw a lush fish that was by the entranceway. Looking at the lush fish, he got hungry and went to fetch it. He licked his lips and started eating the fish raw. As Patu was enjoying his free meal, outside of the sod house he heard someone coming in. He automatically threw the fish down and he had to think fast, so he looked for a place to hide, because Kumak might come in with other people and he didn't want to deal with them.

Kumak had come home late and he was tired and drained. All that night, he'd been jigging for lush fish. Most of the time, the lush fish were caught at night and they were also bottom dwellers. To catch them, his bait was usually at the bottom of the river. The lush fish had large livers and their livers, to Kumak, were a delicacy.

Kumak had caught six lush this night and he was dead tired. His belly was full, because he had just eaten some fresh lush while he was out fishing. When he got to Elai, he gave some of his catch to one of his family members and then went straight home.

When Kumak went inside his home, he immediately noticed his lamps were on. Surprised that his lights were on, he carefully checked around. He noticed the lush fish that he had caught last night was by the bed and it was half eaten. Looking at the lush fish, Kumak thought one of his relatives had come over for a quick bite. He was going to deal with whoever left the lamps on tomorrow. He had enough oil to last him for months, so he went to his wolf fur bed and sat down. He looked around again to see if everything was there. Everything was in place, so he closed his eyes and lay down.

On the bed now, Kumak breathed in and started singing himself to sleep. Everything was fine to him at the moment and what he didn't know was that someone was watching him. Not knowing someone was there watching him, he started singing his name out loud, "Koo-koo-Kumak, Koo-koo-Kumak," from boredom, and usually his friends teased him like that.

On the bed, after he sang to himself, Kumak opened his eyes and gazed at the ceiling and he saw himself there! "Ah!" Kumak screamed out and he quickly sat up. He examined the ceiling again, but he didn't see himself there. *Scary,* Kumak thought and he quickly looked around to see if anyone was around.

Never in his life had Kumak seen himself and that scared him. He decided to check around the house again after that little spooky episode. After checking his house, Kumak calmed down and closed his eyes and lay down again. Slowly, just to make sure he was really all alone, Kumak peeked to see if he would see his body up there again. *Nothing,* Kumak said to himself in relief.

No one was up there, so Kumak closed his eyes again. *I must be dead tired,* Kumak continued thinking, but then he smelled something, something out of the ordinary! His whole body tingled and he slowly opened his eyes again. It might have been the lush fish, but he wasn't sure, this odor was strong and it stank. Something was there. He noticed there was a man on the right side of him and he screamed, "Ah!"

While Kumak screamed his lungs out, the man threw a rope around him and tied him up. Kumak struggled to free himself and began kicking his legs, but the man threw another rope around his legs, so that he couldn't move or kick anymore. Kumak was now roped and he was in terror.

The man who roped him looked down at Kumak and said to him, "Hi Koo-koo-Kumak! It's been awhile since we saw each other and how's your stomach?"

Kumak was very frustrated that he couldn't move. He began to talk, but Patu hit his throat and Kumak couldn't say a word anymore. All Kumak could do now was just stare at Patu. They both stared at each other for a while and then Patu said to him, "Koo-koo-Kumak, I came here to check on my work, the stomach I fixed, and since you didn't give me anything for my perfect service last time, your stomach belongs to me now."

It was time for Patu to operate. Patu gave Kumak his most malicious smile and then took out his knife and tore Kumak's parka and exposed his stomach. Exposing Kumak's stomach, Patu reached down with his knife and made a little incision and exposed his intestines. The perfect incision was all he needed. Then he gently reached down and carefully pulled out Kumak's intestine. The blood was slowly oozing out of Kumak's stomach now. Patu smiled again when he felt Kumak's intestines. The intestines were slippery to the touch and he played with them for a while. Since there was some blood on the intestines, Patu started licking it to clean it up.

"Your people are great at hunting and fishing and I'm really great at my work too, you know?" Patu said as he was nodding his head yes. Next, he had to do a quick curettage and an ablation. Without warning, Patu bit Kumak's intestine and he bit it in half!

Ah! He's opening my stomach! Kumak was yelling at himself. Poor Kumak was in pain, but he couldn't yell or even move. He started sweating heavily and all he could do was watch this evil man and listen to his devilish voice. He had met him before and Patu had told him not to give him anything for his services.

Patu was chewing Kumak's intestines and said to him, "Kumak," and he slowly started giggling. When Kumak looked at him, Patu let him see part of his intestines that was now between his teeth.

Seeing this, Kumak twitched his body to loosen up the ropes, but they were too tight. Kumak knew he was doomed as he gave up and stopped moving.

Patu started chewing some of his intestines and continued, "Not bad Kumak, you taste pretty good, because you keep eating fish and some caribou meat." When he finished chewing, he swallowed part of the intestine.

After swallowing his food, Patu started chanting and then he reached into his pocket and took out a rock and showed it to Kumak. The show for this shaman was on and he had to show the object. Swallowing his intestine was nothing compared to what he was going to do to him. Patu's mouth began to drool, just thinking about it. He wiped it off and looked at his subject. His subject was ready and willing to be used.

"This is what I learned when I was messing around with two live minks," Patu said as he inserted the rock inside the upper part of Kumak's intestine. He then took out a little worm and inserted it in the lower part of the intestine. He then took out his needle, made from a porcupine quill, and sewed Kumak's intestine and his skin back up. The surgery was a delicate process, but he was good at it.

When the surgeon had finished his work, Patu started giggling again and said to him, "I'm the best at what I do, you know?"

Patu smiled at Kumak and told him why he was doing such a horrible thing to him. He had to let him know, Kumak deserved to know and he was his willing patient. "When I did this with two live mink, I fed them both, one with water and the other with food. One mink, which drank the water, lived for a week, while the other mink lived less than a week. The rock that I inserted in their intestine blocked the food, but the water passed through the intestines. The mink that ate the food bloated up real bad and the other, who drank the water, starved to death. The tapeworm that I inserted in the bottom of your intestine will eat the rest of the food and make sure that nothing passes through."

When Patu finished explaining, he hit Kumak's throat again and Kumak could now scream, "Ah!" Kumak screamed for his life.

Patu just smiled and said to him, "Shut up! Kumak, you need to conserve your energy," Patu looked around and continued, "Are the people looking for me?"

Kumak calmed down and cleared his throat. He was mad at what Patu had just done to him, but at least he was still alive. He knew he had to get out whatever this evil shaman had inserted in his stomach. This is why he knew they were after him; this devil of a man was evil. "The people heard what you are and what you did at Tulukar. They're looking for you and if they find you, they will kill you. You are crazy and you shouldn't even live this life!"

As soon as Kumak stopped speaking, Patu hit Kumak in the head and knocked him out, "Shush!" Patu said to Kumak as his eyes closed.

Patu got what he needed and he was hoping no one knew about the incident. He grabbed the rest of the lush fish and went out and left again. This time, he was planning to go back downriver, back to the coast, back to the sea, and back to home sweet home.

The next morning, Kumak's relative came into his sod house to check on him. They found Kumak in his bed, still tied up, and the lamps were out. After being released, Kumak told them what had happened to him and Patu. His people tried getting another shaman to fix Kumak's intestines, but in less than a week, Kumak bled to death. Patu had left another bad mark within that village.

LITTLE RABBIT

That cold crispy morning, coming into Tatu's view was Guk along with two other warriors. Tatu recognized the two other warriors, but he had never really met them or even talked to them. He was a little nervous when they arrived. Guk introduced them to him, Ipuun and Tuma, and they were both from Tulukar.

Ipuun was shorter than the two others, but his chest was wider. He had a mustache and a beard growing on his face. Every time he laughed, he grabbed his stomach for comfort. He was the calm one of the three and he loved to laugh at everything. His parka was made of wolf fur, which seemed to make him even wider. He walked funny, like a duck, his body moved from side to side. Besides his awkward walk, he could run as fast.

Tuma, on the other hand, was the same height as Guk. His face was also tan in color, but he didn't have a mustache or a beard. He was wearing a muskrat parka and said he liked to wear the brand for comfort. In no way was he an average person. He was a little crazy, maybe a little more hyper than usual and he ran on rage, but he was OK. He was a rugged-looking man and he could jump farther than anyone in that area.

Ipuun admiringly waddled up to Tatu and cleared his throat. "So this is the little boy who likes to kill rabbits, but can he run like one?" and he smirked at his friends.

Tatu smiled back to show them that he was friendly. It was nothing really to brag about. It was only one rabbit that he had killed and he didn't know the impact it had on Guk. He was happy that he killed one and he got lucky. He was hungry to catch more, of course, but he was hungry to catch more to please his people. He had to show these men of war his friendliness or they wouldn't like him.

Tuma was holding a pack and he gave it to Tatu. Tuma then told him that he would have to carry it with him and warned him not to lose it or he would break his back.

Getting warned about the pack, Tatu had to check what he was going to carry. He untied the rope and looked inside the pack and saw arrows. He tied it back up and put the pack around his back. The pack felt light to him. *I should be able to carry it all day*, Tatu thought. After Tatu snuggled the pack, Guk gave him a regular bow and said it was his.

The bow went back thousands of years. It was an easy tool for them to use and make. Two types of bows that are made in that area; the sinew-backed bow was favored for big game and war. The regular bow was made from a birch wood tree. The regular bow was mostly used for small game, fish, birds, or smaller fur-bearing animals. The length of the bow depended on the user; it was measured from your arm span from tip to tip of your hands. Any bigger or smaller and it wouldn't fit the archer right.

Once the bow was wet, it lost its strength, so the people made sure they had a bow cased up at all times. To make a waterproof case for the bow and arrows, they made special covers for the bows. The special covers were made of scaled fish, seal guts, or the hides of other fur-bearing animals.

Tatu's case was made of pike skin. His pike skin was first dried, and then dipped into fermented urine to extract the oil and blood. Then after they let the pike skin settles down for a couple of days, they took it out and then they dried it. After drying the pike skin, the women put some oil on the pike skin and wrinkled it, so the pike skin would be flexible enough for the women to work on. Some of the art work on the cases were beautifully designed. The skill with a bow would be shown on the case.

The designs on Tatu were always simple; he colored his arrow case red with the animals or birds that he killed. He was a lousy artist with his hands, so he never really bothered trying to design anything.

The arrow tips these people had were made of ivory, bone, antlers, and stone. The arrow tips that the people commonly saw and used were bone tipped. Some of the arrow tips were made of ivory. The ivory arrow tips were sharp enough to kill big game. The bird arrows had two or three prongs on the tip, also made of ivory or antlers. The stone-tipped ones were mostly used for big game and man. All arrows had three quivers in the end, and if they didn't, the arrow tended to go everywhere when it flew out.

The first arrows Tatu ever used were blunt tipped. The blunt tip was mostly used for small game like little birds or mice. He knocked down a dog once with a blunt tip, but it got up and just whined away. *Finally, I have my own bow!* Tatu said to himself.

"Thank you very much! I'll take good care of it," Tatu excitedly told Guk while he was checking out his new bow.

Tatu's new bow was smooth to his touch, but a little longer than he wanted it to be. Nevertheless, it was a bow and he was very happy! His bow had a design of wolf fangs. The wolf fangs were two triangular designs, colored black, and located just above the grip of his new bow.

"You better take good care of it or Tuma will break your back," Guk warned Tatu.

After Tatu received the beautiful gift, the men at full speed headed out of the village and their journey began. The early morning sun was still creeping onto the horizon as the men were running north. The snow beneath them was hard and they followed a trail that twisted and turned toward the north. At this running speed it would be no sweat for Tatu, but if they ran all day, he didn't think he would make it. In his mind he felt that he could run all day with them, but he was way wrong.

After a few miles out, Tatu decided to slow down and started pacing himself as Guk and the other warriors left him. Then to his relief, the warriors seemed to slow down and finally sat down to rest. He was way behind them, but he finally reached them.

As soon as Tatu reached them, Ipuun questioned him, "What's wrong? Is your pack too heavy for you?"

Tatu was breathing heavily, but told them no. The men got up and started running again. *Please, let me rest for a little bit! I should have said yes, but I'd be lying to them,* Tatu cursed himself with that thought. He had no choice but to keep running after them. He kept up with them for a while, but again, he slowly started falling behind. It occurred to him that he wasn't going to keep up with the strong runners.

The men were now making their own trail. Exhausted after a long run, the warriors finally stopped and rested again. Tatu finally caught up to them at the resting site, where the men gave him some water to drink from their water pouch. He desperately needed the water, so he tried his best to gulp a lot of it down.

When everyone settled down, the men said that they'd run till they saw the spruce trees and that he should track them if he got way behind. Tatu checked the direction they were heading and saw nothing but the endless, viewless snow and some more hills. In his mind he was hoping the tree line was just a hill away. Wrong again.

As the runners gathered their breaths, Guk gave Tatu some encouragement. He knew this little rabbit wasn't going to keep up with them. The straggler was smaller and weaker than they were, "Tatu, you'll be OK and I know you're small, but you must not give up. We step on the tracks that are made in front of us. We follow our own tracks, so anyone who's tracking us won't know how many we are."

Tatu looked back and saw their tracks and then his. Guk reached out to Tatu and patted his back. This run was going to kill the little rabbit and Guk had to give him a confidence that he badly needed. "Are you ready to go, Tatu? Remember to keep up with us," and the men took off.

Keep up? I'll try my best, Tatu thought and he got up and started running after them. After running for a while, he lost his party, but he kept following their tracks as he had been ordered to do. He stopped when they seemed to rest and then ran again. The wind was blowing from the east, as he kept running.

After a while, which seemed to be forever, Tatu saw something dark in his path. Looking at the objects, he recognized what they were; *water and food!* The much-needed energy and water were in his path. Reaching the precious items, he quickly took some gulps and ate a quick bite. When he was finished, he felt better and started jogging again.

The snow was deep in some parts of the trail, and slowed Tatu down. Other times, the trail was hard and it quickened his pace. So far, his energy was OK, but more of this running would drain him completely. He could feel his body stressing to the limit, but he had to keep going.

While Tatu was running, he began to think of what the elders had told him about being alone in the wilderness. The risks that his people took were many and being alone in the wilderness was one of them. Having to hunt and trap in the wilderness, people tended to gamble a lot with death. In the wild, anyone could easily get lost, freeze to death, fall through the ice or get killed by wolves or even by other human beings. Nature had killed more of his people than anything. The more they studied the area, the less risk they took. The elders had drilled them and drilled them in the ways to survive in this area. *It's usually the person's bad calculation of the situation that gets them in trouble in the wild,* Tatu thought, because he knew it from experience.

Overheating, Tatu slowed down and stopped for a while. He opened his parka a little ways and let the cool air in. *Freezing is a cause of death,* Tatu said to himself as he cooled down. As soon as he cooled down, he started running again.

Some people survived through the freezing temperatures to tell about it. When anyone got lost in a blizzard, his people usually searched for the lost ones. Some got lucky and found them OK, but some found them frozen to death. Most of the unlucky ones tended to take their clothes off. Tatu knew hypothermia had the tendency to let the freezing host make bad judgments. The hypothermic person would take his clothes off thinking it was hot outside.

One of the elders had told Tatu a story about a man who survived through the freezing temperatures. It was about a man with a dogsled who got lost in a blizzard. The man was missing for days and being lost, he made a shelter by using his sled. One night while waiting out the weather, he was visited by three women.

In the shelter, the weather was freezing and it was testing this man's limits. As he waited for the weather to get better, the first woman came into his shelter. The first woman offered the man a warm wolf parka and she told him to use it, saying it would keep him warm. Freezing as he was, the man looked at the warm parka, but then he remembered the stories the elders had told him. It was about the situation he was in right now! He looked at the warm parka and declined her offer.

Her offer declined, the first woman went out and a while later, another woman came in and offered him a warm fur blanket. "This will keep you warm," the second woman said to him. Being too cold, the man was about to give in, but the story came to him again and he declined her warm blanket and she went out. The third woman came in with another parka and like the rest, he declined her offer too.

After the three women visited him, he started feeling warm from head to toe. The blizzard and the cold spell were finally over. Finally, when he was able, he dried himself and then went out of his shelter. Outside his shelter, he discovered that his three dogs had died that night. He survived through the ordeal and lived to tell about it to his people. The elders passed down to him the situations that had happened before. If that man had ever given in and not followed the elders' wisdom, Tatu wouldn't know what would have happened to him, but he knew such people were rare.

Tatu was still running when he found himself at his grandpa's porch. He looked around, but then he felt the cold on his cheeks. This was strange and unusual and nothing seemed right to him. *Whoosh!* He heard a whip coming toward him and he jerked up. He opened his eyes and saw the snow and his thoughts of grandpa's porch disappeared. He realized that he was on the frozen ground and his muscles ached all over. He was still in the wilderness and he had just fallen down. *Bad sign*, Tatu thought, and he took a deep breath and stood up.

Tatu looked around and got his bearings and he noticed that he was way off course from the main tracks. Frightened that he got off the tracks, he gathered himself and slowly went back on the trail. On the trail now, he stretched his body and felt better. He checked the main trail and started running again. *That was weird, I must be really tired,* he was thinking to himself and continued, *stay focused or I'm dead for sure.*

Tatu tried his best to focus this time as his environment darkened. It was getting darker when he saw some movement up ahead. Thoughts of his FROZEN BODY in the wild disappeared and he was hoping it was Guk and his party. His heart felt well, but his legs felt heavier than usual. He started to see the pine trees as the shades of gray came upon his world.

"Yes! I'm here!" Tatu yelled out in glee and his dying energy boosted up from just seeing the trees!

When Tatu got closer to the dark objects, he recognized that it was Guk and his crew. His whole body relaxed and he could see the men were already making shelter out of some woods that were nearby.

When they saw Tatu appear in the background, Guk smiled to his men. They were amazed that he showed up this early. All the men got joyous at the moment, for they were worried for him.

When Tatu finally reached the men, exhausted and totally tired, and fell down on his back and just lay there motionless. Once on the ground, he didn't feel like moving his body an inch. Catching his breath, he could not help it, but just lay still.

"The little rabbit made it," one of the men muttered as Tatu was resting.

Then Tuma went over to Tatu and asked him, "Tatu, are you trying to break my arrows?"

Tatu looked at Tuma, but then he closed his eyes again. The run had taken a toll on his body and he was relieved to have made it.

Interrupting Tatu's relaxation, Guk reached down to him and pulled him up. Being tired as he was, Tatu stood up for a while and then sat down. He was now in a sitting position and looking straight at Guk.

Guk didn't like what he saw and said to him, "Tatu, you need to sit as you were taught to and we do it for a good reason. When you lie down on the snow like that, your body gets cold real fast and then your balls shrink."

The men started to chuckle at Guk's sarcasm. Realizing it was a joke, Tatu shook his head no. *I don't think that the balls part was true,* he said to himself. He didn't believe such a thing could happen to anyone. It was funny to him though. Deep inside of him, he was trying to laugh, but he was too drained.

The rest of the crew still had their eyes on Tatu, to see if he had anything left in him. They knew the little runner was drained, but they had to see if he was still strong enough. The little kid had made a long run and that surprised them, but they weren't going to give him any empathy.

Tatu's body was drained and dying. The torturous run was new to him and he wasn't accustomed to it. One more day of running like this and he would be dead for sure.

After telling a joke and not hearing his little runner laugh, Guk had to give him another advice to follow, "Tatu, it is very important for you to avoid lying down on the snow like that. When you lie down on the snow and it's warm outside, your parka gets heavy and wet. Heavy and wet, your parka takes a long time to dry and then your balls fall off." And the men started to chuckle again.

"Now that is not true." Tatu muttered. He couldn't help it and laughed with them. Laughing got his spirits back up, but he was still feeling tired. His legs felt very heavy and all he could think of was resting.

The men offered Tatu some water and he slowly took some sips until he felt better. There was still some light out and he could see the tree lines. Sitting up perfectly, the party were just watching the sunset as the world turned blue and then darkened.

When the stars appeared up in the heavens, Tatu gazed up into the sparkling stars and thoughts of home kicked in. *I hope my family is doing OK without me,* he thought. The hunters were all looking up at the same heavenly stars. The noticeable sign, up in the heaven, was the Big Dipper.

After a little while, Ipuun broke the silence among the star gazers, "The little boy can run."

"Yes, it was a long run for me," Tatu responded and he was feeling much better. He tried his best to give them a smile and hoped his fellow hunters could see it in the dark.

When the night settled in, the hunters went to their makeshift shelter. Inside the shelter, the floor was covered with branches and fur mats. The shelter had room for Tatu, so he squeezed in and closed his eyes. His world suddenly darkened and he fell asleep.

"Wake up!" someone cried out. Tatu thought he had just blinked his eyes and gone to sleep. His mind hollered to his body, "*Wake up!*" but his body couldn't budge one bit and denied its request. He tried desperately to open his eyes, but it felt like it was sewed shut tight. His whole body ceased to obey him and he was in trouble.

"Get up now!" someone cried out to him again.

Hearing the second scream, Tatu forced his eyes open and somehow managed to crawl out of the shelter. Once he was outside the shelter, he stood up, but his legs felt dead and weak and it bothered him. He gathered himself and got his bearings. He looked around and saw Tuma and said to him, "Good morning Tuma, I thought I just closed my eyes."

After observing Tatu, Guk told him to walk around and stretch his legs. As told to, Tatu walked around as best he could and he started feeling better. The soreness slowly disappeared, but his muscles still seemed to be tight.

The men checked on their little rabbit and they liked what they saw. The boy was moving around and not complaining. They knew he was tough and loved him for it. The men were satisfied with him.

Guk had to tell Tatu what the elders had been telling him for years. "You're stronger than you think. We can do unbelievable things. The impossible things can be achieved. We know you're in pain, but you got to keep strong. Don't waste your time feeling the pain; you might learn to love it."

The weak tended to give up and complain a lot and they didn't want Tatu to complain around them. His first two days of training were memorable and he learned that he had to be tough.

The men went in a circle and Tatu joined them. He tried not to moan when he sat down beside them. In the little circle, the men gave him some dried fish and they started talking about the plans for the day. They were going to follow the timberline and make camp again. After making the campsite, they would go up the mountain and get some stones. The sound of, "*trekking the mountains,*" got Tatu weak again, but maybe he could live through it.

The hunters packed up and left that morning. Later on that day, they slowly trekked up to their destination. The hunters found themselves inside the timberlines, in a little clearing area by a small winding river. Inside the timberline, the snow was soft and knee deep, so they trudged their way forward to conserve as much energy as possible. Looking for a good spot, Guk scanned the area and decided that it was a good spot to make a camp.

The campsite being decided, the hunters started gathering wood and brush to make a shelter. The shelter would be big enough for six people. They first had to clear the snow. Once they gathered enough wood, they started off with the walls followed by the roof. The wall frame and the roof were covered by branches and the grass was used to keep the wind out. Grass was difficult to find, but they manage to get enough for the shelter. Lastly, they began to fill the floor with branches and grasses again. The fireplace would be built after they retrieved some stones. The task of building a shelter was grueling, but they got it done. The shelter wasn't comfy at first, but as days went by, the shelter was windproof, warm and cozy from the animals they caught in that particular area.

The next day, the hunters packed light this time and they started heading out toward the mountain. Along the way, Tatu saw some moose and fox tracks, but the hunters left them alone and they kept pushing forward toward their goal. When they finally reached the side of the mountain, they started seeing the stones they were after. The hunters started collecting stones that were smaller than their hands. The stones were big enough to make spearheads, arrowheads and uluaqs.

The stones reminded Tatu of the spearheads the warriors carried with them. His father used the stone knife all the time. His father would grab some meat and cut it up in pieces. His father mostly used the stone knife to shave off a tree bark or willow trees when he made a black fish trap. He also cut the animal furs or willow roots into thin strips to make ropes out of them. It was a useful stone knife to his dad and some of the nice ones had designs on them.

Using the uluaq, Tatu's mom would cut the furs into shapes and made some parkas, pants and maklaks for them. He always saw her cut up the meat with it or prepared fish for hanging. Aan would be furious when she lost her uluaq. She used the useful tool to cut anything.

After getting the stones, the hunters headed back down to the campsite. The stones were heavier than Tatu thought. The hunters managed to make it to their camp before darkness fell. At the campsite, they unloaded their goods and they finally rested.

When the sun set that night, Guk and the men took out the clay lamp and lit them up. After they ate, the hunters started scraping the stones and formed spears and knives out of them. It took them two whole days to make enough spearheads and knives for all of them.

Being a novice, it took Tatu two whole days to make just one stone spear tip. Finally, his staff was made into a spear and he was a warrior now! Tatu was admiring his spear and thinking how he would use it. *Finally, I'll get to kill an animal with it,* Tatu said to himself as he imagined hitting an animal with it.

To clean themselves, the hunters made a little *Maqivik* (steam bathhouse). The little *Maqivik* would be used as a sweat lodge. It was built like the shelter they had made and it was big enough for four people.

The Maqivik's fireplace was placed up front and the entrance was in the back. The hearth was made of stones that were placed in circles. As the wood burned and heated up the stones, they splashed water on the stones by using a dipper.

The competition among the men in this type of sweat lodge was fearsome. He who tolerated the superheated fire got to mock the weak with no remorse. Being the top steamer was lethal. The mocker of the *Maqivik* was constantly challenged by everyone who tried to claim his scorn and shut him off.

The deadliest hard-core steamers tended to have scars on their bodies that looked like veins, but brownish in color. When these hard core steamers steamed, the brownish scars turn fire-furnace red. Some men looked at these scars and thought nothing of it. Other men looked at the scars and started sweating for a challenge.

As fun as it sounded, a lot of people had died in the *Maqivik*. People were told to steam with others, so if something happened to them, the other person could help them out.

The first time when Tatu tried to steam with the men, they said he didn't hit the ground when he scrambled out of there. The men couldn't believe him when he slipped through a crack and did not use the door to get out of there. So mentally and physically, he had to learn to take the pain. Sometimes he almost won the deadly battle, but then he got literally baked.

The *Maqivik*, being hot, relaxed muscles and released the tensions. The heat also killed off the dead skin, thus making anyone cleaner than by just taking a bath. After taking a steam bath, the hunters felt spiritually refreshed. Tatu's people were competitive, mentally and physically, so they loved their *Maqivik*.

THE BLOODY MAN

Meanwhile, Patu was in the trees chasing down some rabbits. He finally caught one and ate some of it. When Patu was full, he stood up and observed his area. The weather was fair and it was getting warmer. For a couple of months now, Patu had been lucky and avoided all human contact. He stretched his arms out and got his bearings, then started walking toward the next village. He knew that he would be killed if he went back to Tulukar, Nanvarnarlak, or Elai. The next village should be safe enough for him and hopefully no one knew about the incidents. He took his chances and kept on walking.

After walking for a while, he got the next village in his sights and Patu could barely see the smoke coming from the Maqiviks. He knew these people loved to take steam baths and the competitions were second to none. He stopped and waited until the night set in. When the people seemed to settle for the night, he was going to pay them a little visit.

As Patu waited, he sat down and closed his eyes and thought about the Maqivik. He started to giggle to himself; what he had done in the Maqivik one time was very funny to him.

One time, Patu had gone to a Maqivik uninvited. Once inside, he met three men and noticed that they were hard-core steam bathers. The owner of the Maqivik was surprised to see him and said to him, "Oh it's you, come on in and we'll see if we can burn the dirt off of you."

Getting invited, Patu took his clothes off and went in with the men. Inside the Maqivik, the fire was burning strong and the stones were red hot. This was a sign of a good steam bath. Sitting by the entrance, Patu felt the heat and his forehead began to sweat heavily. The two men were sitting up front, while one was behind the door. Patu pushed off the guy by the door and moved up to the front. Eventually, everyone settled down and waited for the action. As the men started to sweat and relax, the mocking began.

Patu looked at the owner and said to him, "Hey imbecile," and when the owner gazed his way, he continued, "Did you fuel the fire with grass?"

The owner got insulted and started pouring the hot stones with the water dipper. As the water hit the stones, it sizzled and evaporated, hence creating a super hot steam. As the steam hit the men, the men automatically bowed down and took the pain. The owner checked on Patu and when he didn't bow down with them, he started splashing again. The competition was on and someone was going to get burned!

The owner stopped pouring and gently put down the water dipper. The heat was excruciating as he waited for someone to run out. No one moved and no one ran out, but as it got hotter, they all started to moan in pain. The hot steam always guaranteed that someone cried out in pain.

On the other hand, Patu didn't feel any pain, so when the man stopped splashing, he reached over and grabbed the water dipper and inspected it. When Patu grabbed the water dipper, all the attention was on him now. Patu started giggling and threw down the water dipper and said, "Hey idiot, what a puny water dipper. It's what the women use."

Insulted by this imbecile, the owner grabbed his water dipper. He then looked at the rest of the men, but he quickly changed his mind after sensing the heat and dropped it. When he dropped the water dipper, the rest of the men started chuckling again.

The owner had to defend himself. "Sorry, I had to put it down; I saw Patu's hair sizzle from the heat."

Reacting to the mocker and the excruciating heat, Patu started moving around, but he edged closer to the fire. Patu didn't like anyone mocking him and he didn't tolerate it. Patu reached down for a hot stone and grabbed one!

Holding a hot stone, Patu examined it and replied, "Ha, so cold," and threw it back down to the fire again.

Surprised by Patu's action, the men's jaws dropped. They now knew whom they were messing with and it was a shaman!

Still fuming from the mocker, Patu wasn't done yet and told them, "I'm still cold, maybe if I get a little closer to the fire."

To everyone's surprise, Patu got up and sat down on the burning wood, but he didn't seem to get burned. Watching in total awe and when Patu didn't catch on fire, one of the surprised men had to ask him, "What are you doing?"

Sitting on the fire, Patu replied, "I think I feel a little warm now," and when Patu stopped talking, the men scrambled out.

Seeing the men scrambling out, Patu yelled out, "Wait!" and he got up and chased after them.

On the porch and to his disappointment, Patu didn't see the men around. They had just left their clothes and ran home. Seeing no one around, he started laughing hysterically to himself, as the Maqivik was now empty with no challengers.

Thinking about the Maqivik, Patu's forehead started to sweat. As the night settled in, he got up and started walking toward the village. When he reached the tip of the village, dogs began to bark at him, but he didn't mind. *Dogs always barked at anyone that came in, especially this late, Patu thought* and he knew he was being watched.

When Patu came into the village, he was greeted by three warriors from Anarciq. The warriors were curious about him and asked him what he was doing there so late. Patu just told them that he was going to go to one of the Maqiviks to steam. Little did they know that he was planning to entertain a family.

When the warriors left him, Patu strolled down to the middle of the village and checked the houses. He spotted a big sod house and he got happy and went over to it. At the entranceway, he changed his mind, because the house was too big for him. He began strolling around again and spotted one. He giggled to himself and went over to it and stopped. The sod house was too puny for his entertainment, so he strolled again. Then he spotted one. The house was just right and beautiful. He began to get excited and giggled to himself and crawled in.

Once he was inside the house, the occupants of the sod house were surprised to see him and asked what he wanted. *I want to kill you,* Patu thought as the man asked him. It was unwise to let them hear his thoughts, so Patu just stared at occupants and said nothing to them. *This was too easy,* Patu thought, *way too easy.*

Inside this sod house, there was a man and a woman, and their four kids sleeping. The fire lamps were on and Patu could see everyone in that house. Patu could smell the salmon dried fish they had eaten earlier. The salmon dried fish had lots of energy and his stomach began begging for it.

The couple just sat there and waited for their guest to explain to them why he was here so late. After a while, the couple began inching closer together as they observed the uninvited guest. The man looked at his wife and then to his four kids. His forehead began to sweat from nervousness and then he focused on Patu again.

Uninvited, Patu looked at the man and said to him, "I've been running all day and my throat is dry. Do you have any water?"

The owner of the house seemed nervous and quickly responded, "I don't have water, but my neighbor might have some. Go and ask him, he should be awake right now."

The nervous man looked at him, but Patu didn't seem to believe him. The owner of the house knew Patu and he had heard about his shamanism, but not the recent news. The man didn't know the people of Tulukar, Nanvarnarlak, or Elai were looking for him. He had a funny feeling this night; because when Patu came into his home, his four kids' just fell asleep. The man checked his wife and his kids again and feared for them. He had to get some help real quick and get this shaman out of his place soon.

After a moment of silence and the uneasiness he felt, the man said to Patu. "I'll let my wife get some water from our neighbors," and that was a big mistake.

Patu, sensing the man's nervousness, just sat there and said nothing to him. *Go ahead and feel that feeling. I love it!* Patu said to himself and that was good news for him.

As the man was about to move, Patu, with his right hand, took out a big, sharp-looking needle of a bone and showed it to the man. In his hand now, Patu was holding a bone and the bone was thick as his finger and long as his hand.

After showing the needle, Patu took out his tongue and with his left hand he grabbed it and stretched his tongue out. Then using his right hand, he pierced his tongue with the bone. Getting pierced with the bone, Patu grimaced in pain and the blood started spilling down to the ground.

The man and the woman just stared at him and did nothing as Patu pierced his tongue. When the couple didn't scream, Patu started stretching his tongue upward as hard as he could toward his left eye. Still pulling as hard as he could, suddenly, his tongue ripped in half! As his tongue tore off, Patu screamed out and let go of his severed tongue and it fell to the floor.

Horrified at the show, the woman screamed this time and grabbed her husband. As the woman screamed, Patu waved his hand at them and somehow, the couple calmed down. When the couple calmed down, Patu opened his mouth and showed them the rest of his tongue. His mouth was now bleeding as it was dripped down to the floor. The couple was still horrified from seeing the blood.

After showing them his bloody mouth, Patu then reached down and grabbed his severed tongue and showed it to the couple. After showing it to the couple, Patu took his severed tongue down to the floor again and started wiping it. After wiping his severed tongue on the floor, he brought it up and showed it to the couple again. After showing it to the couple, Patu put his severed tongue back into his mouth and closed it. With his mouth closed, Patu looked down at the floor and started shaking his head violently. After shaking his head, Patu slowly looked up to the couple with his mouth open and showed them his tongue and it was normal again.

Seeing Patu's normal tongue, the couple relaxed a bit and they were happy it was just a trick. They still kept their eyes on the shaman, not trusting what he would do next. Their kids were there with them and they had to protect them. The trick seemed real and it scared them. They hoped Patu would just go out now and leave them alone.

As Patu was looking at the couple and with his mouth still open, all of sudden, the half of his tongue fell off and it hit the floor again!

Seeing what just happened, the woman screamed and grabbed her husband again, but again, Patu waved his hand at her and then they somehow both calmed down again. After his tongue fell down again, this time, Patu raised his right hand and hit his useless severed tongue real hard. After he smacked his tongue, he looked down at it and said, "I need a new one."

Patu slowly looked up at the couple and they seemed more scared than ever before. The impressive impromptu performance for the couple was working for him. Satisfied with the scared couple, Patu with his bloody mouth went over to the clay lamps and blew them out. Sometimes, scared people were too scared to scream or even move.

In the complete darkness, the couple grabbed each other and got closer to where their kids were sleeping, but they seemed gone. The couple started panicking and when they did, they started hearing Patu whispering in the dark somewhere.

"I love it, I love it, I love it," Patu whispered in the darkness and continued, "I want you. I can hear your heart and can I have it?"

The next morning, Patu's thirst was gone and his tongue felt perfectly fine. He had to get out of there, as soon as possible, before the whole village woke up. He went out and checked the area. The sun was on the horizon and all of a sudden a little boy popped out of the neighbor's sod house. He was too late and he was spotted. He looked at the little boy and smiled at him. He gazed back at the horizon and stretched his neck.

After stretching, Patu looked back at the little boy and said to him, "Good morning little runner," as the boy just stood there frozen and curiously looking at him.

When Patu said his good morning, the little boy jumped up and went back into his sod house. Inside the sod house, the boy started waking up his father. The scared little boy shook his father and yelled at him, "Aat! There is a man out there and he's by our neighbor's house!"

The father never moved, but he kicked the little boy. It was too early in the morning for anyone to wake him. He was dead tired and he didn't want to be bothered, "Shut up and get out of my face, I am trying to sleep."

The little boy shook his dad again and yelled again, "His face was covered in blood and the blood was dripping all the way down to his parka!"

Upon hearing about the blood, his dad woke up slowly and didn't believe such a thing was happening. Especially the blood dripping down anyone's parka was out of the question, "You're lying, don't lie to me," and the father went back to sleep.

This time, the boy kicked his father really hard and cried out, "I think he killed our neighbor!"

Hearing the word *kill,* the sleepy man woke up and pushed the little boy to the floor and told him to get his spear and to wake everyone up. The father took his spear and stormed out to see this bloody man.

After waking up all his family, the little boy took a spear and went out of the house. Outside his home, he saw a man with an arrow on his head. The boy gazed slowly to the neighbor's house and saw the same bloody man.

Looking at the boy, the bloody man said to him again, "good morning little runner," and the bloody man started walking down toward the river.

The little boy checked the dead man and noticed that it was his father! The little boy screamed and woke everyone in that village. The bloody man was already gone.

WINTER HUNTING

At the winter camp, the hunters' food supply was getting low. The nippy, merciless days made it hard for the hunters to hunt and catch animals. The men were busy gathering wood for fire, then hunting. When the cold spell was over, the famished hunters started tracking animals for a few days. They finally got lucky and caught a moose. The moose was a young cow and the meat would last them for weeks. Everyone in that little camp felt good about the kill. The much-needed fatty meat was a blessing for them.

The snow was deep in the timberlines. To make it easier for them to move around, Guk decided to make snowshoes for all of them by using the sinew of the moose and the abundance of trees that were in the area. The hunters didn't take long to make the snowshoes. The snowshoes made Tatu float on the deep parts of the snow and he seemed to move faster with them.

On their rest days, Tatu practiced hard with the bow and arrow until he got his blunted arrows where he wanted them to hit. Tuma kept telling him to perfect everything he did with the bow.

The hunters also made a couple of bows from birch wood trees. To make the bow, Guk made sure he got the straight wood from the birch tree. The arrows had quivers from the ptarmigan they caught. The hunters also made enough arrows to last them for days.

On cold days, the hunters told some jokes to keep them warm. The never-ending stories the men told were fun and exiting for Tatu. The men told him that one time they were ordered to track a man who turned into a dog, but they never caught him. Hearing this story, Tatu didn't believe them and they were probably trying to scare him, so he dismissed the idea of that story.

A month passed when a man with a dog team came around their campsite. The hunters were out hunting, so they didn't get to see him. Whoever it was, dropped some food supplies and took off again the way he came. Tatu asked Guk who came by and he said it was Kauki. Kauki was to come by every other week and take the food and the fur they caught and bring them back to the other boys at Tulukar. Kauki didn't take all their catch and he made sure the hunters had enough food and fur for themselves.

A month passed and a dog team came by again. It was Kauki and he was planning to stay for a day. The hunters all helped him unload his sled. The dog musher brought the hunters fresh fish, dry fish and some new parkas, pants and shoes. Most importantly, he brought some berries.

In the summertime, when the berries are ripe, people picked them to make akutaq (salmonberries with oil). The salmonberries are really good thirst quenchers for hunters. To make sure the berries didn't rot, people made grass-woven or from birchbark baskets and stored the berries underground, in the permafrost.

That same day as Kauki came in; he informed the hunters that there were two other boys running behind him. He told them that the boys were from Atmaulluaq and they would be coming in late.

Immediately, Tatu's mind sparked and he thought of Kaluk and Eli. Guk decided to send Tatu's two friends to the winter camp. His village friends were coming and he was anxious to see them. He would feel comfortable talking with kids his age and thinking about it made him feel better.

The hunters started to pack the meat and the fur and got them ready for Kauki, so he could send them to Tulukar. In springtime, the fur would be used to make skin for kayaks. The extra fur would be used to make clothes.

It was getting dark, but the hunters were still outside their shelter and checking the horizon for the kids. It took them two days to get here and Tatu didn't think they would be able to reach this place until the next morning. He could be wrong, because they had been running for months. He was getting faster and stronger and his friends should be too.

As they waited for the boys outside, the men got the fire started and melted some snow. After melting the snow, they roasted some fresh ptarmigan they had caught that day. Guk saved some ptarmigan meat for the kids to eat. Tatu was sure his friends were starving, because long runs got you drastically hungry and thirsty.

Early next morning, when the sun began to peek over the horizon, the boys were seen from a distance. The weather was pleasant and it was a good day to run. As Tatu's friends got close to them, the boys stopped running and observed them. Kauki motioned them to come on in and the boys started running again till they finally reached the camp.

The boys, Kaluk and Eli, were well hardened by their training. They both were happy to see their friend. Tatu could tell they were sore like he had been when he first came here. After not seeing each other for a long time, the kids greeted and hugged each other happily.

Starving from the run, the kids were hungry and Guk gave them the left-over ptarmigan meat from yesterday. The two hungry boys ate and when they finished, they settled down. After a while, before their muscles tightened, they got up and stretched their legs.

While his friends were stretching, Tatu picked up some snow and threw it at them. The three friends grinned at each other and started wrestling each other. They were huffing and puffing as they threw each other around. Tatu knew their legs were sore and he started pounding on their legs. Every time he hit their legs, it made the boys squirm in pain. The three boys were yelling and screaming as they kept wrestling for a while. The men got tired of their little childish games and told them to stop. The three friends finally stopped and started laughing. It was good for them to be together again. The men were happy to see Tatu in a good mood too.

When the boys settled down, Eli told Tatu that he got lucky to get away from Tulukar, because a lot of kids were fighting each other every day. They were training the other boys very hard and they also started to learn the bow and arrows. Pretending not to believe him, Tatu told him that he was lying and Eli got offended.

Eli was going to show how hard they had been training them. He took off his parka and flexed his muscles. Looking at his muscles, the rest of the boys laughed at him and told him he was still small. The rest of the men started laughing too as Eli put his parka back on.

Kaluk and Eli were told to rest, while the rest went out and checked their traps. After a quick bite, Kauki went back to the village with Ipuun this time. Kauki planned to come by within a couple of days to haul some of the meat back.

The hunters stayed behind and hunted with the new crew. They hunted all winter long and as months passed, their furs and food were getting abundant. Soon, spring would be coming and these hunters would be heading back to Tulukar.

BEAR TWITCH

The days were getting longer and that meant one only thing to the hunters-spring was coming! When the weather got warmer, the snow started melting fast. Soon, birds and animals of all sorts would start arriving in the area. The best part of spring was when the tundra changed color from pure white to a variety of beautiful colors. All winter long, one sound of the wind chilled their bones. Then when spring came, many sounds sang songs to them to let them forget the merciless winter. When flocks of birds arrived, they filled the sky with different sounds of brilliant colors. Their spirits changed with the coming of the warmth and with the coming of fresh new life.

The hunter's catches were abundant by now and the kids were learning many techniques to catch animals. They started pairing up in twos and hunted where they pleased. Some of them checked their traps or gathered some wood. As days went by, the hunters started seeing bear tracks.

Then one night, Guk woke Tatu up in the middle of the night. Guk wasn't awake, but dreaming. In his bed, Guk was twisting and kicking his legs uncontrollably and growling to himself. This was strange to him and he got worried for a bit. Something seem to be bothering Guk, because he wasn't sleeping normally.

Tuma woke up from Guk's nightmare too and said, "Oh, he's dreaming and that's a good sign."

Tatu asked Tuma about the, "good sign," Tuma told him that he had been hunting with Guk for a long time and learned when they were about to see a big animal the next day, Guk always dreamed badly and he wouldn't remember anything.

When Guk woke up, Tatu had to ask him, "Guk, did you have a dream last night?"

Guk looked at Tatu questioningly and said, "No . . . why?"

Tuma told him about him dreaming last night. Hearing the news, that same morning Guk gave out extra servings of rations to everyone. The day was going to be full and they would need a lot of energy. After the hunters finished their meal, Tatu was to hunt with Tuma. Tuma wanted to follow the stream west from their campsite.

After the men briefed the boys and when they finished their breakfast, Tatu went out. Standing outside, he closed his eyes and smelled the fresh spring air that seemed to cleanse his body. He opened his eyes and the sun was already warming him up. It was going to be a pleasant day. His stomach was full and he felt great and everything seemed perfect.

The hunters gathered outside and stretched. Guk and the other boys planned to go northward and up the river. The hunters got their weapons ready and took off on their separate ways. Tuma made sure Tatu packed light that morning.

Tuma and Tatu took off from the campsite. As they ran, the snow crust was still hard beneath them and it cracked as they stepped on it. When the sun hit the middle, the top hard layer of the snow softened and it became mushy to their touch. The mushy snow made them slow down a bit, but they were making good progress.

Tuma and Tatu reached the stream and because of the warming of the weather, the little streams were now ice-free and flowing downriver. At the stream site, Tuma decided to head upriver. Going up the stream, the hunters came across bear tracks. Checking out the bear tracks, Tuma and Tatu looked at each other and smiled.

Tuma muttered, "Fresh bear tracks."

When Tatu saw these bear tracks, he felt very excited; because it was the first time he was ever going to see a black bear. His friend had once told him that bears could hear anything they said about them. So he tried not to mention that they were hunting it. That is, if he was lucky today, but these were fresh tracks and they were made early this morning. The bear wasn't going to be far from them.

Their plan was to run and follow the bear tracks until they saw the bear, and slowly stalk it down. Using their bows and arrows, they would wound it and then kill it with their spears. The bear was downwind from them, so the wind was in their favor. They had to be extra careful, because hungry and starving bears usually came out of their dens in the springtime.

While hunting a bear, mistakes were out of the question for them. Tuma didn't like making mistakes and he would have a fit at everyone and even at his friends. He didn't take any excuses from anyone, especially from a young inept one like Tatu.

The bear tracks led inland and then back to the stream again and the animal just kept walking up the stream. As the two hunters pursued the bear, it led them to a large area made of tall cotton grass and there were no trees around. Still, it was a bad sign, because they wouldn't be able to see the bear from afar. Even with the dangerous signs, Tuma kept on tracking it.

Tracking the beast, Tuma was a tyrant when he pursued his prey. For his size, Tuma was very agile and very, very quiet. The two hunters slowly entered the tall cotton grass and without saying anything, Tuma ordered Tatu to slow down and follow behind him and to watch the right flank and the back as well. The tyrant sensed something.

Getting orders from Tuma, Tatu kept his eyes open for any signs of the bear. The area seemed deathly quiet to him. As he stepped on the grass, it seemed to creak out loud, but he knew he was quiet or maybe not quiet enough.

Smelling the air, Tuma stopped in his tracks and then proceeded. Without saying anything, he froze. As Tuma froze, the back of Tatu's hair stood up and he automatically froze too. This didn't feel normal or right to either of them. Something was different and they could feel it. To Tatu's right, in the tall cotton grass, he heard something breathing, but it was too faint to tell.

Tuma turned his head back, faced Tatu, and grinned. Seeing Tuma's grin was a bad sign for anyone who knew him. Quietly, Tatu took two steps forward and something stood up on the right side of him. He took a deep breath when he saw something big and dark from the corner of his eye. It was the bear and it was just inches away from him!

Time ceased to exist as the humans collided with the bear world. Panicking, Tatu yelled out, "Ah!" and to avoid contact, Tatu jumped forward toward Tuma. The roaring bear swung and grazed his right arm and Tatu landed awkwardly on his back. The bear collided with the human world and with deadly force.

When Tatu hit the ground, Tuma's eyes got wide and with his spear positioned to throw, he started yelling at the bear himself, "Ah!" He needed to get the bear's attention and away from his little rabbit, so he screamed again, "Ah!"

On the ground, Tatu quickly turned his head and focused on the threat and braced himself. Luckily, the bear was now growling at Tuma. The bear set his eyes on Tatu again and went down to its paws. On the left side of Tatu's head, he heard a *whooshing* sound as Tuma's spear went past him and the spear hit the bear in its stomach.

Getting hit, the bear made a loud yelp and ran away from them.

That was close! Tuma saved me from the bear attack! Tatu thought and he was relieved, but he was still stunned from the brief attack.

Tuma ran over to Tatu and checked him out. He had seen the bear swing and hit Tatu and that got him worried for a bit. He just needed to see where Tatu got hit and he knew that any damage to Tatu's head or stomach would be fatal.

"Tatu, are you OK? Did you get hit? Are you bleeding? Check your arm." Tuma was talking fast at Tatu.

Tatu checked his right arm with his left hand and he felt a sting at first. He worked his way around the area and everything seemed OK. His parka was torn up and some blood was seeping out of it. He could feel the blood pouring out of him as he pressed on it. His arm felt the pain when he moved it, but he felt OK, it wasn't that bad a scratch.

Knowing that Tatu was going to be OK, Tuma looked at him and said he was going after the bear and he took off with his bow ready. Tuma wanted to get the bear before it went too far. He had injured the bear and he didn't want to lose it.

Even though Tatu's right arm wasn't feeling right, he got up and took his spear and his bow. He wasn't going to waste his time tending his wounds. *Tuma needs my help. Now get up and go!* Tatu thought to himself as he psyched himself up.

Tatu heard a loud roar from the bear and he took a deep breath. He glanced at his spear and started running toward the noise. As he ran, his heart began to pump faster and he didn't feel the pain in his arm anymore. He was running on adrenaline now and he needed it.

In the open tundra, Tatu could see Tuma and the bear. Tuma had his bow ready and shot the bear. The arrow found its mark, but it didn't seem to do any damage. The wounded bear started growling again, but it finally sat down.

Tatu ran toward Tuma and he got there with his spear. As he reached Tuma, Tuma told him to strike it, as he stepped aside. For caution, Tuma had his bow ready and waited for Tatu. Tatu dropped his bow and gripped his spear.

Tatu and the bear were now facing each other and he positioned himself to strike it. When the bear raised it's paws, with all his strength, he thrust his spear into its body. Tatu's spear went in and the bear fell backward. As the bear fell down, Tatu let go and backed away from it. He felt relieved when the bear went down, because it couldn't kill them anymore. The hunt seemed to be over for now.

When the bear fell down, Tuma yelled out, "Wugg' (Awesome)! You got it!"

After Tuma yelled out, he started patting Tatu's back, and every time Tuma hit his back, Tatu was happy, but he grimaced in pain. It was still sinking in what had just happened to him and he started breathing heavily.

That was exciting and *I almost got killed! Wugg' indeed!* Tatu said to himself thankfully. Tatu looked down at the bear and started shaking uncontrollably. He took some deep breaths again to calm himself down.

Tuma hit his back again and told him, "Relax, Tatu, it is down and dying. We got the bear!"

Tatu checked the black bear and he stopped shaking, but then his hands started shaking again from all the adrenaline. Examining his kill, he saw that the bear had a big white spot on its neck. It was a decent size bear and it seemed bigger than him.

"Whew, that was close," Tatu said to Tuma as he started to relax.

Tuma slapped him again and slapped him back to reality. The next thing they did to the bear was scarier for Tatu than the attack.

Tuma got the bear on its back and went on his knees, and with both of his hands he opened the bear's mouth. He then looked at Tatu and told him to put his hand in the bear's mouth!

Tatu was standing beside him holding a knife and he was thinking of dressing it. *Did he just say, put my hand in this bear's mouth?* Tatu questioned himself in disbelief. Tatu looked at Tuma and shook his head.

Tuma's face got serious and said, "You have to put your hand all the way in the bear's mouth. We caught it and if it's your first time killing one of these monsters, you need to put your arm all the way inside this bear's mouth. Hurry up before it dies, and take your parka off!"

Tatu was speechless at getting orders from the killer himself. Tatu took off his parka and placed it down on the tundra. He then checked his right arm again. His arm was still bleeding, but not that bad. He should be able to live for a while.

Tatu focused on its teeth and knelt down beside the bear's head. He hesitated at first, but he reached deep inside of him for courage and took his right hand inside this bear's mouth, while trying to avoid the razor-sharp-looking teeth. His right hand went in and stopped inside the bear's throat.

Again, Tuma told him to put his hand all the way in and again as far as he could. Tuma could see the nervousness in the boy and told him to hurry up.

Tatu was thinking, the bear would come alive and would shut its mouth and tear his delicate arm out. *No, I don't think I will do it, but then Tuma will kill me.* Tatu thought about it and then he cautiously forced his tender arm as far as he could inside the beast. It was kind of slippery and oozy and tight for him as he forced his right hand farther down its throat. He would feel it jerk sometimes or he thought he did as his hand went down farther down to the abyss.

It's going to get up and tear my arm off! It will! It will! Tatu was still imagining the horror of trying to pry his arm out of its death grip.

Tatu's right arm was halfway in and he felt its throat tighten again. That got him worried a little bit. His hand was at the mercy of this bear. His right hand was useful for him; he needed it to punch his friends with it!

"Whoa," Tatu muttered out and he looked at Tuma.

Tuma smiled at him and asked him if he felt its heartbeat. Tatu felt its heartbeat and it was still beating, but getting slower and slower.

Tatu was taking it all in; his hand was inside the largest animal in the world, inside this monster's mouth! The bear brought Tatu back to reality when he felt it jerk again. This monster didn't want him wondering.

"Whoa! I felt that and I think it was the last heartbeat." Tatu told Tuma.

Tuma was smiling at Tatu and told him when the heart stopped he had to get some blood out and drink from it. Finally, Tatu seemed to feel its last heartbeat, so he cupped his hand, which was still inside, and took out his arm and then drank the blood. His arm was free now.

From that day forth, every time Tatu was going to see his prey, his left arm muscles jerked. When his muscles jerked like that, Tatu anticipated seeing his prey. He called it his bear twitch, because it had started twitching after he felt the bear's last heartbeat.

Tuma put his own arm inside the bear's mouth and drank some of its blood too. Both of the men got up and looked around to see if anything was around. They could see a crow fly by and it began cawing. They both could tell the crow was also happy for them as it circled around them in joy.

Seeing the whole ordeal, Tatu started to think, what kind of man would put his whole arm into a live animal with big teeth and feel its last heartbeat? A brave one? A bold one? A hunter? A warrior? and then it dawned on him, it was them, Yup'ik, they were all of them.

After the whole ordeal, the two hunters wrapped Tatu's bleeding arm and stopped further damage. After taking care of his wound, they dressed the meat and prepared it for transport. They used the hide and hauled the meat back to the camp.

After a couple of days, Tatu's wound healed, but he got sick afterward. It took him awhile to recover. When he got better and his wounds healed, Guk told him that he had a story to tell when people asked him about the scar marks on his arm. Jokingly, his friends told him that the reason the bear didn't eat him, but scratched him, was that he smelled bad. Tatu, feeling better after his fever, got up and wrestled his friends. Then he punched their legs with his right hand! The men had enough and told them to stop. They all stopped and started to chuckle.

RUNNING HOME

It was early in the morning when Patu was roasting some meat on a fire. It was a long time since he had seen the Yup'ik people. He was living off hunting and usually, his free meals came from his services. Hunting was not that fun at all, but he needed to eat. The animals he hunted were getting harder and harder to catch.

Patu took a bite out of the meat and savored the moment. He had eaten rabbit and ptarmigan for a while. The change of the menu, with lots of fat, made him feel better. As he took a bite, the fatty part of the meat seemed to melt in his mouth. "Mmm," Patu whispered to himself. Suddenly, he felt something strong in his back.

After two days, when his brother didn't return to his village of Gali, Napaq went out to look for his brother. He told everyone that his brother hadn't returned the following day while out checking his traps. Fearing the worst for his brother, he went off to check on him.

Napaq got ready and took off that morning to check on his brother's favorite trapping spots. As Napaq was checking his brother's trapping spots, some of his traps had caught animals, but he left them alone. *My lazy brother can pick them up for himself,* Napaq thought to himself.

Not too far from his brother's traps, he saw what looked like a smoke fire. Seeing the smoke, he got really excited. *I hope that's my brother!* he was happily thinking to himself.

Getting excited, Napaq started running toward the direction of the smoke and climbed up the hill. When he reached the top, he stopped and scanned the area of the campfire. Beside the campfire, Napaq spotted a man, but he didn't recognize his parka. The man was sitting down and he seemed to be cooking something. He was about to go check him out, but he spotted something out of the ordinary. On the man's right was something that looked like human legs with blood all around it, but he wasn't sure. Napaq looked closely at the leg this time and recognized his brother's muskrat pants!

Napaq felt his stomach purge. *He killed him and I think and I think he's eating him!* Napaq screamed to himself.

Before the man looked around at him, Napaq took off running toward his home as fast as he could, so he could report to his people what he just witnessed. Just running only a few steps, he stopped and vomited all over himself. After vomiting the rest of his meal, he gathered himself and started running again.

By the fire, Patu looked back and saw a man running away. *Fresh meat and not frozen,* Patu maliciously thought to himself. He grabbed the dead man's bow and arrow and started running toward the runner. He hastily climbed up the hill and the man he was pursuing was running away from him. Patu aimed at the man and shot him.

Napaq started running at full speed. Never in his life had he expected to see such a sight. The man was eating his brother and he needed to report to his people and chase after his brother's killer. *Oh my goodness and that guys eating my brother! I need to tell the elders and . . .* Napaq was thinking to himself and before he finished his thoughts, his mind went blank.

Patu hit his target in the head while he was running, "I got him!" Patu proudly yelled at himself. He looked around for any witness that would be awed by his skill, but no one was around and he got mad and yelled, "Come on! Someone should have been watching me!"

Disappointed, he checked the bow and admired its accuracy. After admiring the bow, he started running toward the fresh meat and reached him.

When Patu reached his catch, he noticed the pants, "A brother?"

Without remorse Patu grabbed the corpse. *Fresh meat!* he happily thought as he observed the warm body. Never, in his entire life had he been as lucky as today. He had more meat than he ever had before! *Another day, another lucky day!* Patu thought to himself.

Patu took out his knife and got the man on his back. He hastily started cutting his parka open. After exposing the dead body to the cold, with his knife he cut the man's chest wide open. Opening his chest cavity, he grabbed the ribs and stretched them out. The insides of this man were now exposed. Looking at the rich dark blood, Patu licked his lips and started drinking the blood.

The man's heart was still beating, but finally slowed down and stopped. After eating some roast meat, Patu needed water to quench his thirst. As he was quenching his thirst, the back of Patu's hair stood up again and he perked his ears to listen. Feeling the same sensation, he raised his head and smelled the air.

Patu, hearing and smelling nothing, continued to fill his need. Then he heard a faint noise again and stood up this time. From the path that his victim had been running toward, Patu saw some men coming his way. He looked down at the dead man and spat on him. "You brought some people!" Patu angrily said to the corpse.

Patu raised his legs and stomped the dead man's chest and he could hear a loud crack when he broke the ribs, *crack!* Without waiting for the men to reach him, Patu took something from his parka and ate it. After eating whatever he took, he started running in circles and then ran toward the coast again, away from the men.

Twelve men from Gali kept jogging toward the smoke. They had been sent out by the elders to follow Napaq and help him find his brother. They were briefed about a shaman named Patu. They learned that Patu was the one that turned into a dog and that he was terrorizing villages. Fearing for Napaq and his brother, the men sped up toward the smoke.

Before the men reached the smoke, they saw a man and he seemed to be dragging something. When they got closer to him, they saw what looked like a body on the ground and they spotted a dog running away from the scene and the man was now gone. When they reached the site, they realized it was Napaq and he had been murdered. The men checked the dog tracks and decided to chase it. They had to split into two parties; the other half would go and check the smoke.

Six fast runners were chosen to chase the dog. They were relentless runners and kept up with Patu. After chasing Patu for hours, the men lost him as a blizzard set in and covered his tracks. Patu got lucky this time and escaped from these men or they would definitely have killed him. As the blizzard got worse, the fast runners ceased hunting and headed back to the site where they had found Napaq's body.

After years of running, passing a lot of villages and terrorizing them, Patu finally came to a new settlement. The new settlement was different and he noticed some of the things he used to see in the old land where he was born. So, Patu carefully checked the area and finally walked into the village.

The warriors from that village saw Patu and took him to their qasgiq. Inside the qasgiq, Patu looked at the elders and smiled at them. He saw a familiar face and familiar people. *My people, you finally came for me,* Patu said gleefully to himself.

Patu's people came from another big land from across the ocean. His people were following game. Only thing that stopped them was the big ocean in front of them. Patu figured out that the game had gone toward another land, to this land. So he had taken off and ten seasons later, his people went to look for him.

The men had to row for days to get to this new land and they had finally reached the coast last summer. They killed the inhabitants and settled for a while. There were thousands of them. They called themselves the Teriikaniar People.

SPRING TIME

At the winter campsite, the hunters caught enough bears to make a big skin boat. Unlike the kayak, the big skin boat was wider and rounder. The big, massive, ugly-looking boat was used only once. They carefully made two big boats and they were big enough to haul the meat and the furs back to Tulukar. Finally, when the river was clear of ice, they prepared the big skin boats.

The hunting party was anxious to go back to the settlement and see their friends and especially their families. The spring sun tortured the men endlessly, by increasing its shine and teasing the men to stay awake. When the time was right, with all their gear in the big skin boat, the hunters slowly drifted down the river. The journey to their destination took them about a week, and they reached the lake of Tulukar.

When they finally reached the lake of Tulukar, the hunters were met by two kayaks. The two people in the kayaks had their bows aimed at them and asked who they were. After the hunters told them, the kayaks returned toward Tulukar.

When they got closer to the village, they could see people lined up on the shore. When the hunters finally beached their big skin boat, they were greeted by everyone. The hunters unloaded their goods, while other kids helped them out.

After they unloaded their goods, the five hunters all headed to the qasgiq. At the qasgiq, the hunters settled down and they were greeted by the elders and the other village people. It was nice for them to see the villagers and they exchanged stories of their winter adventures. That night the hunters were going to have their welcoming party.

When the night set in and when everyone got ready at the qasgiq, the festival dance started off with the Tulukar welcoming song. The dancers were women and men and they entertained everyone by trying to make people laugh. They were funny to watch as they competed with each other. There was a lot of food for everyone to eat. The arrival of the hunters was a big blessing for them, along with their successful winter catches.

The women dancers had beautifully designed parkas. The designs on their parkas were of animals they had caught. The designs had birds, caribous, bears, and fish all around their waists. Some parkas had patches of square, circular, and triangular shapes on them and they were colored differently. The ornaments on the parkas were mostly fur, which looked like ropes and some had special beads on them. When the dancers moved with these ornaments, they looked like waves of grass on the wind that caught Tatu's eye. Their head ornaments also were designed and they seemed to sparkle for Tatu. The dance fans, which the dancers held, were mostly made of feathers from birds or furs from caribou. The dancers were beautiful and fun to watch and everyone had a good time.

When the night set in, Guk and his family finally came in and mingled with the people. Atmak was wearing a beautiful parka made of otter pelt and she looked very lovely. She made her way up to the dance floor and danced among the people. Atmak caught Guk's eye and she started teasing Guk. As the dancers picked up the pace, Atmak started dancing toward Guk and that got everyone's attention. People who were sitting beside Guk moved out of the away to watch them. Guk was now smiling and gazing at his beautiful wife. When Atmak reached him, she pulled her husband toward the dance floor.

Getting invited to the dance floor, Guk didn't want to get all the attention, so he motioned his boys to go with him. His brood didn't move, but they all started laughing and just watched him dance. When the song was over, the boys went down to the dance floor and sat down with Guk. The drums started beating slowly again and the singers sang the song of a man who was yearning for his woman. With that in mind, no one could hold it and they started laughing again. Despite the song, the two couples just enjoyed the dance with the people.

When the dancing feast was over, Guk gave Tatu the bear hide and told him to give it to one of the elders. He particularly pointed to a widow who needed one. It was the custom to give more of their catch to the widows and elders.

With the bear hide, Tatu went to the middle of the qasgiq and looked around. He was very nervous as he saw many hands up in the air. Tatu lifted the bear skin up and held it high above him. As Tatu showed the bear skin to the public, little kids started gathering in front of him. The kids were curiously looking at the claws and checked them out. As the kids got too close to him, Tatu scared them off. "Ger!" Tatu growled. . . the kids screamed and backed away from him. One bold girl didn't back off, but she reached out for the claws. Noticing her, Tatu let her touch it. The bold girl touched the bear claws and she smiled at him and said, "So sharp! My name is Arri."

Tatu smiled back at Arri and continued looking around again. Looking at the crowd, he noticed the old woman. The old woman was looking around and smiling at the people. He went over to her and gave her the bear fur.

Getting the attention of everyone there, the old woman took the bear hide and thanked him for it. Receiving such a beautiful gift, she told him that there was more to come his way. She smiled down as she inspected the fur. She then looked around at everyone and showed them her happiness.

The old woman couldn't hold it and said, "So much."

"It almost killed me," Tatu replied.

At that moment, Tatu felt proud and wished his parents were there to see it, especially his Apa. It was a long time since he'd gone home and he missed his family.

After the hunters showed off their catch to the public, they distributed the meat and the fur around. It was a joyous moment for these hunters and to socializing with others was amazing to them.

Later on that night, the old woman whom Tatu had given the fur to, wanted to know more about him. She also wanted to know where he was originally from and wanted to hear about the bear story. After they talked, she said she knew his parents and that she was related to his mom. Tatu's mom was originally from Tulukar and from that day forth, the old woman invited him to eat at her house. Her name was Anuksua and like her grandma, she was a kind woman. Anuksua was fun to listen to and she had many stories to tell him. So every time she was around him, Tatu tried his best to behave.

When the weather got warm and the days got longer, Guk came to Tatu and told him to come with him. They went down to the lake and Guk showed him a kayak that seemed to be brand-new. There were many kayaks in the area, but Guk showed him one and told him that it was his. Guk was to choose three kayaks for Tatu and his friends. The elders gave him first picks, since they had hunted the animals.

Smiling like a baby, Tatu's eyes glimmered as he inspected his new sparkling kayak. He reached out and pressed the skin of the kayak. The skin was so smooth to the touch and it was perfectly sewed on. He placed his eye on the beautifully designed kayak and made sure it was straight. It was perfectly built from the bottom to the top. He took hold of the front bow and lifted it up. The kayak was very light. Any flaw on the kayak and it would slow him down.

He wanted the best, the smoothest, "Yes!" Tatu yelled out in happiness.

SUMMER CAMP

Tatu and his friends were to pack up and leave again. This time they were going downriver to fish for salmon. There was a camp down the Kusquqvak River. Hearing the news, Tatu got excited, because when they went downriver, they would stop by his village. Excited to leave for home, Tatu was restless to see his parents.

That winter, Tatu's parents had come by to see him, but they had been out camping. His parents had left him more clothes to wear. The clothes were especially designed for spring and summer. His new garments were made out of seal guts or pike skin and they were lighter and waterproofed. Whenever Tatu tore his clothes, he would bring them over to Anuksua, whom he had given the fur to, and she would immediately sew it back up for him.

When it was time for them to go, the hunters got ready and headed down the river. On this trip, Guk brought his family with him. It didn't take them long to reach Atmautluak.

When they reached Atmautluak, Guk released his anxious little boys to their parents. Tatu led Guk and his family to his parents' home. There, Guk provided his family some food.

Tatu's parents were very happy for him and told him that he had grown up so big and tall. His grandparents came by and so did the rest of the village people to greet him. Tatu's relatives were eager to hear what he had been doing all winter long. It didn't take them long to hear about the bear that scratched Tatu's arm.

Upon hearing about the monster, Tatu's Apa looked at him strangely. The old man wanted to see the bear scratch, so he got up and told Tatu to take off his parka. When his grandson showed them his bear scratch, he smiled at him and said, "Almost! So close it must have been." His Apa was very happy that his grandson was alive. Losing him would devastate him. His Apa's eyes welled and he hugged Tatu. He was very proud of him and fighting back the tears, he continued, "My Tutgar."

After couple of days in Atmautluak, the boys got restless again. It was a good sign for Guk, because it was time to leave. They bid farewell to Tatu's family and the hunters headed down to the Kusquqvak River. Along the journey, they saw a lot of campsites, but they proceeded to their destination.

The waterfowl were abundant and using three pronged arrows, the men hunted some bluebill ducks and black scooters that came their way. When they caught enough ducks, they beached their kayaks on the tundra. There they decided to make camp and they started a small campfire and roasted the birds.

As they roasted their meal, flocks of birds were everywhere around them. Sometimes, they darkened the sky and they just watch them in awe. The bird songs would never end. After they ate their fill, the boys just lay down and listened to the birds and tried to guess what they were. The loudest ones were the cranes and when the boys heard them call, Kaluk would start flapping his arms and dance funny. They knew that when the sun set, they would hear one bird that would lull them to sleep. Loons being one of the opera singers of the bird world, their call were beautiful and sometimes eerie to hear at night. To the boys, the loon call just jumped out at them and stimulated their imagination.

The next morning, they got ready and continued rowing down the river. As they following the spring sun, their surroundings changed drastically. What was once dead white in the wintertime was now flourishing dark rich green. Taking advantage of the short season, the willow tree leaves and the grass bloomed extremely fast. With the change of the season, the hunter's faces darkened too.

On the third day, they finally reached the Kusquqvak River. The Kusquqvak River was wider than the average river they were used to. This river was half a mile wide and reached one mile at some points. Alongside the river were different types of trees. They could see willow trees, cottonwood, birch, some black spruce trees, and shrubs.

When they reach this particular summer campsite, they saw a couple of sod houses above the beach area. These sod houses belonged to different families from many areas. Alongside the riverbed were ten fish racks that were up and ready. By the fish racks were ten smokehouses. These structures were made of trees and ropes.

The hunters were there to help the households and fish for them. In turn, the women in that campsite helped them prepare the fish. The women cut and hung the fish to dry. When the hanging fish were dry enough, they were moved to the smokehouse. The smokehouse would be smoked daily, using the surrounding trees, until they dried up. It was very important to work together, because the summer season was short.

During his stay and in his spare time, Tatu explored his new and interesting environment. The area was thriving with animals and birds. Their campsite was mostly sandy and it was covered with dead and new cotton grass. Besides the grass, he could see abundant trees loaded with many types of little birds that nested in that area.

As ordered by the elders and men from their new camp, the boys went off and collected dead driftwood for the sod houses. The task of collecting wood was daunting, but they never argued.

Sometimes, a moose visited the area. Occasionally, a black bear came around and they would hunt it. The black bear would terrorize their food supply and sometimes they killed their dogs.

The summer sun would set for awhile and then it came up again. When the sun was in the middle, the heat was excruciating. The summer heat would burn their skin sometimes.

On the other hand, when the sun got low and the air cooled down, the mosquitoes appeared in numbers to kill humans. These vicious mosquitoes were always hidden and when the time was right, they attacked. Though the mosquitoes were an annoyance to the people, they had a purpose. To live, birds and fish depended on these mosquitoes. In turn, people depended on the birds and fish to live. The cycle of life was always cycling and the elders told them so.

When it was time for them to catch salmon, the hunters got up early and got their nets ready. When the tide came in, they went out and set the nets close to the shore. As salmon hit the net, they rowed over and gently pulled them out, while trying not to destroy the net. After they caught enough salmon, they pulled the net out and went home. They hung the net to dry, while the women worked on the salmon.

Tatu got to meet the local men and women there. The boys finally got to socialize with girls too. Checking out the girls, the boys got happy. One of them caught Tatu's eye and her name was Apaq and she was about his age or maybe older.

Apaq was standing by a tree looking at the river. After a long day of work, the people were settling in their sod houses. Tatu had seen her around with the other girls before. This day, Tatu finally got the courage to talk to her alone. Every time he had tried to talk to her, her friends or her family had told him to get lost.

So finally, Tatu went over to her and just stared at her. She had big round brown eyes and her black hair was braided down to her shoulder. Her face was golden brown from the everlasting sunshine. She was from Masercurliq and she was very beautiful.

Apaq also knew this boy named Tatu. All that summer, her girlfriends had been checking the boys out and talking about them. Her mother had warned the girls to stay away from the boys.

When Apaq noticed Tatu staring, she looked at him and asked what he was doing here. He told her that he was just there to fish for the summer. She asked him why he always sat funny and jogged everywhere.

"I don't know. It's normal for me, I guess," Tatu said uncomfortably.

"Hah, it's normal for you?" she said and gave him a smirk.

Tatu gave her his best smile and thought about what he had to say next. Talking to a girl wasn't going to be easy at all, especially a beautiful one.

"Yeah, I walk sometimes and sit normally," he responded awkwardly and felt a little embarrassed. He raised his eyebrows and took a deep breath to see if that was the right, normal word she'd like to hear. To stop her onslaught of questions about him, he had to speak up immediately and continued, "So what are you looking at, Apaq?"

She was looking down at her maklaks and playing around with them. She checked the river and then gazed back at him. She was very nervous too, because she liked him. She didn't want him to know that she liked him. She smiled to herself and looked at him and replied, "Oh, you're still here," but then she blushed. The words just came out wrong. When she noticed herself blushing, she immediately checked her maklaks again. When her blushing seemed to disappear, she looked at him again and continued, "I was just looking at the river and thinking." And she gazed back at the river.

Please don't blush! Please don't blush! she was screaming to herself as she checked the river.

Tatu immediately had to check the river and said to her, "Oh, I thought you were looking at me."

Apaq started blushing again and then she pointed to the river and said, "No, I was looking at the river," and she hesitated to look back at him to see if he knew where the river was.

Tatu had to think and he observed her maklaks and responded, "Oh, I get it-the river is me. Thanks for comparing me to the mighty Kusquqvak River. The Kusquqvak River is basically why people live around here and without it, we are nothing. If I am the river, I'll bring you plenty of fish and birds."

Tatu gave her his best smile again and Apaq blushed again. She had the most beautiful blush he had ever seen before. Her smile was comparable to nothing. The moment of connection ceased to exist when someone yelled at the couple, "Apaq, get over here! Right now! Go home and don't go out again and tell that boy to get lost!"

It was Apaq's mother and she was yelling at her. Apaq quickly looked around and spotted her mother and she automatically stood up. Tatu didn't want to lose the moment, but he had no choice. Her mother was watching and she was mad at them.

"Yaa, I'm coming, Mother!" Apaq responded.

Apaq was walking off and then she abruptly stopped. She was bothered by something he had just said to her. The moment with him had gone too fast for her. She quizzically gazed back at him and smiled and then said, "The big river?" and she turned around and took off toward home.

That summer, Apaq and Tatu got to talk with each other, but not as much as he wanted to. Fall was upon them and the day came for the hunters to leave. Before the hunters left for the summer, Tatu had a chance to talk to Apaq alone again. She was on a riverbank all alone and she was just playing around with her story knife.

When Tatu saw Apaq alone, he crept over to her and spooked her from behind. His objective was to get her attention and it worked for him.

Getting spooked, Apaq screamed out, "Ah!" and she quickly turned around and hit Tatu instinctively. She got angry at first, but when she saw Tatu, she changed her attitude for the better, but she was still fuming and told him, "Oh, it's you! You scared me! Don't ever spook me like that again!" She calmed down a bit and continued, "Are you being mischievous today?"

Tatu sadly told her no and that they were leaving the next day. The summer had been so exciting for both of them. It just seemed to pass by them so fast. Getting to know each other was fun.

Saddened that Tatu was leaving the next day, Apaq took a deep breath and said, "Oh, seems like I just got to know you, you should stay a little longer."

Tatu was sad too and he didn't want to go either. He observed her for a while and then got lost in her eyes. Noticing she was sad too, Tatu said to her, "Don't be sad, Apaq. I will see you next year, then the next after, then the next, until your mom stops telling me to get lost, but tells me to marry you."

Apaq was surprised to hear that from him and she was silent for a while. She couldn't help but smile a little bit at what he had to say to her. She knew he was just teasing her. She decided to go another notch and surprise him too. She scanned around and noticed a little bird not too far off.

Knowing that Tatu was just teasing her about being married, Apaq decided to top it a notch. She quickly said to him, "Hah! No way! She will never tell me that, but if she does say that, you will hit that bird from right here." With her story knife, she was pointing to a bird behind Tatu.

Tatu turned his head around and spotted the bird. It was a seagull and it was a long ways away from them. After looking at the bird, Tatu turned around and faced Apaq. The seagull was way off and he knew it. Being challenged, Tatu's adrenaline kicked in and he got confident. Still looking at her, Tatu had to take a chance and said to her, "So easy."

Tatu was confident and he was drilled to believe that he could do impossible things if he set his mind to it. He then bent down and grabbed a stick from the ground and looked at the stick. The time was now to prove to anyone that impossible things can be achieved. He was ready to hit the bird and the wind was in his favor. Looking at Apaq, he knew it was time. The whole summer was all about them. So without looking at the bird behind him, Tatu threw the stick toward the bird and blurted out, "I got it."

As the stick flew off from Tatu's hand, Apaq's eyes got wide with disbelief.

Looking at her reaction, Tatu knew that impossible things could be achieved. *Impossible things* can always be achieved, Tatu thought and he looked at her face and knew it was an unbelievable shot.

With her eyes and mouth wide open, Apaq looked at him and started laughing. She reached down to her stomach and with her hands she pressed her stomach to try control her laughing and said, "You didn't even come close to hitting that bird!"

Tatu didn't believe her and said, "I got it, is it bloody and flapping its wings?"

"No you idiot, you missed it completely!" she said and she laughed again.

Tatu looked back at the bird and it was alive! He smiled at the bird and turned around and looked at her beautiful blush again, and her amazing eyes. He wanted to see her impossibly beautiful smile, and he'd achieved it. Sometimes, some things are so beautiful that they are worth the moment.

Tatu tried to be serious and disappointed and he told her, "So it's alive." He paused for a bit and continued, "I never missed before, but I'm happy it's alive, because it's alive and alive like us." Tatu was pointing at both of them as he was telling her that.

Apaq stopped laughing and fell silent for a minute, probably thinking about the bird. At this point, Tatu didn't want to see her sad, so he gave her his wisdom of the birds which he secretly knew about them, "Apaq, did you know the birds come here every year to see both of us and to see if we got married?"

Apaq got happy again and chuckled. She stood up and faced him this time and she pushed him gently on his chest. Getting pushed, Tatu moved back and smiled at her. She didn't believe him and that was good news.

"No way, that's not true, the birds come here to nest, you idiot," she said to him as they both started laughing together.

Tatu was looking at her smile and noticed another figure not too far off. It was her mother coming their way and without thinking about it, he took her hand and told her to come with him for a ride in his kayak. She hesitated at first, but then she gave in and followed him. On this last day, she wanted to spend the day with him. It was going to be a long winter and she knew she would miss him greatly.

The couple took off toward Tatu's kayak. His kayak was tight for two, but they managed to fit. That day in the water, Apaq and Tatu were all alone and they just talked about everything. They had a great time as they laughed and told stories. They knew they would get into trouble, but it was worth it.

At the end of their short trip, Tatu just hated to let go of her. He looked at her and said, "I'm going to miss you."

The next morning, Apaq saw him off and the year after, her parka had designs of birds. Since then, every time when Tatu saw her, he would tell her that he was getting her. She'd laugh at him and would tell him to tell her mother, which Tatu never did, but it was good to be alive for him.

That fall, Guk took the boys downriver and they got to hunt some seals. The seal hunters weren't alone in that area. The seal being one of the most important sources of their diet, a lot of men hunted them. Their seal-hunting harpoon tips were made of ivory or the racks of the caribou or the moose. The harpoon tips were designed to pull in the seal when thrown at them. Once the tip was inside the seal, the harpoon tip would turn sideways and grab the meat or the blubber. It lodged in the skin enough for the hunter to be able to pull it in.

Downriver, the hunters beached their kayaks and waited patiently for the seals to show up. The hunters made a small shelter on the land and just waited for the seals to arrive. They sometimes had to wait for days for a single seal to show up. When the seals showed up, they hunted them. That fall, Kaluk got lucky and caught three seals. Eli caught two and Tatu also got lucky and caught two.

Finally, with their catch of the summer and fall, the hunters headed back up to Tulukar. The weather started to cool and the hunters seemed to be more active and alert. The scenery changed slowly again, what was once bursting green, turned red, orange, or yellow and dead. The sign of fall meant the sun set early and darkened the sky. The wind started blowing leaves everywhere. Often, it got cold at night and the humidity kept the hunters restless. Still, they hunted the birds that fattened up during their molting stages.

The hunters finally reached Tulukar and they unloaded their catch. It had been a good summer and fall for them. Tatu got to meet a beautiful girl and he caught seals too. The songs of the birds slowly dissipated and the air got super quiet.

Snow suddenly landed on Tatu's face and melted. "Winter's here," Tatu softly murmured to the wind.

PROFICIENT HUNTERS

As the years went by, the boys got older, taller, and faster. They also became proficient hunters. The never-ending runs and the never-ending hunts made their legs strong and their aims accurate. The competition between three of the boys were fearsome. They were experts with their weapons now. They never trained with the other boys and were now called warriors, but their party was mostly for hunting animals and catching fish. They were learning to shoot the bow while moving through the water. Guk trained his boys hard and they could chase down animals with precision and catch them with ease. As good as they were, Guk didn't want anyone to know that his boys were really, really good at what they did.

Before spring came, the hunters were ordered to get back to Tulukar. Hearing the news, the hunters packed up and headed home. Once at the Tulukar qasgiq, the men began to sing the songs of war.

The songs of war got Tatu worried for his family. Tatu didn't want to go to war with anyone, because living in peace was good. The elders told them that war was inevitable. The shaman had predicted that armies would come down and annihilate everyone in their path. They had only one way to deal with these annihilators.

The Tulukar warriors were great in numbers now as the other village warriors started arriving. Most of the warriors were younger than the three boys, but they were old enough to kill.

The elder council and the leading warriors met and prepared for the first war. The enemy they were concentrating on was the Inuguaq army, which lived up in the mountains. The Tulukar warriors needed high ground to make a stand, so they sent Cung out to scout the area.

After a couple of weeks searching for high ground, Cung and his friends were standing on top of a large hill. This high ground was on a large U-shaped hill and Cung could see the battle playing out in his mind. It was a perfect place and Cung said to his friends, "This is the place and don't let anyone touch the battlefield." He pointed out to an open area and continued, "A lot of people will die on it."

Finding the perfect battle site, the warriors started running back to Tulukar to report their find. At Tulukar, they met with the elders and planned that day. The elders were confident in their young leader. Cung was young and brilliant and the elders trusted his tactics.

At this meeting, their plan was to lure the Inuguaq to this high ground. They needed a scouting party and they were to provoke the Inuguaq and hopefully lure them in to the high ground. Their army was to stay behind on the high ground and wait for them. The plan sounded good and good enough for them to survive. That's if the Inuguaq went for the bait.

Guk volunteered to go with the other scouting party, but the elders had other plans for his group. Guk's party had to stay on the high ground and he didn't want to tell the boys the plan until it was time.

After two days, the Tulukar warriors gathered themselves behind the high ground. There, they were ordered not to step on the battlefield. It was crucial for them not to show their presence, because surprise was the key to their success.

When it was time, the scouting party headed up to the great mountains. It was a bold task and they chose the best of the breed of warriors from there. Most of the chosen warriors were volunteers. The scouting party took a week to reach the mountains. There, they followed trails until they reached the first Inuguaq village and raided it.

Soon, the Inuguaq spread the news that there was an army invading their area. The Inuguaq people prepared themselves to stop these people. Soon, the Inuguaq army gathered and chased after the scouting party. Every time the Inuguaq army seemed to stop chasing them, the scouts provoked them. The scouts did their job and they led them all the way to the high ground.

At the campsite, Guk took a bit of dry salmon and started chewing. The warriors in the camp started moving about and he knew that the enemy was coming.

Someone repeatedly screamed out from the crowd, "A messenger!"

Hearing the news, Guk went up the hill and saw the runner. The messenger was running toward them and he finally reached the camp. The messenger was a young healthy warrior, a fast runner. Seeing the messenger, he quickly headed up to the elders.

The messenger gathered his breath and reported to the elders that the scouts were on their way and behind them was the Inuguaq army. Hearing the news, the warriors hastily got their weapons ready and made sure their weapons were up to the task at hand. The warriors were pretty nervous at the coming of their enemies. The young warriors in particular were very jittery. The older warriors tried to calm them down, but they were also nervous themselves.

At the top of the hill, Cung gathered the warriors and when they settled down, he yelled out, "Listen up! The beast is coming! Tomorrow, when you face the enemy, they're going to be hungry and tired! We have a good chance to win it! Check your weapons; make sure they are in good condition! We trained you hard for this war and tomorrow you are going to smell death! If they run us over, they're going to kill everyone you know!"

With that in mind, Cung let the warriors go. After Cung gave his words, he ordered the top warriors to the shelter to talk to them and Guk went in with them.

After being in the shelter, Guk came out and talked with his crew. His boys were nervous and he could tell. Tuma and Ipuun looked OK, but he knew they were all nervous. This war, with men, was going to be bloody and he knew it. Killing an animal was different from killing a human. Guk had to make sure they were up to the deadly task tomorrow.

Guk was looking nervous himself and said to his crew, "The beast is coming! Did you know that the beast is already here?" Guk paused for a bit and grabbed Tuma and continued, "This beast." He paused again and started shaking Tuma and continued, "This beast is Tuma!" and everyone listening started to giggle at him. When everyone ceased laughing, Guk continued, but in a serious manner this time, "If we get orders from Quuk, the shaman, we will do whatever he tells us to do. Make sure your weapons are in good condition and get as many arrows as you can."

The tension in the boy's faces was now gone after the speech. The men knew that they needed the tension breaker and they were happy to hear them laugh. They were especially happy to be behind the war and everyone knew that if they got run over by the Inuguaq, the villages downriver would be doomed. They had no choice but to win this war.

Since they were going to protect Quuk, Guk and Tuma told why he was important enough to protect him. They told the boys the story of Patu and

Quuk and what had happened in Tulukar and Nanvarnarlak. The hunters were going to follow whatever Quuk ordered them to do.

The warriors settled down to sleep that night. Tatu was restless and he couldn't sleep. To ease his mind, he thought of Apaq. Dreaming of being with her was calming for him. He closed his eyes and saw her. Every year they were anxious to see each other. She was blooming out to be very beautiful and whenever they finally saw each other, they would just feel better.

Tatu remembered when they got lost one day. That day, the kids were gathering around and they had nothing to do. One of the kids wanted to play darts, so they played with them for a while. The dart game got boring to them and so they decided to change the game. Apaq suggested playing hide and seek and the kids agreed.

When they both weren't chosen to be a seeker, Apaq quietly asked Tatu to come with her. When the seeker started counting to ten, Apaq took off to the nearby woods and Tatu followed behind her.

Once they were in the woods, Apaq halted and sat down. Tatu got to her and sat down beside her. She looked at him and smiled and dashed farther into the woods and stopped. Again, Tatu had no choice but to follow her and when he reached her, he immediately said, "I don't think they'll find us here."

"I know," she said and smiled at him and dashed farther into the woods. Every time when Tatu got close, she would go farther into the woods. She eventually tripped and fell down and Tatu fell on top of her.

"I'm sorry," Tatu said and he got very embarrassed and quickly stood up.

Apaq got up and brushed the dirt off from her parka. She sat down and told Tatu to sit down too and told him to stay still.

"Apaq, don't move and stay still," Tatu said and he reached over and kissed her.

They heard someone looking for them and Tatu ceased his affectionate kissing. He listened for a while and said, "I think the birds are calling to us," and smiled at her.

Apaq smiled at him and said, "It's not a bird calling to us, but it's our."

Before she finished her sentence, Tatu kissed her again. He knew it was their friends looking for them. When he stopped kissing her, he said, "Birds," and smiled at her and they both started chuckling.

Hearing their friends calling for them, they finally got up and listened. When Tatu heard his name being called out, he yelled out, "I'm here!"

When Tatu yelled out, Apaq grabbed his hand and took off farther into the woods. Holding hands, she eventually stopped walking. Apaq spotted a nest on a tree and told him to let go of her hand.

"No." Tatu quickly replied.

"Relax Tatu; I'll still be here,"

"You might fall," he said and reluctantly let go of her.

She climbed a little ways up and checked the nest. Inside the nest were three small eggs, "I see three of them," and she climbed back down.

Once she hit the ground, Tatu got a hold of her. She smiled at him and said, "What?" She knew he had something in mind. He wasn't going to let her go and he was holding her tight.

"Three eggs, hah?" Tatu questioned her.

"Yeah," she responded and she started playing with his hair.

Tatu squeezed her harder and said, "So, you want three kids from me?"

With that question, she put her head down to his shoulder and thought. She raised her lips to his ear and whispered, "I think the nest can hold twenty of them," and she pushed Tatu off and once she was free, she gave him a smile and ran farther into the woods, as Tatu ran after her.

Still lost in the woods, Tatu heard his friends calling for him. He slowly woke up and to his disappointment; he was back in the real world and Apaq left him here. So he got up and checked the horizon. The clouds were above them and it was going to be a warm day. Then reality struck them all when someone cried out, "They're here!"

The warriors in that camp got up and started moving around and got their weapons ready. The scouting party arrived and the leader immediately reported to the elders. The scouting party had lost twenty-two men and some were wounded or missing. The other wounded were left behind and they had probably got killed.

The Inuguaq were moving fast and they were trying to catch up with the scouts. At noon, the Inuguaq were seen on the horizon. Like a herd of caribou, the Inuguaq were coming and they had a pretty good size army.

Looking at this army, Cung was smiling as he saw the Inuguaq. He talked to the elders and told them that they had a good chance of winning this war. He knew that the Inuguaq army had been in full pursuit for couple of days and that they should be hungry and tired.

Coming closer to the hill, the Inuguaq army reached the low ground and halted, as the Tulukar warriors lined up on the hill. The other leaders of Tulukar were giving the first line of warriors their last encouragement. Down in the valley, the Inuguaq were also preparing for this battle.

Looking at the enemy, Guk's crew was tense as they just waited on the right side of the camp. "Tatu, are you scared?" Eli asked him as they waited for their orders. Tatu was nervous as they looked at each other, but he didn't say anything. He had never felt this tension before and his hair stood up. Without warning, it began.

The Inuguaq army didn't waste their time and attacked. The yelling and screaming from the warriors began echoing throughout the area. They were calling death and it was listening.

"Archers!" Cung screamed out.

The ground began shaking as the archers raised their bows and let loose. When the earth started shaking underneath Tatu, he knelt down and felt it. It felt like his bear twitch and he whispered to himself, "So many."

The arrows darkened the sky and started dropping everywhere. As the arrows came down, some arrows hit their men and ones that got hit were crying in pain. The healers or their friends instinctively ran over to the wounded and tended them.

After the arrow battle was over, the real heat of the battle started. The Inuguaq weren't ready for the vicious surprise they had coming. The first wave from Tulukar screamed and charged down to meet the Inuguaq army. As the first wave took off, the second wave went up and ran down after the first wave. The ground started shaking more as the two armies attacked each other.

After the armies collided, the crying and the screaming intensified. Guk's group couldn't help it and they had to go up the hill to see what was going on. All they could see was people and their blood.

Tatu gazed over the battlefield. The path the first line of his people had taken was lined with dead bodies. Some of the warriors were crying in pain and he could see arrows on them. Some had gotten lucky and got hit in the legs or arms, but some of them looked dead. Still, blood was everywhere. They were trained for this war and they were going to miss it! He was thankful that he and his friends were not going down to the battle, but he was way wrong.

Watching the battle from the top of the hill, Quuk pointed to the horizon and said to Guk, "Bring me his head!"

In wonder, Tatu scanned the area and saw the head he wanted.

THE HEART STOPPER

At the battle site, looking toward the horizon, Tatu could see a figure of a man. The figure was watching the battle from afar. In his mind, this was a leader of the Inuguaq. The path they had to take to get this person was going to be scary.

Getting orders from the shaman and without hesitating, Guk screamed out, "Listen up! Stick together and watch yourselves! Let's go!"

Led by Guk, they started running down toward this figure. Running downhill, it didn't take the hunters long to reach the main battle site. On the ground, some of their warriors asked for help, but instead of stopping to help them, Guk told them to leave them alone. They had a mission, so the hunters kept on running toward the figure.

As the hunters went through the carnage, Tatu stopped at one of the enemies and checked him out. This man was wearing a black bear fur and his face was covered in black that looked like ash. He could tell that the man was dying as his mouth was gurgling out some blood. As Tatu was checking the man out, Kaluk hit him from behind and he automatically jumped forward. Surprised by the hit, Tatu thought an arrow had hit him, but instead it was Kaluk's hand. Relieved, he realized that he had to concentrate or get killed himself.

"Hurry up and keep going, Tatu!" Kaluk yelled out and he didn't waste time and ran past him.

The hunters continued toward the figure of the man. They eventually reached the hill and the man they were chasing was nowhere to be seen. Instead of seeing the man, they saw a staff and it was sticking out of the snow. They went over and inspected it. The staff had eagle feathers on it and hanging on this staff, what looked like hearts with strings attached. Curiously, Ipuun took the staff and Guk hit his hand, but Ipuun didn't let go of it.

"Don't touch it! They're human hearts!" Guk yelled at Ipuun and continued, "What we are chasing is a shaman!"

The hearts were probably from the scouting party, Tatu thought, but he wasn't sure of that. He didn't know nor did he want to know. The staff has human hearts? Whoever did this was a bad man. Tatu's thoughts trailed off.

After touching the staff, Ipuun finally let go of it and he went down on his knees and started breathing heavily. On his knees, he was now holding his hand over his heart. Ipuun's unexpected reaction caught all of the hunters.

"Ipuun, what is wrong with you?" Tatu asked him worriedly as Ipuun didn't look too good.

Ipuun started breathing erratically and with his hand, he made a beating motion over to his heart. He started sticking his tongue out and he felt uncomfortable.

"I don't know, but my heart's not beating right," Ipuun finally responded and then he rolled his eyes and fell backward.

When Ipuun fell down, Tatu caught him in his arms and gently laid him down on the ground. Immediately, Tatu's heart started pounding funny too and he let Ipuun go. Tatu fell backward himself and landed on his back.

Realizing what was happening, Guk yelled out, "Don't touch him!" but he was too late.

On the ground, Tatu's heart started feeling better when he started to control his breathing. His friends got worried for him and asked if he was OK.

"I'm OK. My heart just started beating funny," Tatu told them.

For assurance, Tatu looked at his worried friends and smiled at them. Whatever had happened to his heart when he touched Ipuun started to worry him. This was not normal and he had never felt this type of power before. Whatever it was, it was strong and evil.

Not wanting any more mishaps, Guk warned his group, "Don't touch it! That staff has a spell from that shaman!"

Concerned for his friend, Guk grabbed Kaluk and told him to get Quuk and explain to him what had happened here. Without saying anything, Kaluk took off and headed back to the front. Whoever was left standing, Guk ordered them to look for the figure. Standing alert, the hunters scanned the area again and searched for this man.

Out in the distance, Tatu saw him again, "Guk, I see him, he's over there." Tatu said to him and pointed in the direction of the man and the figure ran away.

Spotting this figure, Guk looked down at Ipuun and said to him, "Ipuun, I need to get this shaman. I'll come right back for you. Stay strong."

Ipuun was still lying down and his eyes began to close, but with all of the strength he got left, he nodded yes to Guk. Ipuun opened his mouth and stuck his tongue out again. His body was shutting down and he knew it.

The situation was chaotic, Guk quickly told Eli to watch Ipuun and he checked Tatu. Tatu was already up and holding his weapon and he seemed good. They had to get this shaman, so Guk looked at Tuma and Tatu and said, "Let's go!"

Guk, Tuma, and Tatu headed in the direction of the shaman and the hunt was on. The shaman led them to a river and his tracks kept going alongside of riverbank. Then without warning, Tatu's heart started beating unevenly and he stopped and went down to his knees. Noticing Tatu, Guk came up to him and asked what was wrong with him. Tatu told him that it was his heart. Guk immediately told him to go back. They had to catch this shaman, so Guk and Tuma took off without Tatu.

Staying steady, Tatu took a couple of deep breaths and his heart felt stronger. Without following orders, he stood up and continued following Guk and Tuma. *They might need me,* Tatu thought to himself and he found himself alongside of the riverbank.

Tatu then heard a loud cry from that area. Hearing the cry, he stopped to listen. Tatu's bear arm twitched and he froze. *Bad sign!* Tatu thought and he began to worry, because it meant only one thing for him. He was about to confront his prey. His bear arm twitched again and he focused carefully. His breathing slowed down and he waited for the moment. The bear twitch was a curse and a blessing for him. He was hoping that it was just an animal, but he knew what he was hunting for. So he slowly loaded his bow and waited. He didn't like this anticipation that had befallen him.

Standing on the riverbank, Tatu heard someone crying out from a distance again. He knew it was Guk, but he wasn't really sure. The noise was too faint to recognize. Just above him, Tatu saw something move on top of the bank, followed by a whisper, "Ah."

Not knowing what it was, Tatu sat down real fast and aimed at the figure above him. As he sat down and aimed at it, a stick came at him and it hit his bow and ricocheted over his head. *Arrow!* Tatu yelled at himself as it grazed him.

Totally surprised and still aiming at the figure, Tatu let his arrow loose. As he was releasing his arrow, his bow cracked and threw him off balance. Off balance, he fell down backward and he watched his arrow go. His arrow didn't even come close to hitting the figure and he yelled out, "No!"

In a grim position, Tatu was doomed. The figure above him was surprised as he looked at him. Now, the shaman and Tatu were just staring at each other. The Inuguaq smiled at him and reloaded his weapon.

While the shaman was loading his weapon, all of a sudden, an arrow struck him in the neck and then another arrow struck his back. To his surprise, Tatu could see the shaman starting to bleed from the impact. The shaman dropped his weapon and looked at the arrows and collapsed.

When the shaman fell down, Tatu was in a stage of disbelief. With the magnitude of instinctive shock, followed by relief in his mind, Tatu's body collapsed to the ground. Still thinking of what had just happened, Tatu finally breathed out and started breathing heavily. The air felt good in his lungs after the shaman had fallen down without killing him. The unbroken chain of events saved him. He gazed out to the clouds and thanked whoever just saved his life. Realizing he almost got killed, he started sweating heavily.

Getting his breath back, Tatu heard someone calling his name again, "Tatu!"

Still unable to get up, Tatu checked the direction of the noise and spotted Guk and Tuma and they were running hastily toward him. When they reached where the shaman had fallen, they both yelled at him again, "Tatu!"

"I'm down here, I'm OK!" Tatu yelled back to his friends.

Staying down and lying still, Tatu started thinking of what just happened. He had looked into the eyes of death and gotten lucky. He examined his broken bow and took a deep breath again.

Guk and Tuma were both speechless as they looked around the area. The air was quiet and it spooked them. They knew for sure the hunt was over as blood began to ooze out from the dead man.

Still concerned for his little rabbit, Guk looked down and asked him, "You OK, Tatu? Did you get hit?"

Tatu told them *no* and he showed them the broken bow. His trusty bow was now useless, but it had saved him.

Noticing Tatu's broken bow, Tuma grabbed some snow and threw it toward Tatu. He was glad his little rabbit was still alive and kicking and said to him, "Did we ever tell you not to lie down like that and ruin your parka?"

Tatu took couple of deep breaths again and stood up. He shook off the snow and responded, "Yaa, I remember you telling me about that and I really think my balls fell off," and he reached down and checked his balls to see if they were still there. When Tatu checked his balls, Guk and Tuma started chuckling at him. Hearing them chuckle, Tatu realized what he was doing and stopped. Embarrassed now, he gazed at his fellow friends and smirked. Feeling better, Tatu then edged his way up to them.

When the little rabbit reached them, Tuma reminded him again, "You almost got killed!" Then he grabbed Tatu's bow. After Tuma inspected it, he continued, "Hey pal, Tatu ruined your bow."

When Tatu heard him say that, he felt very awkward, but relieved that he was still breathing. As long as he wasn't killed, it was OK. It was hard losing his bow, but it saved him.

Without worrying about his bow, Tatu checked the shaman. The shaman was lying face down and then Tatu asked them who had hit him.

Guk and Tuma were surprised at what Tatu had just said to them. They looked at him and Guk said, "We thought you did." Spooked and alert, Guk and Tuma raised their bows and scanned the area. They couldn't see anyone or any man around. Shamans tended to get men edgy, even the dead ones. Someone was out there and for all they knew, he or it would send another arrow their way.

After looking around for the shaman killer, Tatu checked the dead body again. He wasn't accustomed to seeing a dead body and he felt nauseated and started vomiting. After Tatu vomited the rest of his meal, he examined the arrows on the shaman's back and noticed who the arrows belonged to. He didn't say anything at that moment, because the owner of the arrows was one of them, the shaman killer.

When the area seemed clear, Guk took his spear and was about to cut the shaman's head off, but then he stopped. Holding the spear, he hesitated and looked at his friends. Decapitating a human head just didn't seem right to him.

Tuma noticed Guk's hesitation and agreed with him, "Guk, it's OK, I wouldn't do it either. This shaman was once a man and we are Yup'ik. We have to treat him with respect."

"Let a shaman take care of a shaman," Guk muttered as he eased his spear away from the dead.

Fulfilling their mission, Tatu thought of Ipuun. Worried about him, he took off to where he had last seen them. He saw his friends and a man standing beside them. When he reached them, Eli, Kaluk, and Quuk were there and Ipuun was still on the ground, but he was motionless.

By now, Ipuun had his eyes closed and Kaluk seemed nervous for him. Tatu asked what was wrong with Ipuun. They told him his heart had given out and he was dead. Hearing the news, Tatu's heart started feeling heavy. Quuk had tried his best to save Ipuun, but he was too late. The damage was done and Tatu looked at Quuk and told him the shaman was dead. Upon hearing the news, Quuk headed straight toward the shaman's body.

On top of the hill, the wind picked up. All the boys were on their knees beside Ipuun. They just had no words to describe it. Tatu asked Kaluk if he was OK. Kaluk didn't take it very well and Ipuun was his friend. Tatu could understand that, because he was his friend too.

When Guk and Tuma arrived, they started mourning for Ipuun. Since they were young, Guk, Tuma, and Ipuun hunted together and they knew each other very well. It was unfortunate for their friend to die, but war always had its casualties.

When the time was right, the hunters took Ipuun's body back to the camp. Along the way, they entered the battle area and it was over. Their objective was accomplished, their enemy was destroyed. The battle site was covered with corpses. The warriors were piling the dead in a little pond that was colored red with blood.

The elders said that they shouldn't tell anyone where the bodies were discarded. During the summertime, the dead bodies would sink down to the bog and eventually recycle.

At the campsite, the hunters wrapped Ipuun's body with fur. The warriors tried their best to take care of the wounded. When darkness fell on them, the warriors were drowning in their own memories. Some were crying for their friends and the wounded were either dying or recovering. It was a total shock for everyone.

That night, Tatu was exhausted and mentally drained. He was taking in what had happened that day. They had lost one of his good friends. It was such a great loss for all of the hunters, because they were such good friends. Inside, it was a hollow feeling that he had never felt before. Guk looked at Tatu and said he did well. Whatever that meant, he wasn't happy. That night, the rest of the hunters were talking about Ipuun and mourned for him.

The warriors in the camp began to move around again and someone screamed out repetitively, "Lights! Lights!"

The hunters knew immediately what he was yelling about. Tuma and Tatu stood up and started running up to the high ground to check on the lights. On top of the hill, they saw torches coming from the path where the Inuguaq had arrived. Someone there finally yelled out, "Another army!"

Seeing the torches, Tatu could feel the adrenaline mixed with fear pumping in his blood again. He did not know what to expect now. Not knowing what was to come gave him an insecure feeling that he had never felt before. The warriors lit up their own torches that night.

That night, Tatu's mind was trying to think of something nice after the war in that dark, cold, and mysterious night, but he couldn't. If he did thought of something that night, he defiantly knew it was awful, because it made him cry. Gladly, after what seemed like an eternity, the design of light came to them.

Guk hollered out and woke the boys up. After they woke up, the boys were still sore and groggy. Once they got up, they stretched out and felt a lot better. The boys ate a quick meal, knowing it was going to be a long day for them.

The hunters were in a circle now and Tuma told his group that he was going to check on the enemy. Curious to see how big the army was, Tatu followed him. Up on the hill, they could see the Inuguaq coming, but they were not as many as the first band of warriors.

Observing the enemy, Tuma was disappointed and muttered, "Ha, so few of them," and then went back to the camp.

The second Inuguaq army kept marching at them and then halted. A smaller group from the Inuguaq came closer into their direction and stopped at a safe distance. Without charging, they retreated to the main group and left a spear on the tundra.

As this group retreated, the first line of Tulukar warriors went up to the top of the hill and waited for orders. The warriors looked tired, but they had been trained for this moment. From moving corpses from the battle site, most of the warriors were covered in red. They were confident now and they were ready for another charge. Wounded or dying, they were going to fight them again.

To their surprise, the Inuguaq army retreated, never to be seen again. A warrior was sent out to check the spear and he brought it back to the elders. It was a spear made of spruce tree with a stone tip and falcon feathers. Later that day, the warriors were ordered to go back to Tulukar and thankfully they didn't pursue the enemy.

"What happened to the Inuguaq army?" Tatu asked Guk and he told him that they went back to where they came from.

Receiving the good news that they would not fight that day, Tatu requested for leave to check on his family. All the boys were granted permission to go home.

The hunters brought Ipuun's body back to Tulukar. After Ipuun's obsequy, the boys got ready and went back to home.

BLOODY HAND

I t was the beginning of summer and Patu was sleeping outside. His sod house was too hot for him, so last night, he'd gone out and fallen asleep behind his home. As dawn was coming up, Patu woke up sweating and his face was covered with mosquitoes.

Waking up from the bites, Patu hit the pests that were on his face and then examined his hands. Noticing his bloody hand, he wiped it off on his parka.

The shaman stood up and examined his area. Mosquitoes were everywhere and the area was foggy. The grass was filled with dew and the area was cold. Still sleepy, Patu walked around his sod house and gazed at the horizon of the sea. It was calm and the sea was dead quiet. The elders of the coast had once told him that the sea can see and knew everything, so he respected it. The fog slowly lifted and revealed a red dawn. Seeing the red dawn, Patu checked his bloody hand again and giggled to himself.

Patu walked around a bit thinking how to approach this red dawn. Definitely, he was bothered by it. To conquer this day was going to take all his wits. It wasn't going to be pretty and he slowly went to the qasgiq. Before Patu entered the qasgiq, he glanced at the red sky and giggled. It was a glorious color for him and he proceeded to enter the qasgiq. Patu urgently needed to talk to the leader of the Teriikaniar People. The leader of the Teriikaniar was Qum. This leader always made Patu nervous, so he cautiously crawled his way in.

A tyrant of a leader, Qum was taller than anyone around his tribe. He was an astonishing and distinguished figure to his men. He had a lot of tattoos in his face and his tattoos were lines of the people that he had killed. His black hair was long and he had a long beard and mustache. Born to dominate, he never slept much.

When Qum heard someone coming into his qasgiq, he immediately grabbed his knife and waited. When someone came in unannounced, fearing that he or she might try to kill him, he automatically ordered it to stop.

Hearing that he should stop, Patu stood up at the entrance and waited. It was dark inside and he could barely see anyone in there. Once his eyes adjusted to the darkness, he could see movement on the floor and knew it was men that were sleeping. The air was thick with humidity from the people's breath. He checked the seal gut window and it reflected the red sun. Patu didn't like being ordered to stop. With both of his hands, he reached up to his face and started to scratch his mosquito bites.

From the back of the qasgiq, someone yelled out, "What do you want and what's so important to show yourself this morning, Patu?" It was Qum and his scream woke up everyone who was there.

Standing by the entranceway, Patu stopped scratching and giggled. He cautiously asked him to go out with him. Patu had some important news he liked to address to his leader and it had something to do with the red dawn.

Knowing the shaman, Qum quickly looked around and found a stick and then he threw it at Patu and told him to get out. Once he was dressed, he started kicking his sleeping warriors and told them to wake up. When the other warriors awoke, Qum went out of his qasgiq and his warriors followed behind him.

Once Patu got out of the qasgiq, he walked over to the sea bank and gazed at the sea again. Seagulls were flying around and they were soaring gracefully in the wind. Patu put his hand behind his back and waited for his leader. He was looking directly at the horizon and smiled. What a beautiful sight! *This is going to be interesting,* Patu thought to himself.

Outside the qasgiq, Qum and his men scanned the weather and then they saw the shaman. The day was going to be perfect for Qum and he proceeded to see Patu. As Qum reached Patu, he swung his arm out and swatted Patu on the back of his head. It was intentional what he did to him. Qum didn't like this shaman one bit and he knew this shaman was evil, but he was powerful and useful for him.

Getting hit on the head, Patu smiled at him and lowered his head to Qum and started giggling. Patu didn't mind getting hit and he was used to it from him. Qum loved hitting his people around, especially him. The back of his head hurt a little, but he was going to be OK.

"What's so important for you to get me out of my qasgiq, you filthy animal of a man?" Qum asked Patu angrily.

Patu cleared his throat and pointed at the rising sun. The red dawn was still visible to the eye. When he got everyone's attention on the beautiful sight, Patu cleared his throat again. Everyone there knew what the sign meant, but he had to tell them, "Gracious Qum, look at the red sun, blood was spilled not too long ago. It was not from you, but it was from your new enemy. There was a war recently and the people call themselves Yup'ik. They live out in the open tundra, just up the Kusquqvak River from here. They have many warriors now and now they are battle tested. Upon hearing what you did to their coast people, they are going to come down here and wipe us out!"

After Patu explained Qum about the red dawn; he swallowed hard and showed his prettiest smile to him. Patu knew his prettiest smile was effective and the ladies loved it. Every time when he smiled at the ladies, the ladies would shake their bodies and run away from him. Every time they ran away, Patu had the urge to chase after them and he did it to a couple of them.

Patu looked around the men and they were looking at the same sight. Some began to smile at the sight and Patu knew they were itching for a fight now.

Qum was looking at the ugliest smile in the world and got furious. He faced the red dawn for a brief moment and his mind started thinking, but then he got angry again and punched Patu in the face and broke his nose. From his punch, they heard a loud *smack* and Patu's nose splattered out blood.

From the punch, Patu instinctively covered his face and tried to stop his nosebleed. He was in pain, but he didn't show it to his leader. Any sign of weakness would make his leader mad. *Aka, that hurts!* Patu thought and he tried not to squirm.

After Qum punched Patu and when the shaman didn't squirm, he grabbed the shaman and threw him down as hard as he could. Once the shaman was down, he yelled at him, "Tell me about it, you devil of a man! You always bring bad news to me! I should just kill you right now!"

Qum always dealt violently with others and why should he change now with this curse of a man. He wished that he could just kill this man and get it over with. He needed Patu, because he was always accurate on his predictions. He didn't trust him one bit though.

Down on the ground, poor Patu was hurting. He was about to say something to Qum, but then he changed his mind. Still holding his crooked nose, he had to set it straight. He closed his eyes tight and heard a *crack*. The pain was excruciating, but he wasn't going to show it. His nose was now straight and perfect.

Feeling better, Patu had to tell his reason quickly or get hit again. He cleared his throat and said, "I had a dream, and in this dream, a pack of wolves were chasing me. The pack caught up and surrounded me. The wolf pack began eating me bit by bit. When I woke up this morning, blood was everywhere. Yup'ik protect their people and for sure, they will come down and bit by bit, kill us all."

When Patu finished talking, Qum kicked him in the stomach and made him squirm this time. On the ground, poor Patu gave him the prettiest smile that the ladies would love, but he got kicked again. "Aka," Patu let out a little squirm.

Qum checked the sunrise again and then looked down at Patu. Patu was still on the ground and motionless. Disgusted at the man, he spat on him and headed toward to the qasgiq. The tyrant leader stopped by the qasgiq and told his men to beat Patu up. Without questioning his authority, Qum's men went over and started kicking Patu senseless until he couldn't move anymore.

When the men left him, Patu slid his hands over his broken ribs. Then he silently started chanting to himself. When he stopped chanting, he tried to giggle, but it hurt him. He started chanting again to himself and his hands started tingling. After his hands started tingling, his hands got hot and he could hear his ribs moving into place, but it was painful. The healing process took a whole day for him. When the night set in, he stood up and felt better. He checked his ribs and they were OK and then he giggled to himself. He was definitely fine now.

Later that night, the Teriikaniar People planned to go up to the Yup'ik and wipe them out. Surprise would be their key to success. Qum poised himself with confidence while preparing for the battle. He was good at what he did and that was leading thousands of vicious men.

INTENSITY RISING

In Atmaulluaq, to keep himself cool, Tatu was in the dark shade of the trees. His face was dark tanned and he was starving, because he hadn't eaten all day. He went up to the food cache and took out a piece of caribou meat that he was saving. Once he grabbed what he wanted, he went down to the riverbank and stopped by a campfire area. He took out his knife and started cutting the meat up in chunks. After getting the meat ready, he started collecting wood for the fire.

The campfire was now burning just right and Tatu's meat was slowly roasting fine. It was the beginning of springtime and everyone was enjoying the weather. The sun was out and it was hot, but the cool breeze was comfortable enough for Tatu. His stomach was growling, but he needed to roast this meat real good. The aroma of the fatty meat got him hungrier.

As the meat start to sizzle, Tatu could hear some kids playing close by. The kids caught the sense of Tatu's cooking and surrounded him. The hungry little kids looked at Tatu and gave him their *feed me* look. Looking at these poor hungry kids, Tatu was hungry and felt sorry for them, but he decided not to share this fine roasting meat of his.

"Get away from me!" Tatu yelled at them.

Out of nowhere, a dirty little boy came by the campfire and stood across from Tatu. Tatu smiled at him, because the little kid reminded him of himself. Tatu knew this kid had been playing in a muddy puddle as his face and hair showed the signs.

Observing the kid, Tatu chuckled and said to him, "Ha! You just turned dark from the sun, hah?"

In his own little world, the kid didn't say anything to him. When Tatu was about to tell him to get out of here, the little kid reached over with his own stick and set his stick on the fire. This kid had his own meat and his eyes were glowing as the meat on his stick began to sizzle and crinkle.

Looking at this dirty boy's meat, Tatu thought it was a regular meat at first, but the meat had a tail on it, "A mouse?" Tatu questioned the meat.

Knowing what this kid was cooking, Tatu gave him a funny look. The little boy just stood there and smiled at his meat. He knew what the little kid was cooking, but he had to ask, "Hey boy, what are you cooking?" while he tried his best not to chuckle.

The boy responded, "Meat!"

The other kids that were watching and listening to them started to laugh with Tatu. When Tatu stopped laughing, he got up and grabbed the little kid's stick and examined it. After examining the meat, Tatu took out this special little meat from the kid and replaced it with some caribou meat and gave it to him.

The little kid, with the caribou meat now, stayed still and roasted his new meat again. The other kids took off and they came back with their own sticks. Tatu, feeling sorry for the kids, started distributing the rest of his meat around. All the kids began roasting their meat by the fire.

As Tatu's meat was about to be done, Kaluk jogged over to him and stopped by him. He quickly observed the area and saw what everyone was doing. Then he checked around for a piece of meat, but there was none. Disappointed that there was no meat anymore, Kaluk looked at Tatu.

"What do you want, fire starter?" Tatu asked Kaluk teasingly.

"A messenger is here and he has news for us," Kaluk said to him.

Hearing the word messenger, Tatu looked at him and then to his roast meat and said, "Mmm."

Kaluk reached over and said, "Quyana (thank you)" and grabbed Tatu's meat and ran off with it.

"Ah!" Tatu automatically cried out loud.

Tatu wasn't going to catch him and he knew Kaluk was faster than anyone, so he stayed put and stayed in disbelief. Around the campfire, Tatu could hear the little kids giggling. His stomach seemed to be giggling at him too as it got louder with hunger.

After their first battle, a messenger had come to Atmaulluaq and told them about a menace that was coming up the Kusquqvak River. The Yup'ik called them Teriikaniar People, because they ate everything and even the bones of the fish that the Yup'ik didn't eat.

Last summer, the Teriikaniar People had landed on their coast and raided the neighboring Yup'ik villages. Their whole mission was to destroy and kill them out of existence. The Teriikaniar People came from the sea they said, and they looked like them, talked and dressed the same, but they were very different.

The elders planned to go down and face them this coming fall, but when they were coming up this early, it was a big surprise for them. Being surprised, they were not ready for them and they had to get ready as soon as possible.

As the days passed, people from the neighboring Yup'ik villages from the coast started heading up the river, by the hundreds. Everyone who was going down to the coast was warned about the threat. Even warned, some people proceeded downriver to check on their relatives.

Tatu knew they were going to have to face the enemy. At that moment, Tatu thought of Apaq and her family. He was hoping she hadn't gone to her yearly summer fish camp, but rather headed to Tulukar. The threat was coming and he got worried for his people.

After waves of kayaks headed upriver, Tatu's family got ready themselves and also headed up. In his kayak, he brought his grandma with him. His grandma just entertained him as she sang songs she had learned from her mom. As they rowed upriver, they met Nanvarnarlak people. Since the land was not a good strategic place for a war, Nanvarnarlak people had decided to head to Tulukar. It didn't take them long to reach Tulukar.

When they got closer to Tulukar, the family was awed to see many kayaks in one place. Once they beached, the people assisted Tatu's family with their belongings. The place was overcrowded as the family inched their way up to their relatives.

Everyone was told that Tulukar would be the last stand against the Teriikaniar People. The village was busy getting ready for the menace; most of the wood was gathered up to make arrows and spears.

Since they didn't know which three river routes the Teriikaniar would take. The lower Qusqukvak people either went up to Kasigluq or up to Napaskiaq to make their stand. The upper part of Qusqukvak people went to Kwiggluk to make their stand there.

Of all the people in the world that day, Tatu was looking for Apaq. He walked around the village and found some of her friends and asked for her. They told him that she was around and upon hearing that, he got excited.

Tatu slowly walked around the village looking for Apaq. There were many people around, but then she saw her. She was with her friends and she was holding a water container. She was walking with her friends and they seemed to be heading toward the watering hole. Apaq was wearing a beautiful parka, made of mink skins and her bird designs were going all the around the bottom of her parka.

He caught up to her and started walking beside her. She was looking down as she was walking and she wasn't aware he was there. Then she smiled to herself. Still looking down on the ground, she knew who was walking beside her now. Tatu had a habit of asking her what she was looking at and she waited for it.

"What you looking at Apaq?" Tatu asked her

When Tatu asked her that, Apaq immediately smiled and looked at him. Finally the days glowed brightly for her and she responded, "I missed you," and she shifted closer to him. She just wanted to touch him, but there were too many eyes around, so she brushed him. She had an answer for him this time and she continued, "I'm looking at you," she paused and asked him, "What you looking at Tatu?"

Hearing that from Apaq, Tatu's emotion ran deep inside of him and he said to her, "I can see four beautiful ladies here and they just heard you say that."

Apaq's friends started giggling at them. Apaq was so happy that she forgot about her friends. She immediately stopped walking and told them that she would catch up to them. Her friends told her yes and told her not to get lost in the woods again.

After her friends took off, the couple followed behind them and they talked about their past winter. Just when they thought they would be alone, Eli and Kaluk came by and told Tatu that Guk wanted him. Tatu told her that he needed to talk to her alone tomorrow morning. She didn't hesitate and said yes to him. After a brief courting with Apaq, Tatu took off.

The village of Tulukar was becoming overcrowded and some of the families were making little shelters outside in the open area. The endless preparation was much needed as the tension intensified. The elders and the men met daily and devised a war plan. Guk and Tuma, with the other warriors, were the only men invited to these meetings. The day came when they had a plan to execute.

After the meeting, Guk gathered up his group and they met at the beach. Once they got to the beach, Guk and Tuma told the boys they were planning to send the scouts downriver. If their enemies entered the river, they would confront them. Once they knew the enemy had entered their river, the women, children, and some elders and would go to Taklirlak Lake, just in case they all get killed. If their men didn't come and get them, they would proceed on to Cuukvaggtuliq and keep going toward the west to Qaluuyaaq.

At this little meeting and to Tatu's disappointment, Guk volunteered his boys to go with the scouts. There would be thirty-two young warriors and ten other men to stop the threat if they entered their river. The scouts plan was simple and that was to slow the enemy down. The warriors that stayed at Tulukar would get enough time to prepare for the war. Simple as it sounded, it was a big task for them.

Early next morning, Tatu went to look for Apaq. When he found her, he decided to take her out kayaking in the lake. The couple snuggled in his kayak but it was comfortable for them. She was sitting behind Tatu as they rode off. They slowly rowed out to the other side of the lake and beached themselves on the tundra.

On the tundra, they both surveyed their surroundings in silence. The silence was nice for a change after the constant mumblings in the village. After seeing a lot of people, the scenery was perfect for them. The tundra had a variety of colorful moss and lichen growing on top. The moss looked like leaves colored in white, gray, and sometimes red. The lichens were seen everywhere. Tatu spotted some brown edible mushrooms. Little shrubs of twigs were gathered by the side of the land. The small shrubs seemed to be in millions in one spot. The orange moss then caught Tatu's eye. These types of moss were always wet to the touch. Tatu went over to the orange moss and placed his hands on top of it. The moss was wet as usual. He got up and turned his eyes upon the most significant person he loved.

Apaq was standing all alone and she was looking at him. He noticed she was shining more than the land around him. The beautiful land didn't come close in comparison to her.

"Tatu, so what did the elders tell you?" she asked.

Tatu just stared at her and said nothing for a while. He took a deep breath and looked down. What he had to say next would crush her, but he had to let her know. He raised his head and looked at her again. "They are sending thirty two boys and ten men against thousands of them. I'm going too. I don't think we will be coming back and we are taking off tomorrow morning," Tatu said to her sadly.

His choice of words just sucked the life out of her. Devastated by the news, she was speechless. She didn't like the feeling of losing him. She had her mouth open, but she didn't notice it.

Noticing her sadness, Tatu went over to her and brought her chin up. He didn't like her feeling sad and nothing was down there. Getting her attention, he told her what he thought of her, "Apaq," Tatu started brushing her hair and continued, "You have the most beautiful eyes I've ever seen. Everything you do is beautiful to me. I always seem to dream in your eyes. I just want you to know that I feel just right with you."

The couple was silent for a while and Tatu took a deep breath again. Out of nowhere, a bird came by and landed in front of them. The curious bird looked at them for awhile.

When she saw the bird, her sadness faded. She slowly looked at Tatu and smiled at him, "Every summer, I wait for the birds to arrive and I wait for you," she told Tatu as the bird flew off.

When she talked about the birds, Tatu checked her parka. Her parka had bird designs all over. He noticed that she was getting better at mending furs. He then checked her body, which was also built for long runs.

"What you doing Tatu?" she asked him with curiosity.

Tatu continued looking at his beautiful girl. She was perfect, her designs of birds were perfect, and everything seemed perfect, except for one thing. Tatu was now behind her and observed for a while. Her parka had one single flaw that bothered him.

"I'm just checking you out and the beautiful designs you have on your parka, but you missed something. Don't worry, my mom can fix it, she's good at furs," Tatu said to her and brushed her waist.

She automatically turned around and faced him. It had taken her a long time to finish her parka herself. It was him she was trying to impress and he was not. Hearing this from him was a total surprise for her. She had to know her mistake.

"What?" she asked Tatu quizzically. She had to know, she really had to know.

Tatu gazed at her whole figure and said, "My dog bite," and smirked at her.

Apaq hit his arm and then grabbed him and turned Tatu around. Once Tatu was facing away from her, she reached under his parka and said to him, "Do you mean this one?" and she started tickling him.

They both started chuckling. Tatu faced her again and squeezed her, but what she had to say next crushed him.

"Tatu," she looked down from him as Tatu squeezed her and continued, "My mom is getting me ready for a suitor." After she said that, Apaq quickly looked up at him and continued, "A man came by and talked to my parents and they weren't your parents."

Hearing what she had to say was surprising and crushing for Tatu. He was in disbelief. *No,* Tatu thought as the shock began to creep in him. He couldn't breathe and then he cleared his throat in pain.

Apaq was now in tears and she didn't want another. She loved him very much. Tatu was still holding her tight and he didn't want to let her go.

Seeing her in tears, that was a good sign for Tatu, but he had to ask her, "Is that what you want?"

She smiled and wiped her tears and gathered herself. She wanted the one she had known for years. She wanted the one who showed her the beauty of the birds. She wanted the one who was holding her now.

"No, I don't want to get married to that other man. I told my mom about us," she said to him.

Tatu was curious about what her mother said about him. "And?"

Tatu was wishing her mom changed her mind about him. He didn't know why she didn't like him very much. He didn't seem to do anything right in her sight. Whatever the reason was, he had to know.

"My mom said she doesn't like you and you are not the right suitor for me. She said you're like the weather and very unpredictable."

"Unpredictable?" he asked her quizzically. *Is that all the reason for her mom?* Funny, Tatu was thinking and he couldn't help it and let out a little smirk.

"Yes, she said you are unpredictable," she answered him and smirked back.

Tatu thought about that for a while. It wasn't a perfect, good reason and it was kind of funny. He knew that the extreme weather around here was unpredictable. The harshness of this area made men rugged and their women strong. He wasn't about to give her up and said to her, "Good, I'm very unpredictable. If I was predictable, you'd be very bored with me right now." Tatu then smiled at her and squeezed her waist again. She smiled back and finally relaxed. "Are you bored with me?" Tatu asked.

She looked at him and smiled and said, "I don't think I'll ever tire of you."

Tatu's mind started thinking of ways to have her. After a careful thought, he made up his mind. To have her wasn't going to be easy and he knew it, "I don't think I can do anything, unless I just go over and just get you. The elders won't agree about this, but I have only one life to live. Every summer, I want the birds to see our children," he paused and continued, "I'll also need to talk to my parents and see what they can do first, if they can't do anything, I don't know what I'll do." Tatu gave a piece of his mind.

After telling Apaq about what he wanted to do, Tatu took her hand and they both started walking again. The time of peacefulness that he yearned for over so many years was here with him. Her hand was smooth and small to the touch. When he seemed to wander off, Apaq would pull his hand.

As his arms got pulled, Tatu would look at her and ask her, "What?" And he would gaze away.

"Look at me," she would say to him as he gazed away from her.

She seemed to be worried about Tatu and what he was thinking. She didn't need to worry about anything; Tatu had her in his hands. She didn't know that Tatu never planned to let go of her.

The tundra was soft underneath them as their maklaks pressed gently on the land. Tatu took her to a small hill. There, they both stared at the beautiful and colorful land. As they both gazed out to the beautiful view, Apaq broke the silence. "The first time I met you, I thought you were full of yourself, but since I got to know you more, I want to spend my life with you," she said as she pulled his hand toward her.

Remembering the past with her, Tatu smiled to himself and to that bird he'd left alive. He was glad he left it alive. It was a good choice for him that day, because right now he was with her. He didn't want to lose her. He had to let her know and said, "The first time I laid my eyes on you; I thought I'd never get to talk to you, but your eyes pleased me and pulled me in. We were so young, but now I'm glad we get to talk to each other a lot. This war, which is to come, has brought you to me. Just like the birds that come here every summer, to see us both and to see if we got married yet."

Apaq decided to sit down and then she lay down on the tundra and relaxed. Tatu sat down and stared at the clouds for a bit. Seeing her relaxed and at ease with herself, he decided to lie down beside her. The tundra was soft beneath them. Apaq had to move around until she got comfortable. Tatu was comfortable everywhere, even the ground lump on his back didn't bother him a bit.

"Why do you always think of the good side of things for me?" Apaq said as they watched the clouds above them.

"I don't know, I don't want bad things for us I guess," and he reached over and searched her hand to hold.

Still lying down, Tatu told her to close her eyes. When she closed her eyes, he reached over slowly and gently touched her stomach. Her eyes were still closed and she started to giggle.

"What you doing?" she said softly.

"Don't move, I just want to touch you." Tatu said as he rubbed her stomach ever so gently.

She started to giggle again and moved around. His hands were cold to the touch, but then she got used to it. "It tickles," she muttered and then she started breathing heavily. She felt love and opened her eyes and said, "I want to make love to you," and she took his hands and showed him where to touch.

After they made love, Tatu whispered out, "Birds better not be watching us." She smiled and said, "Yeah."

They lay there and just enjoyed the moment. When they finished, it was getting late and sadly, they had to head back to Tulukar. They got up and brushed off the moss and lichens that clung to their parkas. They slowly headed down to the kayak and they pushed off.

On their way over, the lovers snuggled in comfort. She was behind Tatu and she was holding him tight. Tatu's breathing got uncomfortable for him. He had to let her know, "Not too tight, Apaq," Tatu told her, but she squeezed him harder.

"I don't want to let go of you," she told him.

As Tatu paddled toward Tulukar, he asked her to tell her mom that they had made love already. It was crucial for her to tell her mother and he was sure it was the only way he could have her.

Apaq was thinking about it. It would devastate her mom, but she didn't want anyone but Tatu, "I'm really scared. I don't know if I have the will to tell her, maybe when she and I are alone together," she said.

Tatu told her to relax her squeezing, but she never listened to him and squeezed harder. "You're mine," she whispered.

Tatu heard her whisper, but he didn't say anything. He was relaxing and relaxing didn't come often for him. The smooth splashes from his paddle were comforting, as they headed slowly toward Tulukar. He was hoping to get to Tulukar slowly, but the time seemed real fast for him. Soon, the lovers would get there and back to reality.

On the kayak, Tatu stopped rowing and relaxed his head back. Apaq set her head to his right shoulder. Tatu smiled and closed his eyes. It was a comfortable moment for both of them.

Knowing that it might be the last time with her, he didn't want to ruin it, but he had to tell her, "I'm taking off tomorrow and you need to tell your mom about what just happened to us. I think that's the only way I would ever have you is with her blessing. If not, when I come back, I'm taking you back to Atmaulluaq."

She didn't say anything at the moment. Holding him now was wonderful for her. She then scanned the shore of Tulukar. There were some people by the bank area. She focused closely, because she thought she saw someone familiar. She spotted her father and he was standing by the shore.

"I'll try," she said softly in his ear, trying not to move.

When she said that, Tatu started rowing backward and away from the Tulukar. She hit him on his back and said, "Tatu, you're crazy and go forward. My father's up there watching us," she ordered him.

Keeping emotionally strong, Tatu slowly rowed forward. The water was calm as his kayak seemed to move faster than he wanted to. He didn't want to get there, but they had nowhere to go. He was sad at the moment, but he had to deal with it. He knew he was going to get scolded by Apaq's father.

As the lovers beached, her father started yelling at her and took her up with him. Tatu pulled his kayak in and set it down. He watched Apaq and her father go up the hill and they disappeared. Another man came running down toward Tatu and to his surprise, the man tackled him down.

On the ground, they wrestled for a bit and Tatu flipped him over and he quickly pinned him down. He saw an opportunity to subdue him and choked his neck and squeezed the life out of him. The man began to choke and Tatu eased his squeeze.

Getting pinned, when Tatu stopped choking him, he yelled out, "You better not touch her again or I'll kill you myself!"

Being threatened, Tatu squeezed harder and the man slowly stopped moving. The man, being choked stopped breathing. More of his squeezing would kill this man and Tatu knew it.

The other men, who were there watching the little flurry, separated them. Tatu and the other man got up and they were now looking at each other. The men started pushing them away and telling them that it wasn't worth it at this time.

"She's not yours to have," Tatu blurted out to the man he just wrestled.

Eli came running down to them and stopped by Tatu. He looked at his friend and then to the other man and he knew they just had a fight.

"What's going on, Tatu? Did I miss anything? Who's this idiot trying to pick on you?" Eli asked him as he was looking at the man and continued, "Hey! Who do you think you are? You need to pick on your own size." Eli looked around real quick and spotted a person and continued, "I see one right there and he's your size." He pointed to a person and it was a little kid running around. With his sarcasm, the people there chuckled and the man got mad at him.

Tatu's energy was still flowing and he tried to calm down. When the man finally left, Eli and Tatu went up to Tulukar. Tatu finally calmed down as they walked up. Eli was going to drill him about the fight, so he had to tell him.

"We were just fighting over a girl," Tatu told Eli.

"So who won?" Eli curiously asked his friend.

Tatu told Eli about Apaq and why he got into that particular fight. He gave him a short version of their story. Hearing the story, Eli told him that he was in deep trouble this time.

Later that night, worried about the suitor, Tatu had to tell his parents about Apaq. After he informed them about her, his parents decided to see her that night. To his parents' disappointment, where Apaq was staying, the sod house was closely guarded by two men and they couldn't get in. Hearing the news that no one was invited to see her, Tatu decided to check on her. He went over and sure enough there were guards outside. Without doing anything, Tatu went back to his parents. He wasn't going to cause any commotions, especially with Apaq on the line.

The next morning, the scouts went to their kayaks and started getting their tools of war ready. Tatu was checking his arrows and made sure that he was going to carry enough. Today, he wore his pike skin parka. It was light for him and easier for him to aim accurately with his bow.

As Tatu was tightening his clothing, Apaq came running down to him. When she reached him, Apaq quickly said, "Hi, Tatu!" and she gave him a trinket and continued, "I can't stay long."

Tatu was happy to see her and he quickly inspected what she had just given him. It was a small trinket of a drake and it was made of fur. He rubbed it and as he did, it seemed to sparkle.

"Quyana, that's very thoughtful of you," Tatu said as he admired it.

It was small enough for him to put inside his pocket and he liked it.

Apaq was in a hurry and told him, "If you don't come back for me, I'll look for you," as he was putting her gift away.

"Quyana again and you better wait for me too," Tatu said to her.

Apaq was in a hurry and she didn't want to get scolded again like yesterday. She had to be careful, because there were a lot of people around there watching them. She smiled and ran back up again. Sure enough, someone was watching and the same man who had told Tatu to stay away from her, came running down to him again.

As the man approached Tatu, this time he was ready for him. Tatu ceased what he was doing and faced him. The two men were now standing face to face. Facing each other, they sized each other up. There was going to be another fight and they both knew it.

"I told you not to mess with her. Why are you still messing with her?" the man told Tatu angrily and he tightened his fist.

Tatu noticed the man's intent and he clinched his fist too. A fight usually starts small and it gets big in a hurry. Reckless and getting tired of this guy, Tatu's mind started thinking. I'm just going to punch this guy out. I don't have time for this little guy. The man was a lot bigger than he, but for some reason when he got angry, the man just looked smaller. Tatu wasn't afraid of any man and he was one of them. The man was in his path and he had to crush him.

Tatu had to answer, "I don't mess with things that don't belong to me."

The man didn't seem to like Tatu's choice of words very well and he retaliated, "I can see what you're trying to."

The first thing when Tatu heard him say, "I can see," he punched him in the face and broke his nose. That was all the excuse he needed to hit him. He was mad and he didn't have the patience for him.

"Did you see that coming?" Tatu yelled at him as the man went down to the ground.

On the ground, the man was now holding his bloody face. In trauma and in shock, he checked his bloody hand. His nose was gushing out blood as he kept trying to stop it. The man realized he was hit and bleeding badly.

"A fight!" someone repeatedly yelled from the crowd.

After punching the man, Tatu looked around and saw his friends and the man's friends running over to them, but they were too late. It was already over, as he started walking back to his kayak. Walking away from the fight, Tatu's friends reached him and started interrogating him. He knew they were going to drill him on this current event.

"He could have beaten you up," Eli told him.

"Yeah I know, even that little kid could beat him up," Tatu told him with sarcasm, but deep down inside of him, he felt bad for hitting the man. Punching the man wasn't called for and he should have just left him alone. Feeling sorry for himself, he was surprised the man just fell down. He didn't know this man and he didn't care who he was, but now, he had to know his name.

"What's his name anyway?" Tatu asked his friends.

Both of his friends told him that they didn't know him either. Later that day, the boys got to know his name and his name was Kulun. Kulun was from the Paimiut area, just right above Tulukar.

Tatu's mind was busy worrying about many things. Only thing that was on his mind apart from Apaq was the war. He could take on the suitor, but a whole army was worse than one. He hoped the invaders would lose interest and go back to where they came from. Peace was on his mind and they weren't prepared for this war. Their mission was to slow the enemy down. The people needed the time to get ready for it, because the Teriikaniar People were coming up fast and they were killing everyone that was in their way.

Tatu checked his grubs and Kaluk came by and told him something important that he should know. Kaluk came close to his ear and said, "You have to watch out today." Kaluk said and looked around cautiously and continued, "Kulun got ready and he's coming with us."

Either way, how Tatu ended up today was going to be deadly for him.

LET IT RAIN

When the scouts got ready, the people in Tulukar lined up by the shore to see them off. Most of the crowds were family members and friends of the scouts. As the people gathered around the beach area, the scouts got in their kayaks and went a little ways out from the shore.

There were about thirty war leaders in Tulukar. Ten of them were chosen for this mission. One of these ten leaders had a piece of ivory sticking out, which was under his left side lip, and his name was Cung.

Cung was from Qasgirayak, a village above Tulukar and Nanvarnarlak. In his young days, he had been trained as a warrior and he became a great leader. He was a rough-looking man with a mustache and beard. This war to come was going to be his second. Cung's mind was filled with plans and ideas. The men had confidence in him and they humbled themselves in comfort, knowing that he wouldn't fail them. He was trained by the best, an old elder named Qaluksuk. Qaluksuk died before the boys from Atmaulluaq got to Tulukar. The elders had been training Cung for years and he was their shining one.

Cung's parka had designs of two white fangs in front of his chest and so did the parkas of three other men on this mission. The rest of the men and the boys had no fang marks on them. Guk and another leader named Yuc had one on their parka.

Most of the men and the boys had an arrow ornament on the left side parka. The epaulet was a string-looking ornament. The string was placed on the front left chest of the parka. The other string was attached on the left, back shoulder blade. If someone pulled the two string ornaments horizontally, they could tell it was an arrow.

Most of the scouts were wearing fish skins and bird skins. The fish-skin parka was light and it was good to wear in warm weather like today. The bird skin was preferred by some for they were also waterproof and warm to wear.

On the water, Cung cried out to his men, "Stop and turn around!"

The scouts stopped rowing and faced their people. The scouts could see who they were going to fight for as they began lining up.

"Let it rain!" Cung screamed out.

While in their kayaks, with their paddles the scouts splashed the water way up to the sky and kept on going. They called it the rain display and this splashing of the water up above them was a war tactic to scare and confuse the enemy. Cung finally yelled, "Stop!" and the water sputtered all around them. When it was over, Cung ordered the scouts forward and they proceeded back to the beach.

When the kayaks beached, the people started going down to them. Tatu got out and met his family. Eventually, Apaq and her family walked over to him too. Her family tried their best to be happy for him and they tapped his kayak for good luck and wished him well. Her family knew that today wasn't the day to hate anyone. The people knew their mission was impossible and deadly.

Tatu and Apaq eyed each other. They were now all alone and everyone seemed to disappear around them. Apaq's mom tried to pull her away, but she didn't budge, for she didn't notice her mother. The couple was just in their own little world for now.

Breaking his concentration, Tatu heard someone from the other world calling for him. The people and the noise started appearing and Tatu went back to the real world again.

"Whoa," Tatu whispered to himself, for he was surprised at the experience.

"What?" Apaq asked him as she heard him whisper.

That was a good sign for Tatu, but he was about to leave her and all he wished now was that he could get lucky and come back to her.

"You'll push me off for good luck," Tatu said to her.

"Yaa, if you promise me you'll come back for me."

"Wait for me," Tatu asked, but he didn't say yes to her.

He didn't know if he would come back from this mission. This was a dangerous mission and seeing what had happened to the last scouts, he wasn't sure. He was going to give it his best shot, but he was a marked man and his life was loaded. He had to know if she had told her mother. Not knowing about it would devastate him and he wouldn't be able to concentrate today.

"Did you tell your mom?" Tatu had to ask her.

Without saying a word, she nodded yes to him, but she changed her mind and spoke softly, "You're in big trouble," and smiled at him.

When she nodded to him, Tatu stayed steady for a while and relaxed. These exact words that he had heard so many times in his life, never felt so good, never felt so comfortable.

Seeing the man happy, Apaq had to make sure now that he would come back. It was a dangerous mission, but she needed him to come back to her. Without him, she would be devastated. The times with him were a treasure she didn't want to lose. Everything would be meaningless if he didn't come back.

"You watch yourself and come back for me," she finally said again, but Tatu didn't say anything, he was just too happy at the moment.

Tatu's eyes focused and his breathing slowed down. He looked into Apaq's eyes and he saw what he wanted.

"I'll have you," Tatu blurted out.

With that being said, Apaq blushed and smiled at him. To Apaq's left, Tatu's mom was watching and listening to them. He didn't notice his mom was there and she had tears in her eyes, but she was smiling. He watched her mom for a while and then smiled at her.

Aan wiped her tears, but she didn't say anything. She was very happy for both of them. She didn't mean to eavesdrop on these two lovers, but she couldn't help it. Witnessing the moment was beautiful for her. She wiped her tears again and gave him her best smile.

Tatu talked to his parents and they wished him well. When the people said their good luck, it was time for them to go.

"Get ready! It's time to go!" Cung yelled out loud and tears fell on them.

One by one, the kayaks were pushed back. Apaq pushed Tatu back to where he didn't want to go. Tatu kept rowing back and then he turned his kayak around and started paddling forward. He looked over his shoulder and checked on her and gave her his last smile. He then looked forward and didn't look back again as the scouts headed off.

The scouts crossed the lake and entered the Kuicaraq River. They kept rowing until they reached Nanvarnarlak Lake. The village of Nanvarnarlak seemed deserted, but some people were still there. The people there were probably still packing up. It started raining heavily as they crossed the lake and it slowly subsided. The scouts proceeded to the Pitmigtalik River and they finally reached the village of Atmaulluaq.

In Atmaulluaq, the sun was out and the village was deserted. The scouts decided to eat there. After a quick bite, Tatu took a stroll around his village.

What was once alive with people was now empty. He could hear little kids playing, but no one was there. He walked over to his grandparents sod house and went inside. He proceeded to enter, but changed his mind and stopped on the porch. His first training from his grandpa was still fresh in his mind as he started thinking of the past when Guk came in.

"There you are, are you OK, Tatu?" Guk asked him and found a perfect place to sit.

When Guk settled down, Tatu told him the story of how his Apa had trained him. After hearing his story, Guk moved around and checked the grass mats and said, "No wonder you always move off when we try to hit you." Guk smiled and continued, "We need to get down to the riverbank. We have a plan."

Guk gently patted Tatu's back and then they both went out of there. By the riverbank, Guk and Tatu sat down to listen to their leader and his plan. Cung began to speak when a single kayak showed up down the river from them. Seeing the kayak, the men stood up and began concentrating on it.

In this kayak, whoever it was, was rowing as fast as he could, because they could see the long splashes as he rowed toward them. The kayak finally reached them and the man was sweating and breathing heavily. The scouts walked over to him and gathered around him. The man's face looked very worried and troubled.

The man took a deep breath and knowing the leader, he said, "Cung, the enemy's at the mouth of the Pitmiktalik River and they're coming in!"

Hearing the news, Cung ordered his scouts to give the man some water and food. The men started moving around and they went to their kayaks. They knew they had to go-the enemy was closer than they had thought.

"We got to go now! They are close!" Cung yelled out loud.

The scouts hurriedly got into their own kayaks and headed out to the water. On the water now, the scouts gathered in one spot.

Some people were driven to insanity to achieve perfection. Aiming to win at all costs, Cung had to make sure his men believed in themselves. Cung was nervous too, but he had to comfort his men and yelled out, "Listen up! They're crazy! They just chose the wrong river that leads to us! They don't know anything of our land and they don't know us! I'm guessing they all want to get killed by the best!" Cung paused for a bit and checked his men. They weren't nervous anymore, but now they were itching for a fight and focused on him. Getting what he wanted, he continued and told them of his plan, "We're going to ambush this enemy of ours. We will ambush them twice.

On the first ambush site, you let your arrows loose and try killing as many as you can. Once we lose the surprise, I want you to retreat to this place. If they come after you, just run till they get tired. The last ambush site is here in Atmaulluaq. Someone will come here and drop more arrows for us. Again, we will all meet up here. If anyone of you doesn't show up, you'll be considered to be dead."

After Cung informed them of his plan, he checked everyone for any objections or questions they had. When they all agreed, he didn't say anything, but took off. The rest of the men followed him down the river.

From Atmaulluaq, it was an all-day trip to reach the mouth of the Pitmiktalik River. The scouts followed the current downriver and they didn't say much. They had the advantage, because the current was fast enough for them to ride it down at ease.

Riding the current, Tatu was thinking about Apaq as he stroked his paddle slowly. The rest were probably thinking of their families too. The pressure was on them and that was to slow down the threat. Despite the threat, their families were on their minds.

Cung stopped at the mouth of Kakeggluk, a tributary of the Pitmiktalik River. Kakeggluk was just nine long bends away from Atmaulluaq. Looking at the site, he decided that this place would be the first ambush site.

At the ambush site, Cung had to get ready for the surprise. He split his scouts into three groups. Twenty boys plus six men would be on either side of the river, hiding behind the bushes. The rest of them, twelve boys and four men, would be on the river and in their kayaks. For the ambush to work, he wanted to distract the enemy by using the rain display. On the first rain display, he wanted the enemy to focus and stop. The second rain display was the signal for the men on the sides of the river to fire their arrows and kill as many as they could. As soon as they surprised the enemy, he wanted the people on the water to move forward and attack them. The odds of surviving the attack were slim, but they had the up side and that was the ambush. Once they attacked, they would retreat and head back to Atmaulluaq to face them again.

On the river, Tatu was to be in front with Eli and Tuma. The best archers were placed behind them. Guk and Kaluk were to be behind Tatu with the archers. To be in the front line, Tatu was scared and nervous. His palms were sweating as he thought about it.

"You scared, Tatu?" Eli asked him.

Tatu didn't say anything. They were finally going to face these Teriikaniar People. He was nervous and scared and he didn't like it.

Guk told his men to check their weapons. Guk had to make sure his boys were focused, because the enemy was way too strong for them.

When the day was in the middle, Kaluk was still in his kayak. He drank some water and lay back and basked in the sun. The sun was hot, but he was comfortable and hydrated. The cool wind was comfort to him and if the wind hadn't been blowing, it would have been just horrible. He felt the urge to take a piss. He stood up on his kayak and released his load on the water.

"Kaluk, put that back in," someone told him.

Kaluk turned around and his mind went blank. Whoever was watching Kaluk started giggling at his unfortunate event, because he was pissing inside his kayak. Out of his stupor, Kaluk realized what he just did and stopped. He tied his pants up and quickly sat down again. Without worrying about it, he got his weapon ready.

The scouts spotted their opponents. The Teriikaniar had different-looking kayaks than theirs, but they dressed like them. The front of their kayaks seemed more designed upward than theirs and the front tips were colored black. Instead of a thousand of them, there seemed to be just a hundred of them.

Cung looked at his men and said, "Scouts."

SCOUTS

In the water, the scouts waited for Cung's orders. The Teriikaniar fleet started to line up. It was an eerie moment for them as the Teriikaniar just stared at them. The ire feeling was in the mist and it was creeping into the men. There were just sixteen of them on the water and that didn't look like much of a threat. If the enemy wanted to, they would just come over by force and run them over.

Checking out the enemy and recognizing a man that he remembered very well, Guk finally broke the silence, "Cung, is that Patu?"

Recognizing the name, Cung's eyes squinted and finally he said yeah. Without hesitating, Cung nodded to one of his best archers and said to him, "You have a target, the one with the loon parka, when the battle starts, kill him."

Cung's best archer reached down into his kayak and took out an arrow. The arrow was straight and the tip was made of ivory with a falcon feathers. This arrow was his best and he wasn't going to miss.

"Kill! Kill! Kill!" Teriikaniar scouts started yelling at them.

Hearing their loud roar was weird for Tatu, because it sounded like their own language, but different. He immediately checked his weapon. His right hand reached back and he felt the arrows in the case. He looked around the men and they were checking their weapons as they kept their eyes on the invaders. He put his bow down in front of him and waited.

After the Teriikaniar screamed out, they started hitting their kayaks. They were psyching themselves up and they seemed to be ready to attack. Seeing and hearing their opponents getting ready, Cung grinned and looked at his men. He wasn't going to let the enemy intimidate his men. His men were warriors too and they were trained for this moment. His men were battle tested and they had the advantage.

"Get ready! We are better than them! Kill them all!" Cung screamed out and he raised his spear and yelled out again, "Ah!"

As the warriors yelled out, Tatu's adrenaline kicked in. Soon as his adrenaline kicked in, his bear twitch started twitching, but it felt more violent this time. It was bad timing and it irritated him. He checked his bear twitch and noticed that Tuma was watching him. Tuma raised his paddle and hit Tatu's arm. After hitting Tatu's arm, Tuma yelled out, "Wake up!"

Wake up? Tatu thought and he opened his eyes wider. The water started hitting his face and he looked up to check the rain. *Is this the first water display?* Tatu thought. All of a sudden, from behind him, the arrows flew off. *Oh no!* Tatu thought again and he knew he was in trouble. The battle already started without him, as the arrows started landing all over the area.

The Tulukar front line pushed forward and Tatu realized they were in the confronting stage already. Without hesitating, he started paddling forward as fast as he could. He stopped rowing and his kayak glided over the water. He took his bow and loaded. When he seemed to get close to his opponent, he let it loose and hit the man that was closest to him.

The arrows began coming his way and they were now all around them. Tatu almost got hit a couple of times and some whizzed past his head. His kayak had a couple of arrows in it now. He quickly looked around and found his mark. Finding his mark, he aimed and shot. He could see his arrow go and hit his opponent in the arm. The man he hit got hit couple of times and collapsed dead. Tatu took out another arrow and scanned for another mark.

When the battle intensified, some of their people got hit and killed. The arrows coming from the bank surprised their opponents. The Teriikaniar scouts got confused for a moment. The ambush was working for Cung and it was the reaction he wanted from his enemies.

"Forward!" Cung yelled again and his men started rowing forward toward the chaos.

On the water, Tatu's kayak received more arrows. The closest arrow was just hands away from him and he could reach out and touch it. Some of the arrows lodged close to his feet. With his feet, he had to bend and break them, so he could move his legs freely.

After Cung told them to move forward, Guk's kayak hit the right side of Tatu's kayak and Guk ordered him to go up to the shore. As ordered, Tatu started rowing right, while trying to avoid the arrows. When Tatu beached his kayak, he immediately jumped out and pulled his kayak in. On the bank side of the tundra now, he looked at the battle site and they were still unleashing arrows.

The fight was still on and he grabbed his weapon and went up cautiously. On the tundra, he checked his surroundings. The tundra was flat and he could see that the men who were ambushing the enemy were hastily releasing the arrows at them.

Guk also landed his kayak and followed Tatu up the tundra. When everything seemed clear, he quickly told Tatu that Patu was on this tundra. The shaman was on his kill list and he needed to get him. This was the only time he was able to chase him down again.

Did he just say Patu? Tatu questioned himself with disbelief. The name reminded him of a shaman Guk had told him about. So he scanned the area and saw the running man. The shaman was running away from the river, but he was running slowly.

Keeping his eye on the prize, Tatu waited for Guk's orders. The arrows started coming in toward them. As the arrows started landing by Tatu, he went down as low as possible and then he heard a thud, coming from Guk's direction. From experience, Tatu knew that the thudding sound was an arrow finding its mark.

When Guk got hit, he immediately cried out in pain, "Ah, aka!"

Hearing his leader scream out, Tatu was already analyzing the damage to him. An arrow was sticking out of Guk's left thigh and he was grimacing in pain. He was still breathing and he was going to live. After the initial hit, the arrows thankfully ceased coming their way.

"Go get him! Run him down!" Guk screamed at Tatu in pain.

Without listening to his orders, Tatu ran over to Guk and looked him in the eye. Guk was hit and he had to make sure he was OK.

Guk got mad at him and he pointed at Patu's direction, "Go!" Guk yelled at him again.

Without hesitating, Tatu turned around and started running toward the shaman. He didn't want to leave Guk and he didn't want to run down any shaman on his own. Guk was mad at him and he had to follow his orders. He was going to run down the shaman himself. His parents had warned him a million times, "Don't ever run off alone or the monsters will get you!"

HUNTING EACH OTHER

Following the high tide, they were slowly rowing back to Tulukar. As they entered Tulukar Lake, they could hear the cheers from the Yup'ik. He looked at his fellow warriors and smiled at them. Then one of his fellow warriors yelled at him, "You better erase that smile off your face, Patu!"

Getting yelled at, Patu closed his eyes and looked away from that warrior. He was leading the Teriikaniar scouts toward Tulukar and they were just entering the Pitmiktalik River. Knowing the winding river, Patu knew that it wouldn't be long until they started seeing settlements. Couple of bends later, they saw the Tulukar warriors and they were waiting for them.

Their Teriikaniar scouts were larger than these Yup'ik scouts. Patu observed the Yupik warriors and noticed Cung was with them. He knew Cung was a brilliant tactician and leader and knowing him, Patu had to warn his scout leader.

"Wait for the main army," Patu yelled out.

The Teriikaniar scout leader was checking out his enemy and there were just dozen of them in the water. Itching to test these people, the scout leader didn't listen to the shaman and roughed up his warriors for battle.

Patu was now watching the water display from the Tulukar warriors and he yelled at their scout leader again, "You stupid fool!"

When the battle started, Patu received a hail of arrows and two arrows found his back. When the arrows lodged in his back, Patu groaned in pain and he reached back to dislodge them. The arrows were lodged in good and they were now stuck to him. Knowing that more arrows would be coming in again, even though he was wounded, Patu rowed his way up to the shore.

When Patu beached his kayak, to his surprise, he realized that it was an ambush. He grabbed his spear and got out quickly and lay flat to the ground. He knew the scouts were going to get slaughtered and he had to get away from there. To avoid being detected, he started crawling up to the trees and luckily, no one saw him. Once in the trees, he worked his way up to the tundra and started running away.

The arrows in Patu's back were painful, but they didn't damage him enough. *I can fix the damage*, Patu thought to himself. Right now, he didn't have the time to heal and so he kept running slowly downriver to reach his main army. He wasn't accustomed to running on the tundra and the arrows in his back didn't help much. As his breathing got heavy, he spotted a little puddle of water on the tundra. He needed the rest and the water.

When Patu reached the puddle of water, he carefully knelt down to drink while he groaned in pain. Once his lips touched the water, he started sucking it down. While he was sucking the water, from the corner of his eye he could see two Yup'ik going up on the same tundra as he. After a few gulps, he stopped to catch his breath and then went down again and proceeded to quench his thirst. The water was cool and clean at first, but as he sucked some water out of the little puddle, it started to stir with the dirt.

As Patu started drinking some of the dirty water, he spotted something move on his left side. He could tell it was something small and brown, so he stopped drinking and reached over and grabbed it. In his hands now was an arctic earthworm.

Patu went on his knees and used his spear to stand up again. His back started to feel the pain again. Getting irritated by the pain, Patu hunched down with his spear and looked back at the battle site. To his disappointment, one man was running after him. He checked the arctic earthworm and placed it in his pocket. He was going to need the earthworm later, unless he got away from this man.

If the tundra had not been soft underneath him, Tatu would have reached the shaman in a heartbeat. The shaman was not running now and he seemed to be holding his spear. Observing Patu more closely, Tatu noticed the two arrows in the shaman's back. The shaman didn't wait for him and took off again.

The shaman's loon parka reminded Tatu of some families that wore them. His father wore a loon parka sometimes, but he didn't think much of it. The loon parka was an excellent waterproof parka. It was also warm and cozy for some people. Some people in the village wore them too. *Are we fighting ourselves?* Tatu thought, *I guess they wear whatever is available.*

Tatu continued chasing after the shaman and kept his pace. Then his target changed direction toward the hill. If Patu reached this hill, he knew he wouldn't have the advantage.

The energy Patu had in him was dying as he desperately ran toward a hill. When he finally reached the side of the hill, he started climbing up. Every step he took was agonizing for him, but he needed to get to the top and to get a better view. The hill was not that steep as he slowly inched his way up. After agonizing minutes, Patu finally reached the top.

The shaman was now sitting on the top of the hill. It was a vantage point he desperately needed at the moment. Finally able to rest, Patu closed his eyes for a brief moment and felt the cool air. The cool air calmed him a lot and he began regaining his energy. He opened his eyes again and to his disappointment, the man was getting close to him. He reached behind him and tried to dislodge the arrow from his back. Grabbing hold of one, he tried to pull it out, but it was lodged in good and it hurt him. He gave up and checked on the man. The man was getting close, so he closed his eyes and began chanting. As Patu was chanting, he wasn't aware that he was pounding his spear on the ground.

To conserve his energy, Tatu slowed his pace and started jogging toward the hill. As he was nearing the hill, he realized that he was sweating heavily from the run. His body was burning up and he needed to stop to cool off. To cool down faster, he took off his parka, took a deep breath, and rested. He closed his eyes and felt the much-needed cool breeze. The thing about cool air was that he felt it all winter long and he opened his eyes again. The hill was not far off, so he ran a little ways till he got close to the hill and stopped. He was now looking at the shaman and they were just staring at each other.

The weather was hot and they were both sweating and breathing heavily. Of all the warriors that were with them, it was now just the two, Patu and Tatu, and they were hunting each other. The path they were taking was going to be ugly and one of them was going to die on this particular hill.

On top of the hill, Patu raised his right arm and showed Tatu the big artic earthworm and then he swallowed it whole. Whatever the shaman was doing, Tatu knew he had to take him out as soon as possible and he knew it was for a purpose. He took his bow and arrow and aimed at him. Taking a deep breath, his line of fire was good and he shot.

As the arrow left Tatu's bow, the shaman yelled, "Ah!" and rolled toward the other side of the hill and disappeared from Tatu's sight.

"Come on!" Tatu yelled out in disappointment at missing his mark.

Having missing Patu completely, Tatu took a deep breath again and reloaded his weapon. *This is not going to be easy,* he thought to himself.

It was a decent size hill and Tatu could only see the top and the side of the hill. The shaman could now show up from either direction. Taking caution, he stayed still and checked his surrounding carefully, but Patu wasn't showing himself. Suddenly, the back of his hair stood up and he could feel something behind his back. *Apii?* Tatu thought. It felt like his grandpa's stick coming at him and without waiting for it, he rolled to his right.

The shaman was holding his spear to strike and the worm had done its magic. Patu was going for the easy kill as he struck the man from behind. To his surprise, the man rolled off and he missed him. Instead of hitting the man, his spear hit the ground and lodged in deep. The man was a young warrior and he was quick.

Surprised that the shaman showed up behind him, when Tatu stopped rolling, he stood up and backed away from Patu. He knew immediately that he'd got lucky and almost got speared in the back. At a safe distance, Tatu quickly raised his bow and shot him. "Got you!" he yelled out.

Getting hit by an arrow again, Patu screamed out, "Aka!"

Whoever was going to win this battle was going to have to be quick. Patu had to quickly distract him, "Sorry, I slipped and missed you! It won't happen again!"

Patu then opened his mouth and took out the worm he had just eaten and threw it down. The worm was no use to him anymore and the pain in his back got worse. He wasn't going to pry out the spear in time while this man was loading his weapon. He had to run away again before the man reloaded.

What the- Tatu was surprised when Patu didn't go down as he expected him to do. After the initial hit, Tatu backed up farther and reloaded his bow again. As he was loading, the shaman left his spear and started running up the hill again. Tatu aimed at him and shot him again. His arrow hit the man in the back again and it didn't seem to do any damage. All he heard from him was a grunt.

"Come on!" Tatu screamed out.

Striking the shaman anywhere was not an option anymore. Tatu had no choice but to aim at his heart or even his head next time. His mark was running up the hill, so he ran up after him. Running up to Patu, Tatu's heart started beating fast, because his arrows didn't seem to matter to the shaman. Even though he was scared of him, he was going to get Patu.

Patu reached the top again and sat down. Without a weapon now, he quickly took something out of his pocket and ate it. The man was chasing him up the hill and he didn't have the time. *Come to me, I'm going to get you this time,* Patu was thinking as his breathing got heavy.

Halfway up the hill, Tatu stopped in his tracks and aimed at Patu's head this time. Patu smiled at him and rolled away from his view again. *No! Not again!* Tatu cursed himself. Then cautiously, he went up the hill again and when Tatu reached the top, he immediately looked around. Looking around, to his surprise, Tatu didn't see any sign of Patu. *Patu was hit,* Tatu was thinking to himself, *he should be dying by now.*

Tatu felt the much-needed cool air in his face and he was still sweating heavily. He wiped his brow to clear his eyes, but still, he didn't see Patu anywhere. *I don't think he would go far, he has too many arrows in him,* Tatu thought to himself. He was still searching for the shaman, but he didn't see him. There was no sign of Patu anywhere.

For Tatu, at that moment, the worst sign wasn't Patu. His worst sign was going to let him know that something was coming. His bear twitch started again and he knew he was going to confront his prey, so he slowed his heart and focused. His curse was going to show him his prey.

THE POWERFUL ONE

Patu's people lived in the coldest part of the world. They were really old and his people traveled a lot following game. Being nomadic, they followed game and what stopped them from further travel was the sea. Settling by the sea, they adapted well to the changes. When they learned from the sea, they started hunting sea creatures and also gathered edible plants that thrived in that area.

When the people settled down, a big change fell upon them. One day, in springtime, during a full moon, five women gave birth to three boys and two girls in the very same night and on the very same village. Giving birth on the very same day was very unusual for these people. The people didn't know why such a rare thing happened there, until these babies got older.

As time went by, these five babies grew up. The shaman of that village told the elders that the kids all showed signs of power. The senses of these kids were strong and they were very bright. The odd thing about these five little kids was that they didn't like each other and they kept fighting in their own horrible little ways.

Their parents and the rest of the people kept a very close eye on them. The kids woke up crying a lot, because they would get bruises in their sleep and sometimes they bled. What people didn't know was that this was their way of fighting with each other, in dreams that led to reality. Their bruises and cuts were getting worse as they got older. The parents noticed these scary changes and they decided to tell the elders about them.

Then one really cold day, these special kids were all summoned to the qasgiq. In the qasgiq, without saying anything, the warriors bonded these five special little kids and sent them out of the qasgiq. The kids were led to the graveyard and at the graveyard, the warriors tied them up and left them to die. The warriors made sure no one came and freed them. As the days went by, the kids finally stopped screaming and moving as the cold froze them.

Five days later, after being exposed to freezing temperatures and the endless blizzard, the warriors were ordered to fetch the kids. The kids were all frozen by now, but still, they brought them to the qasgiq.

At the qasgiq, the warriors set the frozen kids down in the middle of the qasgiq and cut their ropes. The people in that qasgiq watched the frozen kids for two days. Finally after two days, the kids started melting. The thawing process took awhile and by the fourth day, all the kids were thawed out and they still showed no signs of life.

At night, on the fifth day, something happened outside the qasgiq. They heard some loud screams around that area. Hearing the screams, the people in the qasgiq didn't want to wander out, fearing they might encounter whoever was out there. When the screams ceased, a man came in and told them that three of the kids' parents were murdered and something was out there killing people. When the man finished his report, showing signs of life, two of the frozen kids started breathing. When the two kids showed signs of life, the people were astonished by this, but one wasn't surprised. One of them was a shaman and he knew this would happen. Miraculously, the two breathing kids were Patu and a girl, while the other three kids were dead.

The shaman ordered the people to pick up their drums and start beating. He knew that when the two kids heard the beats of the drums; their hearts would get stronger and stronger. So the drummers began slowly and eventually they got into the rhythm of their hearts.

In the middle of the qasgiq, Patu and the girl finally opened their eyes and looked at each other. The girl closed her eyes and she reached for Patu. Seeing her reach for him, Patu closed his eyes and stayed still for a while. He then opened his eyes and groaned out loudly and forced himself up to his knees.

On his knees now, Patu closed his eyes and felt the drums. His heart was getting stronger and stronger and he felt better. He opened his eyes and searched the area and spotted what he needed. With the strength he got left, he started crawling toward a warrior, who was holding a spear. When Patu finally reached the warrior, he asked for his spear.

When Patu asked for a spear, the people didn't move, but instead just focused on him. When the warrior didn't budge at his request, he grabbed the spear himself. The warrior let go of his weapon and the weapon was in Patu's hands now.

With a spear in his hand, Patu slowly crawled back to the middle of the qasgiq. With all his strength, he slowly got up and raised the spear high up above him. Everyone knew what was going to happen next, but they never moved and watched him thrust the spear into the girl's head and the drummers stopped beating.

Still, the people in that qasgiq didn't move nor did anything as they witnessed a killing. The girl that got speared started shaking for a while and stopped. The blood slowly started oozing out of her head and she was dead. Still, the witnesses to this horrible act didn't move or say anything.

After Patu killed the girl, he looked at his people and said, "I'm the one," and he fell down on the floor and passed out.

Seeing Patu pass out, the men finally began to move and checked on them. Patu was still breathing, so they moved him to one of the beds. They also buried the other kids that didn't make it. The people started moving around again, because it was over.

The warriors were sent out to check on the killer or killers, but they didn't find him or her. When the accomplices were not found, the shaman told his people that the parents, that were killed, were probably killed by a demon. The parents, that were dead, were shredded to pieces. The parents of these kids that lived it out that night weren't lucky either. They were also killed in a week and also shredded to pieces. The people in that village never found out the killer or killers, so they were edgy about it for years.

As Patu grew older, he was taught by another shaman. Patu was already powerful at his young age and killed his master. His master caught Patu summoning his demon. Patu's master was surprised that he could summon the most powerful demon in the world. When his master learned that Patu was diabolical, the master had a knife in his eye the next morning.

At a young age, Patu noticed game crossing over the sea and never return. He started observing the sea and learned a lot about it. Finally, he figured the reason why the birds weren't coming back and he talked to the elders about it.

When Patu reached his teen years, he got beat up by other kids, who were the chief's sons. The chief of that village had many sons and to show the people that they were a strong breed, the chief's sons picked on the powerful shaman. With deadly consequences, Patu ended up killing two of the chief's sons.

The chief sentenced Patu to death for his actions. Somehow, two days after his presumed death, Patu revived and came back to life. The arrows that were lodged in him were still there when he showed up. The people in the village were stunned to see him walk in and they left him alone for they were very scared of him.

Coming back from the dead and after he recovered, Patu talked to one of the chief's strongest sons and they made a pact. If Patu killed the chief, the chief's son would start ruling the people. After Patu killed the chief, the elders sentenced him to death. The son who had made a pact with Patu decided to send him off to the other side of the ocean to check on the game. The chief's son was named Qum and he would wait ten seasons and then he would cross the sea to look for Patu.

Being nomadic people, they were anxious to leave that forsaken land. It was said that the most powerful shaman would show them a new hunting ground and Patu was the powerful one.

DECEIVER OF EYES

On top of the hill, Tatu was still looking around for Patu. All he could see was the tundra and no sign of the shaman. He knew the shaman was around somewhere. He focused his eyes for any movement. After a moment of searching, he began to worry. *He can't disappear like that,* Tatu said to himself. Despite getting nervous, Tatu kept moving left and right. He still had to be focused or get killed. He didn't like that feeling of nervousness. He had to trust his bear twitched. Making a mistake or not, he had to yell out to Patu and get him to respond.

Tatu made up his mind and yelled out, "Patu! Come on! Show yourself!" After yelling out, he heard a soft growl behind him and he automatically rolled to his left. He had to move now or get killed. "Ah!" Tatu yelled out as he rolled away.

As Tatu was rolling away, something bit his left ankle. Instinctively, once he felt the bite, he kicked outwards to shake it off and a black figure flew off his leg. Whatever it was, it just tore up his pants. Tatu immediately questioned himself as he took a quick glimpse of it, *a dog?* Shocked for a bit, when Tatu landed on his back, he came up in a sitting position and he immediately raised his bow and aimed at the thing.

When the figure landed down the hill, it made a yelp and rolled to a halt. Confused, at what he had just encountered, Tatu checked it closely as he lined his arrow on it. *It's a dog?* Tatu thought. Focusing this time, he noticed the dog had some arrows on its back. There were about four arrows on it and it dawned on him that it might be the shaman that he was hunting!

Tatu murmured from the surprise, "Patu?" and he was still confused at this dog.

Realizing that it might be Patu, Tatu shot it and it hit its hind quarters. The dog yelped again, as the arrow found its mark. It began crawling forward in pain. He put another arrow on his bow and shot it again. This time, he hit its stomach and it stopped moving. After hitting the dog, Tatu reloaded and stood up. He started looking left and right again. He knew it was a dog, because it yelped out loudly. Right now, he was looking for the shaman.

It's not him, it's a dog, Tatu thought as he focused himself back on hunting Patu. Tatu checked his back, but with the same results, nothing. In the far distance, he saw three people running toward him. He had a shaman to hunt and turned again to check on the dog. When he turned around, his eyes got wide from just seeing it.

"Ah!" Tatu yelled and jumped up at the biggest surprise of his life!

The dog Tatu thought he hit was a man on his knees. The man had a long tongue and he was breathing heavily. He scanned for the dog, but he didn't see it. There was a long black tail on the man's back and he was looking straight at him. *What the…* Tatu thought and his heart was already shaking in terror.

Tatu had to get back to the game and he grinned to himself. He then took a deep breath and aimed at Patu's chest and fired.

When the arrow hit Patu's chest, he checked it and tried to reach up to take it out. Having arrows stuck in the chest was agonizing. All of a sudden, two more arrows hit him.

Tatu wasn't going to take any chances this time and he sent more arrows at him. He expected Patu to go down and die as Patu got hit several times. For some reason, this shaman didn't want to fall down. Patu was still on his knees as Tatu went down to him with caution. With fear in his mind and surprise, every step Tatu took, he felt it. When Tatu reached the shaman, he yelled out, "Patu!"

With arrows sticking out of him, Patu looked at Tatu and gave him his prettiest smile. He was starting to breathe heavily now and then he started gurgling up some blood. As Patu tried to breath, he coughed out some blood. Looking at the arrows and the blood, he was disappointed. He tried to move his arms, but he couldn't move anymore.

Patu wasn't dead yet and with what Tatu had just witnessed, he started walking around him and unleashed his arrows. The arrows were flying out at Patu's body and Tatu could hear loud *cracks* every time his arrows hit Patu's bones. With the last arrow in his back, Tatu faced the shaman.

Patu was bleeding badly and didn't look too good. He gave this man a smile and said to him, "Ha, a little boy, so cute you are, can you give me a little smile?"

Looking at the condemned man, Tatu couldn't believe Patu was still alive and talking. This man, whatever he was, was evil, but he had to ask him, "What are you?"

Patu began to speak, but an arrow hit his forehead and he fell down backward. Tatu knew what Patu was, but the shaman didn't hit the ground as he expected him to. He reached back to his arrow case again to see if he had more, but it was now empty. Realizing that he was out of arrows, he calmed down a bit.

Tatu noticed that he had put so many arrows into Patu that the man didn't hit the ground. He observed him for a while, just to make sure he was dead. Finally satisfied, he went down to his knees to catch his breath and wiped the sweat from his eyes.

Tired from the hunt, Tatu checked the corpse again. He replayed the moment when he thought he saw him change. It was a weird sight that he would never forget. Patu was dead and he knew it.

Still shocked at what he just saw, Tatu murmured, "That was too much, so weird."

"Tatu!" someone yelled out to him as he was catching his breath.

Tatu looked up the hill and saw a man. The man was on top of the hill and he was getting his bow and arrow ready. The man, for some reason, aimed in his direction. When the man aimed at his way, Tatu thought about Patu and he quickly checked his body. Patu was still down and he still looked dead to him. He looked closely at the man again and saw who he was and it was a bad sign for him. Up on top of the hill was Kulun and he was aiming straight at HIM.

"Oh no," Tatu whispered to himself.

On his knees and empty-handed, Tatu was out of arrows and his body began shaking now from pumping a lot of adrenaline. He was trying to calm down, but then he let his adrenaline flow again and got up to face Kulun.

Tatu and Kulun just stared at each other now. Tatu looked at Patu's dead corpse and saw his arrows. *There were two others behind him*, Tatu thought and he needed to stall Kulun.

"She's mine!" Tatu yelled at Kulun.

Kulun had Tatu in his sights and his intention was to kill him. All he had to do was sent an arrow down. He knew that they were in a war and people got killed and he let go.

The arrow flew off Kulun's hand, but missed Tatu as he jumped off. Avoiding the arrow, Tatu could hear the arrow hit the ground and he knew he was still in a hunting mode. He'd got lucky and Kulun missed him.

"She's mine!" Tatu yelled again as he faced him.

In a grim position, Tatu had to concentrate on everything and try slow everything down and wait for his arrow. He knew he'd had luck with the first arrow. He could have tried pulling an arrow out of Patu, but arrows tend to lodge in and they were hard to pull out, even the ones on the ground.

Tatu tensed his body and got ready to move when all of a sudden he heard a thud and Kulun fell down. When Kulun collapsed, Tatu could see two arrows in his back. After a brief moment, the other men showed up on top of the hill and he recognized them.

On top of the hill, Eli cried out, "Tatu, are you OK?"

Realizing it was Eli and Kaluk, Tatu finally took a big breath and relaxed. He went down on his knees to catch his breath again. *Quyana*, that was close, Tatu said to himself.

Without hesitating, his friends ran down to check on Tatu. When they reached him, they quickly checked him out for any wounds that he might have received.

"Tatu, are you OK?" Kaluk asked him worriedly.

Tatu looked at his friends and smiled at them and that was a bad move for him. When he smiled at them, the two friends pushed him off and he fell down to the ground. They were both happy that Tatu was alive and unscathed. They both knew that he almost got killed by Kulun. Realizing that there was a dead man beside him, they both got curious and checked on the dead man. Eli went over to the corpse and his jaw dropped.

"Ah! Hey Kaluk! Come over here and look at this man!" Eli yelled out.

Kaluk checked Tatu again and when he seemed OK, he went over to Eli. Kaluk's jaw dropped too when he saw the shaman. Kaluk and Eli were silent for a while and they kept looking at the shaman and their friend in disbelief.

"That's crazy! Look at that! Tatu, what did you just do? This man has so many arrows that he didn't even hit the ground!" Kaluk said in disbelief.

The two friends didn't say anything for a while as they examined Patu's dead body. Eli started counting the arrows, but then he gave up when Kaluk kicked him.

Tatu was replaying what just happened and noticed that he was very thirsty from running and running into this mess. He knew he'd got bitten by a dog, but it wasn't or was it? He was still confused at what he just witnessed. His throat seemed really dry at this point and he needed water.

"My throat's dry," Tatu blurted out to his friends.

Eli was still standing by Patu and he looked at Tatu and then back to Patu. He knew his friend was thirsty, but he was still busy looking at Patu from all possible angles. He had never seen such a thing before and this was something new and interesting for him.

"Unbelievable, I'll never forget about this one and I'm never going to let you forget it, Tatu," Eli said to Tatu out loud.

Kaluk was shaking his head at seeing such a thing. He too was in disbelief, because he had never seen an awful kill before. To kill a man, he just had to hit the man in the heart or the head. The odd thing about this kill was that the shaman had eight arrows in the heart area and five were in his head and a dozen on his back. This sight was a total mess to him and he had to let his friend know about it.

Kaluk went over to Tatu and kicked his leg and said to him, "Tatu, you're crazy and you wasted arrows! You just shredded this man to pieces!"

Tatu's friends started chuckling and lifted him up to his feet. Tatu looked at them and asked them what happened in the battle. He had left Guk wounded and he was worried about him and he had to know.

"The battle is over and we won. A lot of us got hit and some died. Guk got hit, but he's down there tending his wound. Guk sent us out to check on you. We didn't see Tuma and I think he's dead. The rest of the scouts are dead and Kaluk's right, you're a poor shot." Eli informed him.

Finding out that Guk was OK, Tatu was happy, but learning about Tuma, he calmed himself and wished for the best. The three friends went up the hill together, but then Tatu started worrying about his friend, Tuma. It was crucial to find him OK.

"We need to find Tuma," Tatu told them as they climbed the hill.

At the top of the hill, Tatu checked Kulun's body and looked at his friends and asked, "Who killed him?"

Kaluk looked at Tatu and just smiled at him and he knew it was Kaluk's arrows that killed him, but he had to ask.

"We heard you yell something about 'She's mine' and then we saw Kulun reload again. We heard you yell again, so Kaluk sent arrows on him." Eli told him.

Tatu was glad that Kaluk had saved him or he would end up like Patu, dead. This was the second time Kaluk had saved him and he had to let him know.

"Quyana for saving my life, he was trying to kill me too." Tatu thanked Kaluk.

After Tatu thanked Kaluk, Eli grabbed Tatu's shoulder and turned him around toward the river and said, "They're here."

BLACK TAIL

At the top of the hill, the boys could see the river that led up to the ambush site. At first they saw a single kayak and then it was followed by many more. The Teriikaniar army was going up the small Pitmiktalik River and they were going toward their scouts. Looking at them, they knew that this was their main army. The three friends had to get out of there fast.

"Let's go," Tatu said softly to his friends.

Without saying a word, the boys turned around and started running toward their kayaks. Along the way, Tatu picked up his parka, while running back to the scouts. They could see some men on the tundra and ran toward them. Getting closer, Tatu slowed down when he realized that they were dragging the dead up to the tundra.

When they reached the battle site, Tatu observed the area and saw a lot of the dead floating around. Some of their warriors were gathering the much-needed arrows from the dead. The kayaks had some dead bodies in them and they were driven to the shore.

The enemy was quickly coming up to them and they told the men what they had just seen. Tatu thought there would be many more of them, but half of them seemed missing. Once they saw Guk, they reported on what they had seen and what had happened.

Guk looked in the direction of the hill and asked Tatu, "Tatu! Did you kill the shaman?"

Tatu nodded and at that nod, Guk said, "Good, let's go home."

"Guk, you should see the," Eli was in the process of talking, but he got cut short.

"Let's go!" Guk yelled again, not wanting to waste time.

Once in the water, Guk screamed out to the remaining scouts, "Men, they're here! Leave the dead, we got to go now!"

Leaving the dead, the scouts went down to their kayaks and got on the water. Tatu went over to Guk and asked him where Tuma was, but he didn't say anything. There was no time to waste there or the main army would get excited and chase them.

"Let's go!" Guk screamed again and he rowed away toward Cung to report.

The scouts didn't have the manpower to face the main army. They were in a rush or else they'd get slaughtered. One other leader named Yuc didn't seem to be around and he was also declared dead. Fearing that Tuma was dead, Tatu didn't say anything.

Once the scouts got ready, Cung led them back upriver to Tulukar. They killed the Teriikaniar scouts, but half of his men were left. Tatu was still shocked about his fight with Patu, so he didn't say anything to them, thinking they wouldn't believe him. His people might think he was crazy anyway for the way he put so many arrows into Patu.

As the scouts rowed back home, they didn't talk much after the battle. They were just taking in what had happened at Kakeggluk. The shaman sequence was playing through Tatu's mind at times as they rowed hastily upriver.

It was getting dark when the scouts reached the village of Atmaulluaq. At Atmaulluaq, they replenished themselves. Of the thirty-two men and boys that had gone to face the enemy, there were only four men and eleven boys left. The second ambush was called off, because they didn't have enough warriors for it. There was a whole army behind them and they didn't waste time and took off again.

It was dark when the scouts reached Tulukar Lake. They could see the torches from Tulukar and Cung lit one of his own and proceeded. As the scouts got close to the village of Tulukar, they were met by two kayaks and they escorted them to Tulukar.

When the scouts got to Tulukar, the curious men immediately asked what had happened and who died. Cung and Guk were led up to the qasgiq to report to the elders. The rest of the scouts were given food, while some of them tended their wounds. The other warriors asked them a lot of questions about the battle.

Tatu kept to himself. It had been a long day for him and he didn't feel like talking to anyone. He had lived through the scout battle and all he wanted to do now was to see Apaq, but he learned that Apaq had already left for Taklirlak Lake. He had hoped to see her and tell her that he had lived through it, but it was best for her to leave. Disappointed, he walked around the village for a while and then he searched for his friends. He found them by the hill that overlooked the lake. The boys had their own campfire going and they were just lying still and thinking deep thoughts.

After the meeting, Guk came out of the qasgiq and searched for his boys. When he found them, he sat by Tatu. The rest of his boys were curious to hear what he had to say so they gathered around him.

When the boys settled down around him, Guk began to speak. "You boys did well today." Guk looked around and continued, "The elders want to talk to Tatu."

"I told you, Tatu. You were crazy to kill a person like that." Kaluk said to him.

"Tell the elders that you want a bed of arrows, Tatu!" Eli said and they started chuckling and continued, "You're in big trouble now."

Tatu just smiled at his friends and stood up. Guk told his brood to shut up and he took Tatu away from them. They started walking over to the qasgiq and along the way, Guk told him that they wanted to know about Patu. Since he was going to face the elders, Tatu told Guk everything that had happened on the hill with Patu.

Inside the qasgiq, the elders were talking to each other, but they ceased when Tatu showed up. One of the elders ordered Tatu to sit in the middle. There were other warriors in the qasgiq and they were all concentrating on him. As Tatu gazed at the rest of the people, they shied away from him. This meant they were worried for him or they might just be scared of him. Tatu proceed to the middle and sat down.

In the middle of the qasgiq, the clay lights were burning brightly. The fire blurred Tatu's vision when he stared at one spot, so he looked away from it. He patiently waited for their questions. He knew they had to ask him on how he had killed Patu.

An elderly man cleared his throat and asked him, "We all know that today was a long day for you, Tatu. We have been talking about the battle and we heard that you hunted down the shaman. So, did you kill Patu?"

Tatu noticed that the elder was concentrating on him very carefully. He could tell everyone was listening and watching him. The quietness of the qasgiq was eerie for him.

"Yes," Tatu answered the old man.

The elders seemed nervous as they looked at Tatu. He was the shaman killer and he didn't blame the elders for how they felt about him. Looking at the elders seemed to make them nervous, so he looked down at the floor and waited for more questions.

"Tell us how you killed him," one of the elders asked him.

Tatu told them about the hill sequence of Patu and him and how he saw a dog and then Patu. Even though they might not believe him, he told them about his big long tongue and his black tail and then how he put so many arrows into him afterward.

When Tatu finished his story, one of the elders said to him in disbelief, "You're lying to us."

When this elder didn't seem to believe him, Tatu looked at Guk. When Guk nodded to him, Tatu reached back and showed them his arrow case. Holding his arrow case, he reached inside and took out a black-looking fur and threw it down on the floor.

"That's his tail. When I went down to Patu, he still had a tail. When I pulled the tail, it just fell off him. This tail wasn't attached to his body. Then I put so many arrows in him that he didn't hit the ground," Tatu answered the nonbelievers.

Everyone who was there and listening to him breathed in and they all looked at the mysterious black tail with curiosity. The elder who had said Tatu was lying, smiled at him and said, "Quyana, you can leave now."

So quick, Tatu was thinking. Being ordered to leave, Tatu got up and he was quickly escorted out. The warriors that were escorting him out started asking what it was, but he didn't say anything to them.

In the qasgiq, the elders checked the black tail and examined it. It was the tail of a dog. Then Quuk, the shaman, came out of the crowd and placed his hands on the tail, but before he touched it, he stopped and looked at the elders.

"It's evil, burn it!" Quuk ordered the elders.

After examining the tail, the elders agreed and the warriors burned the tail. The tail slowly simmered in the fire. It was the end of it; the black tail was no more.

I SEE YOU

After Tatu was interrogated by the elders, he went to see Eli and Kaluk that night. His friends were sitting by a small campfire and he hesitated to accompany them. He knew that after being summoned to the qasgiq, he was going to get onslaughts of questions from his friends. The boys were drained and sore from the events of the day. Guk remained at the qasgiq and he was tending his wounds. Tired and drained, Tatu went ahead and sat down by his friends.

As the boys were resting peacefully, Kaluk looked at Eli and shook his head and said to him, "We need arrows, Eli."

Eli started laughing and when he stopped, he said, "Yeah, we'll get some arrows from that man that Tatu just killed."

Tatu's friends started laughing hysterically, but he wasn't laughing at all. They were going to keep teasing him about it, so Tatu told them about Patu and what had happened at the hill. After the shocking story, his friends didn't say a word to him.

As their thoughts wandered off to the unknown, Guk came limping by and sat down with his boys and that brought them back to reality. Guk then asked Tatu if his friends knew about the shaman and him and Tatu told him yes.

"I'm glad you took the tail and told me about it. I had to tell one elder about it and he was the one that said you were lying. I'm glad you showed it to them. You should have seen their eyes," Guk said to him and tried to chuckle.

The rest of the friends didn't know about the tail and they both began to look at Tatu funny. They had to know more about it and asked him why he didn't show it to them.

"You should have let us see the tail!" Eli angrily told Tatu.

Disappointed that their friend hadn't shown them the tail, they both started pushing him around and asking him what else he was hiding. When they didn't find anything, they stopped searching Tatu briefly. Still disappointed, Tatu's friends started wrestling him. Being double-teamed, Tatu knew he was going to lose this battle. He was sore from rowing and running. The battle at Kakeggluk drained him, but still he had these two to wrestle.

"OK, stop it!" Tatu yelled out as he began laughing uncontrollably.

Guk looked at them and shook his head. The two friends of Tatu were going to give him a hard time for not letting them touch or look at the tail. Guk got irritated and he made sure they stopped messing around.

"Boys," Guk muttered.

When the boys stopped fighting, they stood silent for a while. Guk then told Tatu to sit in front of him and he grabbed his front collar. Surprised by this, Tatu tightened, but Guk told him to relax and he showed them a white triangular patch and he started stitching one on both sides of his chest. When Guk was placing the patch, he told them that this was the mark of a wolf fang. Then he told them that wolves hunt in a pack and tomorrow, he wanted them to stick together.

After the boys got their patches sewed on, they talked about Tuma all that night. As the night got deep, the warriors were singing the songs of old and the songs of war. When everything got deathly quiet, the boys lay down on the tundra and just stared out to the stars.

As they quietly drowned in their own thoughts, Tatu heard a whisper in the dark, "A black tail, you should have let us seen it." After someone whispered, he also threw some dirt on Tatu. Whoever threw it and whoever was listening started giggling.

Tatu's eyes were tired, so he closed his eyes and thought about Apaq. The ground was hard, but he felt comfortable. Loneliness set in as it always seemed to do when he thought of her. The world seemed dark and lonely at first, but the loneliness disappeared when he thought of her more. Apaq was at Taklirlak Lake and his mind was pulling him to run that way. He wanted to get away from the battle, away from everyone, but to her. He reached into his pocket and felt the trinket that she had given him. His eyes felt heavy and he fell asleep and dreamed.

In this dream, Tatu was on the same hill where he had fought Patu and he was all alone again. The area was dark and gloomy this time and he got frightened. He checked for his weapons, but he didn't have any on him. He started hearing growling noises, but nothing seemed to be around. Then he heard a crow calling from a far distance and he looked around and saw the crow.

The crow was coming toward him and it brought dark clouds upon him. All of a sudden, as the crow passed him, the ground beneath him began to move around. Surprised that the ground was moving, he looked down and saw what it was and it scared him!

Tatu was standing on top of what looked like a dead man. The ground started moving again and he could tell the ground was just covered by corpses.

As he was looking at this horrible sight, a hand reached out from behind him and grabbed his mouth and threw him down to the ground. On the ground, he looked at the man and it was Tuma and he was looking straight at him.

Tuma then said to him, "Shh!"

Looking at Tuma, Tatu realized that he was supposed to be dead. He got scared and woke up. Waking up from the nightmare, he could still see Tuma's face and the ground with dead bodies moving. It was an awful nightmare and it was scary. Then he noticed there was a hand covering his mouth. The man who was covering his mouth was looking straight at him.

"I see you," the man said to him and Tatu looked at him and recognized who he was and that was Quuk, the shaman. Quuk was looking at him and continued, "Shh!"

When Tatu calmed down, Quuk gently took his hand off his mouth. Still surprised, Tatu just stared at him. Quuk slowly got up and left and left him breathing heavily.

When Quuk left, Guk walked over to his boys and told them to get up and stretch. As ordered, all three of the boys got up and stretched their legs. It was daylight already and they slept all morning. A man came running by and dropped arrows, food, and water by them. They all took the rations until their bellies were full.

After the meal, the hunters all got up and went to the bank side of the hill. At the bank, the rest of the men were scanning the lake. They immediately knew who they were looking at. Curious, they had to check it themselves.

Tatu scanned the lake and saw the Teriikaniar army. The enemy had beached themselves on a large tundra island, but he couldn't see all of them. This war to come was going to be massive and he knew it. He could see some of their own kayaks going to them. The kayaks were probably trying to spy on them and to see how many heads they could count. As the bold kayaks got closer to the enemy, they got chased back. All they could say was that there were thousands of them.

The warriors of Tulukar were already lined up on the beach and they used their kayaks for cover. Everything seemed to be set for them. Tatu could tell most of the warriors there were with their relatives.

The words they dreaded were cried out, "They're attacking!"

MAN HUNTERS

Like a flock of thousands of geese migrating to their land, the invaders were heading toward them. Seeing this, the Tulukar warriors at the beach started moving erratically. The warriors seemed to get nervous and excited at what was to come. They started checking their weapons and made sure their garments were on tight. While they were in chaos, on top of the hill a scream was heard.

"Listen up!" someone yelled out.

Everyone stopped what they were doing and looked in the direction of the elders. At the highest point of Tulukar, the elders were lined up sitting and watching them. There was one warrior among them and he was holding a spear. This warrior was wearing the markings of a fang and it was Cung. Cung was holding Qaluksuk's spear and everyone calmed down.

Cung raised the spear and with his deep low voice, he yelled out again, "Listen up!" and his loud cry could be heard by everyone.

By now, everyone was quiet and they calmed down. The terrible thing was coming upon them, but the whole army was silent. These men were named after people that had died before them and the time was now to shake them up from their fears.

"Man hunters!" Cung screamed out.

Tatu's skin chilled to hear those words. Cung was calling to him, calling to everyone that was there.

"Show me your war legs!" Cung screamed again.

Receiving orders, all the warriors automatically raised one leg up. As soon as his men raised their legs, Cung screamed out again, "Wake up the dead!"

Together, the warriors stomped once on the ground and the ground shook beneath them. It sounded like thunder, thousands of them. They woke up whoever was dead or alive.

When the earth shook under Tatu, it gave him goose bumps all over his body. It also gave him the courage to face the enemy now. The warriors had all been scared and confused at first, but when this leader of war told them to wake up the dead; he made them feel as one.

Cung told them to wake up the dead again and the thunder struck a thousand times and shook the earth again. Satisfied with waking up the dead, Cung raised his spear higher and screamed out, "Man hunters!" He paused for a bit and continued, "Show me your war hands!"

All the warriors raised their weapons and so did Tatu. Cung looked around at his people and gave them his last order.

"Kill them all!" Cung screamed out and the warriors roared and now they were ready for a battle.

After the encouragement, the warriors, who had seemed to be excited at first, calmed down. They seemed to be more focused this time, including Tatu. *Kill them all?* Tatu thought, and he looked at his enemies and noticed that they had stopped, because they were getting ready themselves too. He could hear their screams.

Tatu and the rest of his friends were just standing with the archers. They were all lined up on top of the hill when a little boy came around and asked if the hunters needed anything. The little boy seemed younger than the rest of them.

Looking at this little boy, Tatu stopped him and asked what he was doing here. The little boy looked at him and said that he was helping out everyone.

"Why aren't you at Takllirlak, with the other little kids?" Guk asked the little boy with curiosity.

"I'm a hunter, I killed a duck," the little boy responded.

"Little hunter?" Eli questioned him and they all looked at each other and shook their heads.

The little boy was way too young to be in the middle of men that bled and died. The little boy took off and asked the other warriors if they needed water. They felt sorry for him, but they couldn't do anything now. Now was the time to concentrate or get killed.

On the beach, the Tulukar warriors got into their kayaks. The first group of kayaks went out and lined up in a line, while the second group went behind them. The last line of defense was ordered to stay on Tulukar. Once the enemies breached their fleet, they would have to defend Tulukar.

Tatu observed his enemies and they seemed to have more warriors than they had. The Tulukar warriors were thousands and still they seemed to be outnumbered. The pressure and the challenge this day were enormous.

While watching their fleet go out, a messenger came by and told Guk to report to Quuk. Receiving orders, the hunters grabbed their gear and went over to the top of the hill, where the elders were staged. At the top of Tulukar, there were about a dozen elders lined up and they were all watching the lake. If their enemies decided to beach, the hunters were ordered to fight them.

The elder who had said that Tatu was lying last night, told him to come over. Tatu checked with Guk and Guk told him that the elder's name was Nuk and told him to go over and see him. As ordered, Tatu jogged over to the elder Nuk and stopped beside him.

Nuk was old, but he didn't have a lot of gray hairs like the rest of the elders. Nuk's eyebrow was thick and he had a mustache and a small beard growing. The elder told Tatu to sit down by him.

As Tatu sat down beside him, Nuk didn't say anything to him, but he motioned his head to the lake. Tatu turned his head and scanned the area. Their kayak fleets were now closing in on the enemy. The old man cleared his throat.

"A wolf fang. Guk must think highly of your abilities. That man is hardly ever wrong you know?" the old man said, and paused for bit and continued, "Tatu, would you rather be hunting every year or kill this enemy of ours?"

Tatu knew it was a trick question, because if he wanted to hunt animals, he would have to kill this enemy first. So he just watched the event that was about to unfold and thought about it. Making up his mind, he had to tell him.

"I don't know, I'd rather come back to a girl I want and we've known each other for years. Like this war, I want something and I want her," Tatu answered him and he was nervous about it, but he had to tell him.

Tatu's answer seemed to surprise Nuk and he looked at him and smiled. As the old man smiled, his wrinkles multiplied because of age. At his age, nothing surprised him much, but Tatu's answer was unexpected. At a time like this, no one seemed to think of love, but survival.

After smiling, the old man replied, "That's a nice thought and a good reason for you to live then, but your parents will choose a suitor for you and that's if you live this day." Nuk, squinted and scanned the horizon and continued, "Tatu, we have been endlessly teaching these warriors for this war. You can't be a good leader without feeling some pain. If we all get killed today, they will blame it on the elders for killing our people. We are the responsible ones and if we get crushed today, we failed."

When the old man finished his sentence, Tatu's hair stood up and he focused. Nuk stood up and so did everyone in that area. There was a faint scream from the direction of the battlefield. The battle started and Tatu could see the rain display from their men. The Tulukar fleet kept displaying the rain and when it was over, all got deathly quiet and then gasped, "Agaaa!"

Above the battle line, Tatu could see a black cloud forming and then it just dropped! Tatu *gasped* to see such a deadly sight.

"That black rain cloud just killed hundreds of them and hundreds of us. You will see it again," Nuk said to him.

Tatu took a deep breath and tried to calm down. *That was something else,* Tatu thought. After the devastating black rainfall, Guk yelled out to Tatu. Getting Tatu's attention, Guk waved his arms for him to go over. Tatu looked at the elder and when he nodded to him, he went over to see Guk. He jogged over to Guk and when he got to him, he asked if he needed anything.

"We got orders to protect Quuk," Guk told Tatu.

Quuk looked at Tatu and smiled at them. Without thinking about it, Tatu asked him what he had seen this morning when he covered his mouth. Quuk just nodded his head toward the enemy and replied, "Them."

Tatu looked around and checked the elders. Surrounding the elders were warriors and most of the warriors were strong leaders. He felt out of place to be with them. He looked back to the battle site and saw the second black rain cloud again.

"Come on!" someone yelled out seeing the sight again.

In the water, the Teriikaniar fleet started attacking. The Tulukar fleet took off and they clashed into each other. It was a fearsome sight and it seemed to take them forever until the rest of their kayaks started retreating to the stronghold.

On the beach, some of the Tulukar warriors got into their kayaks and went to meet the retreating men. As the warriors reached their retreating kayaks, they also retreated to Tulukar themselves. The slow kayaks from Tulukar stopped rowing as the enemy overcame them.

Cung stood up again and ordered the warriors to get their weapons ready. The warriors on the beach began lining up. As the warriors lined up, their leaders were walking the line and they were giving their warriors the last encouragement they needed. Still the Teriikaniar fleets were coming by thousands. The Tulukar Lake water was higher than usual, because there were so many kayaks on the lake.

As the invaders started rowing toward them, the elders ordered the torches to be lit up. Tatu didn't know what it meant then, but soon he would see what it was for.

As the Teriikaniar fleet was closing in, the elder looked at Cung and said to him. "Do you see them?"

Cung looked to the horizon and said, "Yaa I see them, they are coming."

Tatu observed where Cung was scanning. From the other side of the lake, he could see another kayak fleet coming into view.

As the hunting group gazed at this great sight, the boys started checking their weapons again. They were ready, everything they needed was there, but they had to check again.

"Wugg' (Awesome), so many of them," Eli said to his friends as he was looking at the enemy.

The three friends looked at each other and nodded. The invaders were many and that was for sure. These two armies were going to battle and one was going to remain. Guk hit Tatu's arm and got his attention.

"Is your arm twitching?" Guk asked him.

Tatu grinned and replied, "It's been twitching all morning and it hasn't stopped yet. It's the big one and many hearts are going to stop this day."

Guk gave him a fake smile and said, "Good, it's killing time. You guys are going to kill many of them," Guk paused for a bit and continued, "Save your arrows and hit the ones you can hit and stick together."

Tatu wasn't worried about the arrows they had, he was worried about the Teriikaniar army running them over and killing their women and children. They were the last line of defense and they had to focus or they would all get wiped out.

Guk checked his boys and noticed their tension and he yelled out this time, "Wake up!" When he got his boys' attention, he continued, "Get ready! When Quuk gives his orders, you guys go! I have a bad leg and I can't run with you! You watch yourselves and we have the advantage. We are on land and they can't shoot properly on water! Don't let them beach on our land! They're not worthy to touch it! Only time they'll touch it is when we bury them!"

The boys didn't say anything to him and just nodded. The moment for them had come and the time to be focused was now. The energy in the boys was too strong for them. Tatu started kicking his legs back to try shaking it off. The magnitude of the moment was much too great. He checked his friends and they started doing the same thing.

While shaking out the nervousness and out of the blue, Kaluk muttered, "So many, I want to see tomorrow."

Tatu noticed Guk was observing them and his face reaction didn't seem good. Hearing what Kaluk just muttered, Tatu could tell Guk got mad at them. Realizing that Kaluk was going to be grilled, Tatu pushed him off and said to him, "Yeah, me too! So I can punch both of you tomorrow!"

"Ha! I love it. I want to see tomorrow, what a crazy thing to say at the moment." Eli muttered out with a big grin and hit Kaluk in the arm.

Everyone could feel the excitement and Eli couldn't hold it and yelled out, "Tatu! Kaluk!" and when they both saw him, he screamed again, "Let's rip them apart! Tear them to pieces and shred them to nothing!"

Eli was emotionally charged and the boys focused now. Guk's tension faded and he knew his boys were ready. The boys had only one thing on their minds now and that was hunting time.

"Archers! Get ready!" someone yelled out.

The battle was about to begin on their turf. The enemy was close enough for the archers now.

"Go!" someone cried out and they unleashed the deadly black rain cloud.

As the arrows took off, in turn, the warriors on the beach received arrows too. There was yelling and screaming down at the beach. The fight was on and it wasn't going to stop till everyone was dead.

A lone arrow was flying toward the elders. They didn't see it coming in until it got close. The warrior, who was beside an elder, pushed him off at the last moment and the arrow struck where the elder had been and the push had saved him.

"That was close!" one of the elders, who were watching, yelled out.

All the elders who just witnessed the incident started nervously laughing for some reason. The arrow that almost hit one of them was unexpected. One elder got up and told them that he was going to his home. Hearing this, the rest of the elders started laughing more.

The warrior, who saved the elder, took the arrow and looked at it. It was a decent-size arrow and it was blackened to the tip. He quickly gave it to the elder, he saved, and let him inspect it.

Distracted for a bit, Quuk hit Guk in the shoulder and pointed at some kayaks that were to the right side of the battle. These stray kayaks were heading toward the beach. Guk looked at his boys and said, "You watch yourselves," and his boys took off in the direction of the strays without saying anything.

The boys started running down toward the beach and along the way a small bird passed Tatu and followed him. Tatu closed his eyes and saw Apaq and she had tears in her eyes, but she wasn't crying, but then she smiled. He opened his eyes again and he was back at Tulukar. The boys were still running down the old trodden path and they reached the beach area. He wanted to see Apaq before he started this battle. He looked at the bird and it flew away.

"Quyana," Tatu said to himself silently and he loaded his bow.

BLACK RAIN

Running in line, Eli was leading the boys down to the belly of the beast. The hungry arrows were already coming their way. Seeing the sight of the arrows, their eyes got wide with surprise and they now knew how it felt to be the prey.

"Ah! Watch out!" Kaluk yelled out.

Eli hit the brakes and so did the rest of the boys. They looked up at the wall of arrows-they were coming upon them fast and they had to move.

"Ah! Forward, toward the water!" Eli screamed out.

The enemy was targeting them and they were aiming high. The boys burst toward the water at full speed and the arrows started landing over their heads, where they had just been.

It didn't take the boys long when they reached the beach. Eli turned right by following the water line and sped up. As they ran along the beach, Kaluk raised his bow and Tatu saw where he was aiming. They all knew that this first man was going down.

Kaluk carefully aimed for the middle of the man's heart and released his arrow. He could hear the *whoosh* sound as it took off. It sounded smooth and perfect. He carefully watched it go and then it was joined by two arrows from his friends. The two arrows hit the man in the heart, while one hit his eye and he just dropped dead. As soon as the man dropped dead, they all yelled, "Got him!"

After dropping the first man, the three boys kept running along the beach. Then three other warriors joined their run. The boys knew these warriors also received orders to kill the strays. Without stopping, they all kept on running toward the strays.

"Kill what you can hit!" Eli yelled at them.

The enemy that was closest to them met their arrows and there were many of them. Eli changed his direction by running farther up the waterline and Tatu could see why. The whole Teriikaniar army had changed their direction and they were heading toward them. The boys kept running toward the strays and they were getting close. The six strays saw the boys and fired upon them.

"Watch it!" Kaluk said as the arrows flew all around them.

Weaving and curving, the boys tried to avoid the arrows. Suddenly, Eli stopped and the boys ceased to run. As they stopped, Tatu heard a thud behind him and he knew it was an arrow finding its mark. The warrior behind him didn't utter a word, but gasped out his breath. The rest of the boys, hearing the thud, looked back and saw him. *Ah!* Tatu thought as he saw what happened to the warrior.

The warrior that got hit was still standing and he was looking upward. An arrow was lodged in his eye. The arrow tip was out of his head and it started dripping red. Tatu was waiting for the warrior to just drop, but he just stood there and said nothing. He finally collapsed and died.

Guk was up on the hill when his boys took off. He watched them run down to the beach. To get a better view, Guk got up and went to the edge of the hill and observed them. Then his whole body tensed up. *Run forward!* Guk yelled to himself, as his boys were about to receive a hail of arrows. His boys stopped and ran toward the water. Guk was relieved as the arrows missed them. *Whew, that was close, good move, boys,* Guk was thinking to himself.

To the left of Guk, an elder yelled out, "No!" and slapped his thigh in disappointment. The elder who was watching the battle was also probably watching his own boys. Guk looked back to his boys and his boys were now shooting and hitting their marks. His boys were good and fast and he had trained them well. *Keep going boys and shred them to nothing,* Guk was thinking. When his boys sped up, they disappeared from his view. Guk wasn't running with his boys, but he was sweating.

Checking the enemies' movement, the boys had to get out of there or get killed, knowing that if they stayed in one spot, they would attract more shooters.

"Let's go!" Eli yelled out.

Without hesitating, they all started to run again. When they got close enough to the strays, Eli ceased running and aimed at them. The enemies were a good distance for them to start shooting.

"Go!" Eli yelled out.

The boys went down to their knees and shot the six strays and hit three of them. Disappointed, Kaluk turned his head to the other two warriors and yelled at them, "What happened? You guys are worthless!"

The rest of the strays started turning away from the beach, but they got hit and one got lucky and fled. The lucky man screamed his lungs out as his fellow men got hit. He had no choice but to turn back.

Eli yelled out to Kaluk, "Rip his lungs out!"

Kaluk's arrow was already on its way and the enemy fell down to the water dead. The last stray had gotten killed and from the direction of the Teriikaniar fleet, the arrows started falling all around them again.

Tatu checked the direction of the arrows and the sight wasn't good. He saw the whole Teriikaniar fleet pushing for the beach. Knowing their intentions, the boys started unleashing their arrows at them. They were staying in one place too long and one of them got hit in the leg.

Tatu quickly checked on the warrior and realized that he was going to be OK. They had to move, so Eli got up and they all started running up the hill and away from the threat. The other two warriors followed them, but one was limping badly.

Once on top of the hill, Eli screamed out at them, "Come on! We'll bury you!"

The invaders noticed the Nunapicuar and Kasigluq fleets charging them from the rear. Seeing the fleet behind them, half of the Teriikaniar fleet turned around and charged. Confusion began to get hold of the invaders.

"Let it rain!" someone screamed and the boys raised their bows and shot up toward the enemy. At first, five arrows got up in the air and then hundreds of them joined in as Tatu lost his arrow in the black rain cloud. The cloud formed and dropped on their foes. Whoever was under this cloud got their flesh and bones torn open.

Still, there were enough Teriikaniar warriors that lived through the black rain and they finally beached. Unfortunately, they were met by the Tulukar warriors with their spears, bows, and arrows.

In the water, the fleet from Nunapicuar and Kasigluq clashed with the rest of the Teriikaniar fleet. It took a while, but the battle was over as Tatu watched the rest of their warriors finish off the live and the wounded.

Showing signs of defeat, some of the Teriikaniar warriors gave up and just stopped moving. The horror of defeat was too much for them. Their mission failed and they knew it as they watch their men die in front of them.

On top of the hill, Tatu gazed over the battle area. Some of their warriors were badly wounded and bleeding. He scanned the once beautiful lake and it was filled with red. Many kayaks of the Teriikaniar People had dead bodies in them and some of them were still wounded. Their wounded met the same fate as the rest of them. The area was filled with death and he didn't like it.

The battle was over and Eli, Kaluk, and Tatu looked at each other and sat down. The boys were sweating heavily from head to toe. Moments like this, they had nothing to say, there were no words to describe it. *We lived and we're alive!* Tatu said to himself as he finally relaxed. It had been a long day for them. Exhausted and relieved, the boys fell down on their backs and splashed on the water. It was tundra, but it felt like that at this particular moment.

"Ah, it feels good," the boys said in sync.

The boys were looking at the blue beautiful sky and catching their breaths. Tremendous relief hit them and breathing had never felt so fine for them. After a moment of silence the boys got up and threw their bows down to the ground. The friends looked at each other and broke their bows. They had no use holding on to pieces of this war. They knew they had to move on and their bows meant nothing to them but death,

After breaking their bows, they felt a lot better. With happiness in his mind, Kaluk broke their moment of silence. "Remember when Tatu threw the pink mice at the old woman?" he said to his friends.

Eli hit Tatu on his shoulder and replied, "Yaa, I remember." Then Kaluk continued, "I think that old woman cursed us that day. She jumped so high that-"

Kaluk got cut short, because they heard people yelling. The boys slowly walked to the edge of the land to see what the commotion was all about.

"Man hunters!" someone yelled out loud and the earth shook again for the very last time.

Tatu gazed upon the warriors and in his mind, he hoped they wouldn't have to fight again. The brutality of killing a man wasn't in him. Eli noticed Tatu was thinking deeply and asked if he was OK. Tatu looked at his friends and tried to smile at them.

"The arrows got pretty close today," Kaluk told them and continued, "I hope we don't have to do this again."

The boys just took a deep breath and Eli said, "Let's go."

The boys walked down to the beach and they saw a dead guy with an arrow between his eyes. This man was nothing compared to the other dead bodies they saw.

TEN DEAD

When the war was over, Guk limped his way down the beach and searched for his boys. When he saw his boys, he gave them the biggest smile they had ever seen from him. They didn't notice him and seemed to be paralyzed. Guk stopped and carefully observed his boys and they all looked OK. They were moving a little bit, but not that much. He had to test them to see if they were really OK.

"Run!" Guk yelled at them.

Out of their stupor, all the boys jumped up in the air and when they landed, they all ran toward him. His boys were good and they were fine, Guk was thinking and he was happy now.

After the boys briefed him on what they had done, Guk had them help the warriors. One crow landed by Guk that day and by the end of the day, there were hundreds of them. It took them two days to separate the dead and on the next day, every ten dead of the enemy were marked with a spear, pierced through their bodies. The casualties of war totaled over five thousand of their enemy and over thousands of their own. There were so many dead that day and they tried their best to bury them.

After burying the dead, being restless to find their friend, Guk, Eli, Kaluk, and Tatu went down to Kakeggluk to bury the rest of their scouts. They also wanted to find Tuma's body.

When they reached Kakeggluk, they found the bodies near the small scout battle site. Sadly, they found Tuma's body among them. Disappointed that Tuma had died, Guk started crying. Guk and Tuma were the best of friends and they had hunted everywhere since they were really young. The boys felt badly for both of their leaders-one was dead and the other was alive. Tuma had been a good teacher for the boys and a good hunting partner.

The bodies were gathered up in one spot and the hunters buried them together, along with their belongings. After they took care of the dead, the hunters marked that place with a stick. Years later, the stick they put up rotted and disappeared. Then they headed home to see the rest of their families.

After they took care of the dead, Quuk gathered all the warriors he could and ordered them not to tell the story of this battle or someone who did would end up dead. After a couple months of this war, a warrior told the story about this war to his family. The warrior ended up dead the next day.

Tatu couldn't keep a story like that inside, so he told his family about it. He couldn't keep it inside of him and he had to tell them how his friends had died. After telling what happened in the war, nothing happened to him, but still, he was edgy about it.

LIGHTS!

A couple of years later, after the war, Tatu was alone outside his village. It was nighttime and he was just looking up at the stars. The bright stars were blinking at him and the fresh cool breeze was gently blowing his hair. He could see his breath as he exhaled. Seeing his breath usually meant it was really cold out. As Tatu was deep in his thoughts, out of the dark, two men came up to him and grabbed him.

Getting hold of Tatu, the men quickly tied him up with a rope. One of the men looked at him and told him his name was Qum. Without warning, he punched Tatu in the stomach. As Tatu got hit, he gasped for air and grimaced in pain.

After the attack, the men dragged him to the closest sod house and brought him inside. The occupants of the house were nowhere to be seen. The fire was lit as they laid Tatu down on the floor. When they settled him down on the floor, they let go of him.

Tied down, Tatu asked them what they wanted, but they didn't say anything to him. Qum and the other man went out of the sod house and came in again. This time, the men brought Patu's dead body with them and they laid him down in front of Tatu.

Seeing Patu's dead body, Tatu started screaming for his life, but it was no use. Patu's head was facing the floor and the arrows were still sticking out of him. Tatu tried his best to break the ropes, but they were too strong for him.

As Tatu struggled to get free, Qum looked at him and gave him his most evil smile and said to him, "I'm letting you live to watch over my pet!"

After telling Tatu about his pet, Qum began pulling the arrows out of Patu's head. When Qum finished pulling the arrows out, he stood up and kicked Patu's head really hard.

Seeing this savagery, Tatu could hear a loud *crack* coming from the gruesome kick. Qum looked at Tatu and then back to his dead pet.

Qum reached down to Patu's face and raised his dead head and cried out to him, "Wake up, Patu!"

After yelling at the dead man, Qum threw Patu's head down and got up. Qum kicked the dead man in the head again and after kicking Patu in the head, Qum smiled and he slowly walked out of there.

Wake up? What does he mean by wake up? Tatu thought and he checked Patu's dead body very closely. The house was silent and Patu was still motionless and dead. Outside, the dogs began barking, but they slowly started whimpering in pain.

Tatu's hands were still tied up behind him as he went on his knees. He quickly looked around the house for any sharp object, but there was none. Then his bear twitch moved. Feeling his bear twitch, Tatu jerked up and yelled out, "No!"

Feeling his warning sign, Tatu checked Patu again. At first, Patu's hand slowly started twitching and then it stopped! *I saw it move,* Tatu was thinking and he looked carefully this time, because his eyes might have deceived him.

Then Patu's head jerked up again. Jerking up, he gasped for air and blood started dripping out of his mouth.

"No! It can't be!" Tatu cried out, "No!"

Patu was still looking down on the floor as the blood started oozing out of his head. Then he started coughing uncontrollably. The blood splattered down as he coughed. When he stopped coughing, he began to giggle.

"Water, I'm very thirsty," Patu said to himself.

"*Ah!*" Tatu yelled out and he knew he was in trouble.

Tatu pulled his arms outward and tried to break free, but the ropes were still tight and strong. He stopped moving around and checked Patu again.

Hearing Tatu's scream, Patu slowly turned his head toward him. His left eye was still pouring out some blood. "I see you." Patu said and his voice trailed off.

Hearing Patu talking to him, Tatu's whole body jerked violently! He had killed Patu and there was no way he could have lived after he killed him. He looked at the evil shaman as Patu started trying to inch his way toward him.

"Ah!" Tatu suddenly woke up and he was sweating from a bad nightmare. "Shush, you're going to wake up your baby," a woman's voice said to Tatu.

Tatu focused his eyes and the area was still dark, but he noticed it was Apaq. He stood up and checked his surrounding. Everything was there and everything looked OK. Once up, he dressed and walked out of his sod house.

Outside, Tatu stretched and looked at his skeleton kayak. He started feeling the cold and the chill in his bones. A little hand took his hand and he looked at her. The young girl looked like her mother and he smiled at her.

"What you looking at?" Tatu's baby girl said to him.

Tatu quickly smiled at her and her hand was warm to the touch. Feeling the warmth of her hand, Tatu felt better. She always made him feel better when he looked at her.

"I'm looking at my beautiful baby," Tatu finally said to her.

Apaq came out of the house and she was holding a newborn baby. She was in her warm new parka with her bird designs. All her kids had the same parka designs.

"It's cold out here! Bring her back to the house," Apaq ordered Tatu.

"No, I want to stay out here, Mom," his girl automatically declined.

They looked around the village and there was another boy outside his grandpa's sod house. Tatu raised his baby up above him and made her squirm.

"Let go of me, Daddy," she cried out, not liking the height.

The boy looked at them and smiled. It was Tatu's son and he was checking the weather.

"Wake up!" Tatu yelled at the boy as he set down his baby girl.

The little boy turned his head toward him and responded, "It's going to be a nice day."

In that last war, no arrow ever hit Tatu, but he felt the pain of one. Many restless nights like this one kept him uneasy, but after looking at his kids, they calmed him down and made him feel better. He had his lights and they could take the darkness away from him. His grandfather was right; you could never forget the unsuspected moments.

Pamyua

REFERENCES

Steven J. Langdon: The Native People of Alaska
  Fourth addition
  Greatland Graphics
  Anchorage, Alaska

http://www.yupikscience.com

Steven B. Young: To the Arctic: An Introduction to the Far Northern World
The Center for Northern Studies
Wiley Popular Science
John Wily and Sons, Inc
New York*Chester*Brisbane*Toronto*Singapore